"History does not record in its annals any lasting domination exercised by one people over another, of different race, of diverse usages and customs, of opposite and divergent ideals. One of the two had to yield and succumb."

— *Jose Rizal*
National Hero, Philippines

Reno Ursal

ENLIGHTENMENT

BOOK ONE
THE BATHALA SERIES

PACIFIC BOULEVARD

PACIFIC BOULEVARD BOOKS EDITION
MARCH 2019

Published in the United States by Pacific Boulevard, a division of The Imojin Group LLC.

This is a work of fiction loosely based on the myths and legends of Filipino folklore. Names, characters, businesses, organizations, places, events and incidents either are the product of the author's imagination or are used fictitiously. Any resemblance to actual persons, living or dead, events, or locales is entirely coincidental.

The Library of Congress has cataloged this edition as follows:
Ursal, Reno

Enlightenment: Book of the Bathala Series / Reno Ursal - First Edition

Pages cm

1. Filipino folklore-Philippines - Fiction.
2. Coming of Age-Dramatic-Young Adult - Fiction I. Title.

Pacific Boulevard Trade Paperback ISBN: 978-0-9844-4081-8
ebook ISBN: 978-0-9844-4080-1

Cover design by Damonza

Printed in the United States of America
10   9   8   7   6   5   4   3   2   1

TERMS OF CONSEQUENCE

1. Alibata *(Ali-bah-ta)* – The original writing script in the Philippines prior to Spanish colonization. Also known as *Baybayin* script.

2. Amanikable *(Amani-cob-lay)* – The god of the sea in Filipino folklore, also the god of hunters. Known to have a temper.

3. Anitun Tabu *(Ani-toon Ta-bow)* - The wind goddess in Filipino mythology.

4. Anak *(ah-knock)* - A term of endearment when a parent speaks to a child.

5. Apolaki *(Apo-lah-key)* - The sun god in Filipino mythology.

6. Apritada *(Ah-pree-ta-da)* - A tomato sauce Filipino dish usually consisting of chicken, potato, carrots, bell pepper, green peas, garlic and hot dog.

7. Aramaic – One of the three languages the original Bible was written and said to have influenced Arabic script.

8. Aswang *(Os-wong)* – Beautiful white-skinned creatures who turn into monsters at night according to Filipino mythology.

9. Ate *(Ah-tay)* – Tagalog term of endearment for "older sister."

10. Balikbayan *(ba-lick-bye-yan)* - A Filipino visiting or returning to the Philippines after a period of living in another country.

11. Bathala *(Bah-ta-la)* – Supreme god of the Philippines in Filipino folklore, the father of *Mayari*, *Hana* and *Tala*.

12. Baybayin *(Bye-bye-yin)*– The original writing script in the Philippines. Also known as *Alibata*.

13. Brand – An emotional connection between two Danags broken only through death.

14. Brunei *(Brew-nigh)*– A kingdom in the southern islands.

DOROTHY AND ADRIAN

2018 A.D.

ޑޮރޮތީ އާ އެޑްރިއަން

had disappeared. She started to turn her proas boat, but stopped when she was consoled by Panginoan, her closest Kinalakian friend. Panginoan reminded Urduja that the Mongols had outnumbered them and had most likely killed everyone in Tawalisi.

The rajah had ordered Urduja to make the sacrifice to not fight knowing it would be painful, but necessary to save her life and preserve the secret traditions of the Tawalisian kingdom.

She tried to remember the rajah's orders to keep sailing regardless of what happened, frustrated and angry with her father for being stubborn, even if his orders had significance and wisdom.

With sorrow fracturing her heart, Urduja kept her fleet on course to the south. She and her women warriors sailed in silence, praying to Amanikable, the god of the sea, and the Supreme *Bathala,** that they weren't the last of the Tawalisian people.

---

*   *Pronounced Ba-ta-la. Considered the most powerful of the gods in Filipino mythology. Bathala is the Tagalog name for the highest deity. Other islands have other names for the highest being, but this novel will use the name Bathala. Term #11 in Terms of Consequence.*

PROLOGUE

The *Tawalisi** horizon slowly faded as Urduja's fleet of proas boats sailed south out of Dosol Bay.

Urduja[†] navigated the outer edges of the Luson Sea towards Brunei, making sure to travel slowly and methodically through the dangerous waters of Seludong, claimed by Tondo as their own waterway.

Once they passed safely by Hubek Bay, Urduja felt a rush of sadness as her fleet sailed further from Tawalisi, the only home she'd known. She gazed at the rising sun, *Apolaki,[‡]* and closed her eyes to stay connected with her father, the great Rajah Tawalisi. He had stayed behind to defend Tawalisi from an imminent attack from their biggest enemy, the *Yuan dynasty Mongols[§]*. Tawalisi had rebuked trade offers from the Yuan dynasty for years. Now the Mongols had gathered their entire navy fleet to attack Tawalisi, the last remaining unconquered kingdom.

Urduja held hands with her *Kinalakian[¶]* women warriors, praying to their ancestors that their people's fighting abilities would be enough for victory. But she began to weep when she no longer heard the rajah shouting orders to the Tawalisian army. She yelled for her father, but the energy between them

---

*	*Fabled land said to be in modern-day Pangasinan.*
†	*Urduja is a fabled woman warrior of Tawalisi, leader of the Kinalakians.*
‡	*Apolaki is the sun deity in Filipino mythology, son of Bathala, brother to Mayari, Hana and Tala.*
§	*The Mongols empire was close to its end in 1347.*
¶	*The women warriors of Tawalisi, experts in archery and horseback riding, led by Urduja.*

Urduja of Tawalisi

1357 A.D.

ᜇᜓᜇᜓᜌ

We reached the land of Tawalisi, it being their king who is called by that name. It is a vast country and its king is a rival of the king of China. He possesses many junks, with which he makes war on the Chinese until they come to terms with him on certain conditions. The inhabitants of this land are idolaters; they are handsome men and closely resemble the Turks in figure. Their skin is commonly of a reddish hue, and they are brave and warlike. Their women ride on horseback and are skillful archers, and fight exactly like men.

— *Ibn Battuta*
Moroccan world traveler, 1347 A.D.

TABLE OF CONTENTS
(continued)

TABLE OF CONTENTS

27. Mandalagan – An area in Negros Island, Philippines.

28. Muta *(moo-tah)* - Tagalog word to describe gummy secretion around the eyes.

29. Mayari *(Ma-yah-ree)* – The moon goddess, daughter of Bathala, sister of Hana & Tala.

30. Pencak Silat *(Pen-cock See-lot)* – This term is used today to describe an Indonesian martial art, although it was used historically known as a martial art from throughout Southeast Asia.

31. Tala - Goddess of the stars, daughter of Bathala, sister of Mayari and Hana.

32. Timawa *(Tim-ah-wah)* – Warriors class of Danag society who escorts others into Mandalagan and on the frontlines of protecting humans, yet inferior to Tumaos in ancient times.

33. Tawalisi *(Ta-wah-lee-see)* – The fabled homeland of woman warrior Urduja, rival of Tondo and the Yuan dynasty Mongols. Most likely the province of Pagasinan in modern-day Philippines.

34. Tumao *(Too-mao)* – The royal class in ancient times made up of datus and rajahs families.

35. Urduja *(Ur-doo-jah)* – Fabled woman warrior of modern-day Pangasinan. Daughter of Rajah Tawalisi and revered for her beauty and connection to the Filipino god Bathala. It is said she longed to give birth to a daughter.

36. Uripon *(Ur-eee-pan)* - The commoner class in ancient islander society.

37. Visayan *(Va-sigh-yon)* - Region in central Philippines. Natives speak the dialect of the same name. Also spelled *Bisayan*, but spelled with a V in this novel for consistency.

38. Waysaypayan *(Why-sigh-pie-yan)* - A Visayan term that means *you're welcome*.

15. Danag *(Dah-nug)* – Secret society in the Philippines that dates back to the days of warrior Urduja of Tawalisi.

16. Diniguan *(De-ne-goo-an)* - Pig blood soup originating from the Philippines.

17. Drift – When a Danag *kindred* visually sees the thoughts of a fellow *kindred*.

18. Duwende *(doo-when-day)* - Mischievous goblins/dwarves in Filipino mythology. This term used to describe similar beings in various other cultures around the world, particularly in Latin America.

19. Eskrima *(Es-cream-ma)* – Filipino martial art utilizing knives, bamboo sticks and daggers, banned by the Spaniards upon colonialization and practiced in secret by Filipinos. Also known as *Arnis* and *Kaliradman*.

20. Kaliradman *(Kali-rod-man)* – Same as #19. Shortened to "Kali" in modern times.

21 Hana - Goddess of the morning, daughter of Bathala, sister of Mayari and Tala.

22. Iha *(E-ha)* - Term of endearment parents use for their daughters. Masculine form is *Iho*.

23. Inday *(in-die)* - Visayan term of endearment when speaking to a young girl.

24. Kindred – A Danag's special connection with another. No Danag has more than five kindreds and no one can explain why.

25. Kolipulako *(Koh-lee-poo-lock-oh)*– A tribal leader from the 1500s who resisted conversion to Christianity. Known as *Lapu-Lapu* in Filipino culture, a national hero of the Philippines. A rival of *Humabon*.

26. Kuya *(koo-yah)* – Tagalog term of endearment for older brother.

CHAPTER ONE: DOROTHY

﷽

Stella and I were at Tao Nightclub dancing to a dope EDM set by DJ Asia. Out of nowhere, a middle-aged man emerged onto the dance floor. He wasn't interested in the scantily-clad go-go dancers on raised platforms, shaking their butts around us. Instead, he ogled DJ Asia as she cupped headphones against her ears, her long hair and curvy silhouette hovering behind a laptop in the elevated DJ booth. When his view was blocked by a crowd of party-goers, he looked in our direction. He approached us, his musty scent forcing me to hold my breath. I turned away.

"Hey there," he said in a raspy voice.

Stella nudged me, a signal it was my turn to take the lead. She'd done the honors last night at Club Lavo in the Palazzo Casino.

I reluctantly turned back. "Hello," I replied, hating that my voice sounded more polite than intended.

"So you two alone?"

"Our boyfriends went to get us drinks."

The man shifted closer. "Your boyfriends are idiots for leaving you two by yourselves."

Stella gave me a get-rid-of-him look before disappearing into the crowd by the bar. I tried to think of any reason to get out of the conversation. "They'll be back, but thanks."

The man reached for my arm. "I guess it's you and me. Your friend left."

He somehow wrapped his arm around my waist and twisted me into him.

"What do you think you're doing?" I said in a rising voice.

"Come on now," he breathed in my ear. "Let's make this a night you'll never forget."

"Frickin' let go of me! You're like fifty years old. I could be your daughter!"

The man reached for my arms. "You can't believe I'm old enough to be your daddy, can you?"

A crescendo of sharp energy rose through me once I heard the word daddy. Perhaps being abandoned by my father at a young age had actually affected me, or maybe it was because of this guy's creepy demeanor. Whatever it was made me twist his hand and pin his neck against the wall with my forearm.

"I'm only eighteen!" I yelled. The look of shock on his face gave me a moment of satisfaction as I fought off a sudden urge to lick and bite his neck. Why did I want anything to do with his neck?

"Feisty," the man replied hoarsely, my arm still pressed against his Adam's apple. The color drained from his face, and I almost smiled at that, but the scent of his skin overcame me.

"Who are you!" I growled. And why did my throat feel like it was starting to burn?

The man strained for a breath. "I've never seen you before in my life!"

"Why did you walk up to me?"

"You were staring at me! And it's hard not to notice girls who look like twins!"

It was a bullshit response, even if Stella and I did look like twins, at least on this night. We had decided to wear matching black halter tops and skirts, while I added three inches thanks to my only pair of wedges. Stella soared like a model and her skin had a golden radiance; I was never in her league, but tagged along when she begged me to go out on the strip. And because I had given in, I had to confront this creepy guy who had noticed us in the Tao Nightclub's strobe lights.

"You shouldn't even be looking at girls our age!" I yelled.

My hold on his neck loosened when my stomach inexplicably convulsed in a split second of pain. I cursed the impeccable timing of female cramps as the man staggered away. A blue vein spiraled from his neck into his shoulder blade. I leaned closer to touch his skin until two powerful arms grabbed the guy's collar.

Harvey, a bouncer at the club, looked at me with a shocked expression. I backpedaled, suddenly aware an altercation had started because of me. Smoke seemed to rise from Harvey's face and over his bald head. There was absolutely no way the guy had a chance now. I took a deep breath, the burn in my throat quickly extinguished. What. The. Heck.

"What's going on here?" Harvey yelled in the man's face.

The man pointed in my direction. "She attacked me!"

Harvey tugged the man's collar and pulled him towards an exit sign. "You got to be kidding! She's barely over a hundred pounds!"

The stranger tried to push him, but his arms caught air against Harvey's six-foot frame. Once they disappeared down a dark corridor, chills ran through me.

Stella emerged and held my hands. "What was that about?"

Exactly. Why did I growl and jump on the guy? I leaned towards Stella's ear. "I'm not sure what just happened!"

Stella held my shoulders. "Oh my God! I ran to get Harvey when he reached for your arm. But that's before you pinned him against the wall!"

"I had to defend myself!"

"Shit! Maybe it's time for me to take martial arts like my girl Dorothy Dizon! You kicked his sorry ass!"

I could still smell the trail of the man's scent. "I feel...gross!" I absolutely wanted to take a shower to make the ickiness go away.

"Don't let that loser ruin our night! Come on!" Stella pulled me to the dance floor where she attempted an exaggerated running man in her flats, which somehow made me laugh. I tried *not* to get into the cheesiness of classic dance moves, but Stella's enthusiasm broke me down. Harvey emerged and motioned us to the bar in the middle of my halfhearted Roger Rabbit. He asked if I was okay. My insides squirmed at the reminder of the man's arm around my waist, but I assured him I wasn't hurt. Then a fight broke out.

Harvey sprinted up the stairs to the second level. He pushed a drunk and pointed at another guy to stay at the end of the bar. There were verbal threats between two guys with high-pitched yells from their girlfriends, making the scene even more dramatic. By the time Harvey and his crew had handled the situation, Stella and I had agreed to call it a night.

After a pit stop in the ladies' room, we waved bye to DJ Asia in the booth and accepted Harvey's offer to escort us to my car in case the creepy guy was loitering in the casino. Once we found my Mercedes in the self-parking garage, we thanked him for kicking the guy out. He said it was nothing and watched us drive off before he went back in the Palazzo.

After hitting all the greens on the strip, I accelerated into traffic and started to feel normal, especially when our favorite Cardi B. song played on the radio. But after dropping Stella off and promising to text her from home, my hands quivered on the steering wheel as I swallowed a strange craving at the back of my throat. I focused on keeping my trembling hands from driving me off the road as the image of the guy's creepy smile made me nauseous.

Who the fuck did he think he was?

I pressed my forehead against the steering wheel and took long breaths after parking in the driveway, trying to settle the queasy feeling inside me. I texted Stella that I was home and walked in the house.

I checked on my mom upstairs. She was snoring. Loudly. Which meant she would be knocked out until late morning. I closed her door quietly and threw my smoky halter top and skirt in the hamper. I took a long-ass shower, making sure my entire body was slathered with body soap. After toweling off and brushing my teeth, I changed into my favorite Golden State Warriors jersey and shorts and plopped on my bed, cringing at almost licking the sleazy man's neck. No girl should ever want to lick that man's neck!

After a half-hour of tossing and turning, I fell asleep listening to Coldplay's "Viva La Vida" on repeat in my earbuds, hoping I wasn't losing my mind.

CHAPTER 2: ADRIAN

ಹಲಹ

The Philippine Airlines Boeing 777 sat on the runway as I patiently waited for takeoff. I wanted to scream at how this had all gone down. I had been training comfortably in *Mandalagan** when Kaptan summoned me.

"You are the one," Kaptan had said in our mother tongue, his authoritative voice knifing through the jungle. A sudden breeze had rustled the palm leaves on the ground and swayed the coconut trees around us. "You're the one to protect the girl from *Sitan.*†"

The girl in Vegas. Dorothy.

Frustration swelled in my stomach, but refusing Kaptan was not an option. He accepted the *Danag*‡ principle of protecting mortals, which meant underlings like me had to adhere to the values inherited from Urduja, the woman warrior who preserved Danag culture by leaving Tawalisi before the Mongols attacked. She had sailed the Luson Sea for the greater good. Urduja's legendary sacrifice reminded me that I had nothing to complain about.

---

*	*Mandalagan is both a fictional and actual place in the Philippines.*
†	*Sitan is a mostly-evil figure in Filipino folklore. It is said he led mankind to evil using his four agents, but understood mankind's importance.*
‡	*Danags are referenced in Filipino folklore as beings who lived in harmony with humans in ancient times. Term #15 in Terms of Consequence.*

Kaptan's booming voice echoed in my memory. "You are the strongest. No other Timawa has defeated you in combat exercises, so this is your calling. And you know as much as I do there is only one way to get a break from missions. And you haven't *branded*[*] yet."

"My love life shouldn't matter," I murmured.

Kaptan laughed. "A Danag's love life *always* matters! It's central to one's existence! Once you brand, you'll never want to leave Mandalagan again. But until then, you're off to Vegas. Sitan is probably a step ahead of us. And Dorothy has no idea what's coming. Indeed, this may be a most important mission."

Most important was translation for *most dangerous*. There was a handful of Timawa warriors capable of taking my place, but I was still the lead warrior assigned the most important missions.

Apparently, the safety of Dorothy was important. *Dangerous*.

Within hours, I stared at the receding landscape of the coconut trees and rice fields of the Philippines as my plane ascended over the Pacific Ocean. I leaned back and tried to relax. Sitan could attack me now and I would only have my fists to defend myself. My Timawa abilities were minimized by the increased altitude, a phenomenon called *Anitun Tabu*[†] by my people in tribute to the wind goddess exerting her power over our earthly abilities.

---

[*]   *An intense, emotional and physical connection with another being in Danag culture. Terms #13 in Terms of Consequence.*

[†]   *Anitun Tabu is the wind goddess in Filipino folklore. Term #3 in Terms of Consequence.*

I settled in for the sixteen-hour direct flight, leaning my first-class leather seat back into a comfortable position. I closed my eyes, sensing the passengers on this flight were mostly tourists excited to visit family in the United States (and gamble their money away in Las Vegas). Everyone on this flight was mortal.

Except me.

Once the in-flight meal was served, I had finished my evening prayer to Allah for a successful mission and tried to push away the burn of being away from home.

CHAPTER 3: DOROTHY

بسِّمِ

I hoped no one noticed Stella's zombie-like demeanor, her Gucci sunglasses hiding the bags under her eyes. "Stellz! Can you make it more obvious we were out last night?"

"Don't worry. No one assumes you were partying on the strip. As for me, I don't care what people think."

We entered the quad of Valley High. "Can you keep your voice down? At least try to pretend you're not sleep-walking! Everyone knows we do everything together."

"Besides Tae Kwon Do and basketball," Stella replied. "And you never go to Mary K's with Eric and me."

"Fine. Quite a few exceptions. But otherwise, we're always together."

"Yup. We're attached at the hip all right."

"Don't make it obvious we were out. Okay?"

Stella ran her hand through her shiny hair and adjusted the front ruffles of her pale pink Ted Baker summer dress. "Again. Don't care what people think. And besides, it's our last month of high school! An F on a test wouldn't matter!"

Stella was right, but I didn't want her to know it. "I still need to be focused, you know?"

"No, I don't know. I think one day, you'll snap."

Like last night. My insides shifted at squeezing the man's neck. "You know I've always been a focused student. I will not let my GPA slip because of senior-itis."

"My Filipina sisters!" It was Darcy Franklin, one of my basketball teammates. She was rockin' her familiar blue Adidas jumpsuit and old-school white Adidas sneakers. She was the only girl I knew who could make such an out-dated outfit look so cool.

"Hey Darcy!" We hugged, which meant being temporarily suffocated by Darcy's chest. She was over six feet tall, our starting center on the varsity basketball team. She wrapped her long arms around our shoulders.

"Not to freak you out, little Dor, but Billy's pretending not to care you're in his line of sight," Darcy said in a low voice.

From my peripheral vision, Billy Schaedig looked our way. He had grown between his junior and senior year, his body catching up with his gangly arms and legs.

"I don't date baseball players," I replied, recognizing Darcy and Stella's give-him-a-chance look.

"Correction," Stella said. "You haven't dated anyone."

She said I was too selective, a legitimate accusation, even if I denied it all the time. My one kiss had come in seventh grade when Bobby Rivera planted one because of a stupid dare. Once our lips separated, I spit in his face and kicked him in the balls. Ever since, boys didn't approach me after seeing my martial arts abilities in the flesh. I didn't mind people knowing I kicked butt.

"I haven't found the right guy," I blurted out.

"Nor have I," Darcy said. "You know I have a thing for athletes, but there ain't any guys at this school willing to take me on."

I gave Darcy the stank eye. "OMG! Tons of guys have asked you out!"

"But not anyone I vibe with!" Darcy took out her phone. "The immature football players are childish. Hence, they are boys in my book. Not like the older guys online."

"Darcy! Be careful who you meet online!"

"Little Dor, don't be a hater. You know this girl has it locked down!" Darcy always referred to herself in the third person when she was defensive.

"Social media gets people in trouble," I said.

"Don't even," Darcy replied.

"For real." Stella was wiping her sunglasses, revealing her droopy eyes. "Guys meeting high school girls online are losers."

Darcy thumbed and scrolled her phone. "Most girls aren't like you, Stella, with the hot and gorgeous boyfriend."

Stella dated Eric Garcia who had transferred from San Diego last year. Girls had swooned over his muscular build, bronze skin and black shoulder-length hair that somehow stayed in place when he ran his hands through it. He looked like a Filipino WWE wrestler and surfer mixed together. When he asked Stella on a date, she became the envy of all the girls at Valley High.

"Like Bruno Mars says! That's what I like!" Stella exclaimed. "The real question is, what's Dorothy's type? Is it Tae Kwon Do fighters named Christian? Or tobacco-spitting baseball players like Billy?"

"Yeah, that's the real question," Darcy teased. "Who is little Dor into?"

"Guys. Stop."

"Sparring with Christian doesn't do it for you?" Stella feigned a look of shock. "His hot sweaty body isn't to your liking?"

"Christian is only a friend."

"Who went to every game to watch his favorite

point guard play ball," Darcy said. "He needs to fucking man up and ask you out!"

"Darcy! You better watch your mouth or you ain't getting the ball in the post."

"Whatever, little Dor! Your threats mean nothing anymore! Our high school basketball careers ended two months ago!" Darcy broke from us to turn towards another hallway. "Love you my *Pinay** sisters! See you laters!"

The mention of basketball made my stomach churn. I loved playing ball, but hadn't received any college offers, even with a killer crossover dribble and a lights out three-point shot. My basketball career ended the day I accepted an academic scholarship to UNLV. You would think not having to run sprints anymore would give me added energy. But I was more lethargic than ever and still skipped out on Tae Kwon Do.

I slung my backpack over my shoulder. "I'm abstaining from going out for a while. I should get back to working out."

"I feel the same, except for the working out part," Stella said. "I need sleep."

"Especially after last night," I replied. When I had almost killed someone. The mental image of the man holding my waist made me want to hit something, until my life changed with the life-altering sight that awaited me.

෴

---

*   *Slang to describe people originating from the Philippines, particularly used by fellow Filipinos and non-Filipinos involved in the community.*

We had turned the hallway corner when a piercing white light blinded me. Strange tingly sensations spread through my body. Once my eyes adjusted to the brightness, a stunning guy emerged with black and red neck tattoos spiraling in various directions beneath his The North Face shirt. His biceps strained against his golden skin. His hair was nicely combed to one side and his sculpted jaw had me staring when his eyes connected with mine. I couldn't hold his stare, turning away as if I had been looking at the sun too long. It wasn't until the guy walked off, bobbing his head to music in his earbuds, that the tingles in my arms and legs subsided.

"Are you okay?" Stella asked, incredulous.

This guy—whoever he was—had made me dizzy. When he looked at me, he seemed to take pleasure in seeing me lightheaded. If I didn't know better, I would have said that he had laughed when he walked off. As if he enjoyed seeing me suffer.

My legs were jelly, forcing me to lean on Stella for balance. "Yes. I'm fine."

Stella pulled me down the hallway towards the band room for my next class. We stopped near the entrance, my self-confidence crumbling by the second.

"You are soooo not okay," Stella said, her glamorous eyebrows raised in genuine concern.

"Who was that guy? The guy with the frickin' tattoos?"

"I have no idea." Stella's gloss-covered lips curled into the familiar smile she had when she was crushing on someone. "And from how red your face looks right now, I think that guy literally took your breath away."

Stella waved as she separated from me and backpedaled to her math class. "Cleng. I will see you at lunch. Okay?"

I nodded as a sudden chest pain had me stagger

in the band room and to my first chair position with the clarinets, my lungs feeling compressed.

As Mr. Gonzalez asked everyone to take their seats. I tried to focus on the "America the Beautiful" sheet music until I realized I had looked weak and vulnerable and hadn't even said one word to the guy.

When Mr. Gonzalez raised his arms in conductor fashion, I blew into my clarinet, shaken by the incredibly handsome stranger who had stared as if he already knew me.

CHAPTER 4: ADRIAN

ॐ॒॒॒ॐ

The truth is I didn't like Valley High, the home of the Vikings. The school's motto had me wanting to punch someone in the gut. *Ensuring a better world through academic excellence and global vision.*

The school administrators and faculty had no idea about *global vision* or how to prepare its student body for the real world. If they did have a clue, they would know my people had protected humans for centuries from Sitan and his cronies constantly on the prowl for purely evil reasons.

A part of me didn't have a high opinion of mortals, although I understood the importance of their survival. Humans had flaws; a sense of entitlement being the biggest. Of course, this was my humble opinion. Mortals had to be protected for the deities to survive, an absolute truth never to be questioned.

What I did question was the location of my next class. Room A130 was not next to Room A128 as it should be. I stood in the gap between A132 and A128, remembering what Gus had told me about Valley High. *It's a big school so don't get frustrated when you get lost.*

Gus had picked me up at McCarran airport the day before. I was reunited with my Vegas family, the family he married into and the people who had a room for me when I visited. Frank and Lilia were the patriarchs, the parents of his wife, Anna. I hadn't seen them since the birth of Abraham, Gus and Anna's son.

They had *lumpia, pancit and lechon**** ready for me when I walked in the house and they surprised me when they introduced Abby and Alana, the three-year old twin daughters. Abraham held their hands and the three kids gave me a warm hug. The last time I visited, the family had given their hearts, but would never remember the heartache they endured.

I made sure they would never remember.

We ate throughout the evening, catching up on each other's lives. I told them what they should hear about my family. My parents were close to retirement from Metrobank and my brother and sister were doing well as call service supervisors in *Bacolod*†.

For now, that's all they needed to know.

༄

In the morning, Anna had dropped me off at school. She would pick me up in the afternoon and drive me to the Ford dealership to pick up my Shelby. I couldn't wait to get my own wheels.

I was thinking of speeding the Shelby through the Nevada desert when Dorothy and Stella emerged in the hallway. I smiled when I saw how easy they were on the eyes.

Dorothy was shorter than I'd thought, barely over five feet tall. Her nicely shaped eyelids

---

*   *Popular Filipino dishes served in various styles in Filipino households.*

†   *Capital of Negros Island, Philippines.*

angled downward at each end, her excessively long eyelashes disguising the natural beauty of her brown eyes. Dorothy's round face was almost like a circle in my opinion, but adorable underneath her feathered bangs and wavy hair tied elegantly in a ponytail. Perhaps *elegantly* wasn't the right word, but the ponytail made her face naturally shine.

Dorothy's lime, drapey popover shirt and maroon wide-leg cropped pants hid her petite, athletic body and differed from Stella's burnished skin glowing underneath her pink dress. Stella soared and moved like a fashion model, her baby bouffant hairdo and curvy body making teenage boys turn when she walked by. Stella was fashionably accessorized with pink retro runner shoes and a glacier ipomoea shoulder bag, her rainbow Christian Dior bracelets fitting effortlessly on her wrist.

The luxury designer obsessed females in Mandalagan had particular tastes, but I hadn't expected Dorothy and Stella to be swept up into these luxuries at such young ages. It was a shame they had given in to societal pressure to stylize and groom, even if their golden skin were more authentic than women in the Philippines who stayed indoors to keep their skin as white as snow. The modern-day Filipina strived for porcelain skin, even if they posted social media photos of sunbathing poolside or on the beach.

Dorothy and Stella had distinct caramel-colored skin tones, just like most of the females in Mandalagan. For mortal males, Dorothy and Stella had to be mesmerizing.

A female voice snapped me back. "Are you lost?"

I looked over my shoulder. Stella and her dark, brown eyes were looking up at me. "I'm afraid I can't find Room A130," I answered.

She tucked a stray hair behind her ear. "That's the one room that isn't in sequence. It's down the hall, next to Room 154."

Students walking by were side-eyeing us. The first bell rang and the hallway began to empty. "Thank you. I should be able to find it now."

"Right down there." Stella pointed to her right. "The school changed the number my freshman year for some unknown reason. No one knows why."

"It definitely doesn't make it easy for a new student like me to find it."

"It sure wouldn't, I would imagine." Stella had raised an eyebrow, which somehow gave her high cheekbones an extra glow.

I smiled. She looked almost as physically stunning as a Mandalagan female. Almost. "Well, I better get going. See you around."

"You too." She rubbed the back of her neck, her pink dress conforming to her curvy body. "And if you don't have anyone to sit with at lunch, look for me and my boyfriend. We usually sit with the girls basketball team."

"Are you a basketball player?"

"I only wear these runner shoes for fashion reasons. I'm not an athlete, but my best friend is. You'll meet her if you sit with us."

"I appreciate you looking out, " I said. "But maybe later in the week. I have to meet with an academic counselor at lunch today."

"If you want any counselor, make sure to ask for Mr. Hopp. He's super funny and he'll get you the right classes if you aren't in them already."

"What does he look like?"

"Bi-focal glasses. Gray hair. Has a stomach. You can't miss him."

"Thanks for the tip. I'll look for him. And I'll look for you in the cafeteria one of these days."

"Sounds good, stranger."

I wanted to introduce myself, but the way her hair flipped and settled against her shoulders had distracted me. She turned and walked into room A128 just before the final bell rang. I turned away, hoping no one noticed that I had stared until she sat at her desk.

I ran like a human to Room A154, apologizing to Mr. Sims for being late. He wasn't upset, pointing at a desk near the window. I sat, ignoring the stares from my new classmates. A blonde girl snapped gum in her mouth while looking me over. I stared straight ahead, pretending not to notice.

Mr. Sims motioned towards me. "Ladies and gentlemen. Our new student is Adrian Rosario. A junior exchange student from Bacolod, Philippines. Please welcome him to Valley High."

Students blatantly stared before looking to the front of the class once Mr. Sims turned on the projector. I clasped my hands on the desk, trying to look like a legitimate FOB, or fresh-off-the-boat, Filipino teenager.

࿇

After school, Anna was waiting for me in the parking lot with Abraham, Abby and Alana sitting in the back of her Toyota Sienna minivan.

"How was your first day?" She asked as I slipped into the front seat.

"It went as expected."

She pressed on the gas and turned onto Eastern Avenue. "This is a preview of when Abraham goes here in a few years."

"I'm going to high school here?" Abraham asked.

Anna peered into the rearview mirror. "We can't afford private school, so you're going to be a Viking."

"Aw, man! I want to go Palo Verde!" Abraham whined.

"Too far from our house," Anna replied. She leaned towards me. "I didn't even know what high school was when I was his age. Kids these days are so aware."

I turned back to Abraham. "You'll like being a Viking," I said. "The girls are pretty!"

"Pretty as mom?" he asked.

"Almost," I said. "Remember. No one is prettier than your mom."

"Adrian!" Anna exclaimed. "Don't worry about pretty girls, Abe! The only girls you have to worry about are your sisters."

"Awe, man!" Abraham said with a sincere pouty face.

We had merged onto Interstate 95, the traffic stop and go. I turned up the volume of the radio station and head-nodded to the latest Drake song "In My Feelings." Abby and Alana started singing the lyrics. Abraham had his arms crossed, his pouty face receding as the rhythm of the song took over the minivan.

"Did you know Kiki is rumored to be Kim K?" Anna said.

I laughed, the sincerity in Anna's voice making me think of how lucky the kids were to have a mom so down with pop culture.

ॐ

We pulled into the Friendly Ford parking lot and within minutes, I was behind the wheel of a new silver and blue Ford Shelby. I reviewed the lease agreement to make sure my father hadn't missed anything important, like the time he forgot to include an extended warranty when I was on a mission in Paris. When I had totaled the car in the midst of evading capture from Sitan's goons, my father was not a happy camper. Forget the fact I had almost died. Why he was concerned about the bill for a totaled car we could easily afford was beyond me.

As I looked at each line item on the paperwork, Anna drove off to pick up outdoor patio chairs for the family barbecue they had planned. For some reason, the chairs were only in stock at the Target on Rainbow Boulevard. I couldn't convince her to let Abraham ride with me. She made it clear she didn't trust me behind the wheel of a sports car.

Finished with the paperwork, I sped away from the dealership ready to rock 'n roll, the Vegas traffic lights forcing me to test the vehicle's braking system with sudden starts and stops. Each light took an eternity to turn green. Once I made it onto the freeway, I hit ninety miles per hour, slowing when I sensed highway patrol. I merged onto Interstate 11 and exited East Desert Inn Road to get to my Vegas family's home, salivating at the promised *apritada* dinner Lilia had promised me.

Yes. I was hungry after my first day of being a high school student for the first time in decades. They knew me as a high school student, even if I hadn't physically changed since the last time I saw them. My people's influence over their perception tugged at me, but it was necessary to keep them in a happy place. Otherwise, they would panic and perhaps contact the authorities. The guilt of changing Lilia and Frank's memories of their oldest daughter's death was starting to surface, which made me even hungrier.

Long ago, Mandalagan had made a declaration to stay under the radar until human enlightenment was reached. This meant we had to use our power of persuasion. We tried not to abuse this power, but I have to admit it was tempting in certain situations.

But with Frank and Lilia, it just felt wrong.

But I reconciled this guilt knowing I was following the great Kaptan's orders. No other leader had gotten us this close to capturing our greatest enemy, Sitan.

I parked the glimmering Shelby in the driveway, convinced I was a Timawa warrior doing the right thing, hoping one day I could tell Frank, Lilia, Gus and Anna the honest truth.

CHAPTER 5: DOROTHY

بِسْمِ

The daddy-long-legs spider on the wall hadn't moved since I flopped on the couch. Once I stopped staring, the spider would escape and be gone forever. I stared and stared until the door slammed.

An out-of-breath exhale and my mom's high-pitched voice broke through the house. "Cleng, I'm home!"

Dorothy is my birth name, but mom called me *Cleng**, a nickname only a Filipino family gives a girl named Dorothy. Mom said my father had given me the nickname as a derivative of my middle name Claire, but I didn't understood how Claire became Cleng. Dorothy wasn't even close to Cleng.

"Mom, I'm in the living room!"

"Can you help me with the groceries?"

I walked in the kitchen as mom patted her forehead, her skin glowing with perspiration. "Okay, mom. I'm here."

She lifted her foot and slipped off her sandals. "No matter how long you live in Vegas, you don't get used to the dry heat. Thank God for air conditioning."

"For real." I peered into one of the grocery bags. "You feeling okay today?"

She hung her keys on the rack near the garage door. "I'm fine, *iha*†. I showed two homes to my

---

*   *It is not unusual for a son or daughter in a Filipino family to have a nickname completely different from their given name.*

†   *Term of endearment from parent to child.*

pocket clients. I'm pooped."

My mother was a finalist for Las Vegas Realtor of the Year, a nomination bestowed upon her by *My Vegas Magazine* for being in the Top 10 in home sales in the area.

"Cool."

"And how about you? How was school?"

This was the daily question that would stop in June once summer break started. "School was fine, mom."

I opened the freezer door and placed hamburger patties, frozen fries, and ube-flavored ice cream in the freezer, knowing mom would reorganize later. She had crumpled a grocery bag and reached in another, taking out string cheese, mayonnaise and a bag of tomatoes.

"That's all you've said since basketball season ended. The word *fine*."

"Mom. I know for a fact I say more than 'fine' to you. I actually said, 'school was fine.'"

"*Susmaryosep!** A total of three words! It's not like I've provided for you. A five bedroom house and wait! You drive a Mercedes! Humor your lamo momo and give details about your day. And get the big pot from the cupboard please. I'm making *diniguan†* for dinner."

"Fine," I said. She brought up the material blessings in my life whenever she thought I was acting like a spoiled brat. I was blessed, not spoiled.

---

* *A common Filipino expression to show excitement, fear, confusion. Somehow, the parents of Jesus, Mary and Joseph, became a slang term similar to "Oh my God!" in English.*

† *A filipino soup dish consisting of pig's blood and pork belly. Many Westerners are grossed out until they taste it. This author recalls the blood curdling pig squeals across from his Uncle's house in Cebu when a pig was drained of its blood the night before a party.*

Mom handed me bok choy wrapped in plastic. "Let's try again. How was school today?"

I played along. Through the years, I'd picked my battles with her very carefully. I took out the pot she asked for. "Okay. Where do I start? The lecture on Shakespeare? Or the mind-numbing graduation rehearsal?"

She handed me two cartons of orange juice. "How about both?"

"Fine. Othello is depressing, and I can't believe Miss Woods has us reading it until the end of school. What a downer."

"Mmmm hmmm," she murmured, nodding her head. She handed me a carton of almond milk.

"And why do we have to rehearse graduation? I know Stella's my partner and I pretty much know how to walk in an auditorium."

"Okay."

"And…there was this guy at school."

Mom's eyes widened. "A guy worth mentioning to me? He must be something." She crossed her arms with a smirk on her face, waiting for me to elaborate.

An ache of regret settled below my abdomen. I wished I hadn't said anything, but now I couldn't hold back from my mom. The guy's triangle-shaped jaw, his deep brown eyes, and his caramel skin adorned with Asian tattoos flashed in my mind.

"I don't even know his name, but when he looked at me, I lost it!"

Wrinkles formed at the edges of mom's eyes. "What do you mean you lost it?"

"I lost my breath and got dizzy. It took all my strength to keep standing when I first saw him. And Stella totally made fun of me!"

Mom straightened her lips. "He's Filipino?"

"From what I could see from a distance. And

why do you have that funny look?"

As if overwhelmed by a cold breeze, she crossed her arms. "It reminds me of your no-good father the first time I met him."

"Really?"

"*Sus!** It took all my strength to keep myself together when I met him at the grocery store. He kept repeating my name after I told him. Meredith. Meredith. Meredith. The way he said Meredith made me feel special." She took a breath. "If I had known he would abandon us, I would have walked away."

My mom's venting over the years made her words go through one ear, skip over my brain and exit out the other ear. There had to be other reasons my dad left. Maybe something about mom? Something about me?

"He's a missing person, not a deadbeat dad." I turned on the faucet and filled the big pot with water.

She looked back at me. "That's what the police says. But a part of me suspects he went back to the Philippines to forget about the wife and daughter in the States."

"Mom. Please. Can you get over it?"

She let out a big sigh, squirming like she was the teenage girl scolded for talking back. "Fine, but if this Filipino boy hurts you, he'll have to answer to me."

That's how it was between us: mad and angry one second, laughing and joking the next, with the sensitive topic of my father lying beneath the surface.

"Mom. I haven't even said a word to him."

"You haven't spoken to him yet? Oh, *anak*†."

---

*   A shortened version of Susmaryosep.
†   Tagalog term of endearment addressed to a son or
        daughter.

My rapid heartbeat made my breath shorten. Great. A guy I hadn't even spoken to was making me hyperventilate. And that's when mom laughed.

"Mom! What's so funny?"

"With you hardly going out, I was worried you wouldn't meet anyone!"

Except the man at the club. "Mom! You thought I wouldn't meet anyone?"

"Sorry, *anak*! It's different to see you have an actual romantic interest in a guy. They're either your Tae Kwon Do or basketball bros. And with my liver, I want to see you love someone before I die." She wrapped me in a hug.

The warmth of her arms enveloped me like a blanket, arms there for me every day of my life. "Mom, I'm not sure what to do. And please don't talk like that. Your doctors said your cancer is treatable."

She tightened her hold. "Doctors always say it's treatable. You see it on TV all the time. And the next thing you know, they're shocked when the patient dies!"

"Mom! That's on TV! Not real life!"

"Cleng. I have liver cancer. It's inevitable I'm going to die."

I wiped my eyes and broke from my mother's embrace. "You are not going to die! Just...Stop talking that way. I don't like it when you talk that way."

Mom ran her hands through her hair. "Okay, Cleng. No more talk about my untimely death."

"Mom!"

She laughed. "Back to this Filipino boy. Maybe say hello to him?"

I must have looked silly in the hallway; I promised to be stronger next time I saw him. "Say hello? Of course I can do that."

"I know you can. But let's come up with a game

plan over dinner?"

I moved the pot onto the stove. "That sounds awesome, mom."

We were preparing diniguan, a stew of pig's blood, affectionately called chocolate stew by Filipinos. We prepared the meal in a comfortable silence, the cutting and pouring of ingredients being our therapy from a long day. I turned the heat to high after filling the rice cooker with jasmine rice. Mom minced pork into small pieces. I poured thawed pig's blood in the big pot, mixing in the pork belly. The water boiled and simmered as the pig's blood, pork, garlic and onions settled together into a brown, chocolate-looking stew. The spicy sour aroma filled the air, making me salivate.

Diniguan smelled soooo damn good.

After I reminded mom to take her meds, we shared a quick prayer before I satisfied a ravenous hunger not felt since pinning the creepy man's neck against the wall the night before.

CHAPTER 6: ADRIAN

ఌఌఌ

Living among humans wasn't bad, except for having to protect a girl in Sin City. *What happens in Vegas stays in Vegas.*

The casinos easy money was impossible to access when pretending to be an eighteen-year-old kid. And since eighteen-year-olds aren't allowed to gamble in Vegas, I was out of luck. The adrenaline rush came from defeating the odds. My ability to predict the probability of things was considered a subtle intuition for my kind. But in Vegas, I could profit from the casinos and return home with something to talk about. Stupid human laws.

It wasn't about making money, the most useless invention ever created. The greenback a valuable commodity? Anyone with half a brain knew money was simply pictures and numbers printed on paper! From trees! The real commodities were platinum, gold and silver stored deep in the earth's core. But humans still hadn't realized the value of utopian wealth. Society's sense of value was strictly tied to one's annual gross income.

I didn't like babysitting in Vegas of all places. I had done too much to be a babysitter. Maybe not me per se, but my family. Didn't my great-grandmother insist we remain in the Philippines instead of branching out like Sitan? Now he was our biggest enemy. What would have happened if we followed him out of Mandalagan?

For the time-being, I was stuck in Vegas pretending to be a Filipino-American teenager in the name of protecting Dorothy from an impending

Sitan attack. I played the part of a teenager well, naturally oblivious to human authority while catching up on the latest music by Drake and Post Malone. My host family said I looked like a rapper, especially with the tattoos on my body. In America, Asian tattoos were portrayed as cosmetic novelties on TV shows. It was beyond frustrating that mortals didn't understand the true power behind the tattoo.

Unless...

It was impossible. There was no way humans would ever reach the level of enlightenment to see the world altruistically.

How sad.

Since my arrival in Vegas, the only entertainment was the girl staring in the hallway. Since she had no idea who I was, I didn't feel bad about overwhelming her. Most humans—especially females—interpreted my energy as a connection, an attraction, and perhaps even love. Dorothy was trapped in her narcissistic human perspective and simply didn't know any better. So typical. Yet I was told she was not a typical girl. I tried to remember Kaptan's words.

She will see the truth through her own eyes once she is ready.

The row of lockers shook when I slammed my locker door. As the vibration dissipated, a nervous energy resonated behind me. The girl.

ॐ

Dorothy's crooked smile disappeared as soon as we locked eyes. Based on the extra shine reflecting off her forehead, she looked like she was perspiring. She walked past me athletically in a cream side-button tunic and black ankle-length leggings, her brushed-out wavy hair bouncing with each step, her bangs now to the side. The smell of artificially flavored berries lingered in the air from her perfume.

Conscious of my strength, I ground my teeth to keep from overwhelming her. I stared at the hallway's linoleum floor, wishing I had the willpower to balance my energy. I hadn't given her enough space to perceive me without her feeling a connection. Yet she smiled at me. Didn't she? Why did she look away when I smiled at her? My influence over emotions should have affected her, but she had the strength to break free. Maybe I pulled back too much?

And that's when a staggering frustration overtook me. Humans were emotional, crying and whining over things like money and love. History had proven mortals didn't comprehend the true significance of their existence. This was true with Dorothy.

After the nightclub incident, she had somehow tapped into her ancestry that humans would consider to be a Filipino cultural connection, not able to perceive that race and ethnicity was a facade that hid our truest form. There was no doubt the truth would shock mortals into unrelenting panic. But it wasn't my place to worry over the human condition.

The only thing to worry about was the safety of Dorothy Dizon. She had nearly suffocated a guy at the club, sending signals to us in Mandalagan. I had to stay focused in case Sitan had received the same signals.

We didn't know if Sitan knew she existed, but I couldn't let my annoyance at being assigned to her distract me from my mission. I was her protector, regardless if I liked it or not.

I walked by her classroom as she opened her chemistry book. She looked back and our eyes connected. She broke our staredown when her teacher closed the door.

Her class had just started, which meant I had to hustle to make it on time to Algebra a few doors down. I got to my desk just as the bell rang, wondering how Dorothy managed to look away from me when I purposely stared at her beautiful face to control her topsy-turvy emotions.

CHAPTER 7: DOROTHY

بسم

A headache had me pressing my fingers against my temples during lunch. I didn't feel hungry, even as my stomach curdled.

I felt totally out of it.

The cheerleaders mingled near the cafeteria water fountains. The science kids huddled on the opposite side with open math books next to their food trays. The skaters and goth kids had come together somewhere in the middle. Since freshman year, I had somehow found a niche with Stella, my band friends, and of course the girls on the basketball team. Today, Darcy had ditched us to sit with girls from the team eating lunch with their boyfriends.

Stella looked at me with one eyebrow lifted higher than the other, dangling half of a peanut butter and jelly sandwich in front of me. "Hungry?"

I curled a stray hair around my index finger, staring over Stella's shoulder. "No, not really."

My appetite had decreased the last month, except for mom's diniguan. I didn't count the hunger that overtook me when the blood drained from the creepy guido's face at Tao. That was...I'm not sure what that was. Perhaps a momentary state of madness. Although the incident occurred the other night, it was quickly fading with each passing second.

The only vivid image on my mind was the beautiful guy in the hallway. His muscular build and baby face contrasted from the mysterious tattoos twisting through his neck and his arms. But beyond the obvious physical attraction, I was drawn to him by something I couldn't pinpoint. And this morning in the hallway, I had literally ran to my classroom when he looked at me. It took all my energy to find my desk with any self-dignity.

A hand waved in front of my eyes, snapping my thoughts. "Hello? Dorothy Claire Dizon? Anyone home?" Stella held a celery stick. "You need to eat something."

My response to Stella's sincere concern was grabbing the celery and taking a loud, crunchy bite. And that's when two muscular, tattoo-filled arms engulfed my line of sight to the right of Stella's uneven smile. The guy from yesterday sat a few tables over, his magnificent brown eyes glancing at me with an adorable confidence. His biceps exploded through his white Hanes t-shirt. The tattoos on his arms, a combination of unrecognizable Asian symbols, were hard to ignore as they spiraled below his neck. A lot of guys had tattoos, but not like these. A shiver shot through me that made me tremble, my heart suddenly beating double time.

"He's staring at me," I whispered to Stella and Eric through my teeth.

Stella tried to catch my gaze. "Who is?"

I pointed with my lips. "He is. Over there, but don't look!"

Stella looked over her shoulder. The tips of my ears suddenly tingled. "Stella!"

"Sorry. I couldn't help it. But I recognize everyone sitting there."

I pointed again with my lips without looking; there was no way I wanted to make eye contact with him. "Stella, over there."

"Like I said. No one I don't recognize."

The familiar faces eating lunch had me relieved until a smooth, velvety voice startled me from behind.

"Is this seat taken?"

"No, it's not taken," Stella said with an I-can't-believe-this-is-happening grin. My shoulders slumped and my arms felt heavy until a sudden flood of energy shot through me. I hid my face with my hair.

"Hello everyone." The sound of his voice made me clench my fists. Another jolt of energy made my stomach roll.

"Hello," I mumbled. I rubbed my sweaty hands in an attempt to dry them, but it had the opposite effect—they became more clammy and wet.

Stella curled loose hair behind her ear. "I'm Stella and this is Eric. And you are?"

"Adrian. Adrian Rosario."

Eric reached out his hand. "Nice to meet you, bro. You're new. Right?"

"Yeah," Adrian replied, his voice smoother than before. "Looks like I'm finishing high school here."

My hands trembled, my mouth dry as a desert.

"A late-year transfer?" Eric asked suspiciously.

"I'm a junior, so I have a few days to see the school I'm attending my senior year. You are undoubtedly Stella's boyfriend?"

"Yeah, I guess I am." Eric patted Stella's thigh. "She's a keeper."

Stella rolled her eyes and playfully punched Eric in the shoulder. She responded in a high-pitched tone. "You're lucky I keep you around!"

The exchange made me laugh, which turned out to be a mistake. Everyone looked at me when I laughed.

Stella gave me a soft kick under the table. "And this is—"

"Dorothy," Adrian interrupted, his voice inflecting downwind. "Nice to meet you, Cleng."

An immediate awkward silence gave me time to realize he'd used my nickname. Cleng. No one called me Cleng except my mom, Stella and Tita Yasmin. How did he know my nickname?

"Nice…to…meet you," Stella said slowly, her eyes darting between me and Adrian. "She says…she says nice to meet you."

Since Adrian sat to my left, I didn't have to look directly at him. I looked straight ahead without making eye contact. I wanted to say, "Nice to meet you," or, "A pleasure to make your acquaintance," something that sounded casual and proper, but instead, my mouth had stopped producing saliva which prevented me from saying a word.

Inexplicably, my stomach gurgled. The sound of my stomach slowly dissipated into another awkward silence. I crossed my arms, embarrassed by my body's incredulous timing.

"Dorothy's tired," Stella said, trying to cover for me. "And not herself lately."

"This time of year can especially be stressful for the valedictorian of the class," Adrian said.

Heat rose to my face and chills shook my upper body until an intoxicating scent flooded my senses. "Coco—" I sniffed to make sure my senses weren't betraying me. Unable to restrain myself, I sniffed towards Adrian's neck. "You smell like coconut." Somehow, my nose was inches away from the side of his throat.

Did I just sniff him?

Adrian rubbed his neck. "Is my cologne that noticeable?"

OMG! I did sniff his neck! Like a dog!

I curled strays of hair behind my ears. "Yes, I can smell it," I said to Stella and Eric. "Can you?"

Stella shifted towards Eric. "Nope. Don't smell a thing except the chicken nuggets on my tray." She tugged Eric's arm and stood up. "Adrian. It was nice to meet you. Gotta get ready for class, but we should hang out soon."

"Hold on," Eric said to Stella in a low voice. "Are we leaving Cleng alone with this guy?"

"She'll be fine," Stellas insisted. She gave me a funny look before pulling Eric from the table. No frickin' way was she about to leave me alone with Adrian, but she was already a few feet away. She turned back and gestured for me to calm down before walking out of the cafeteria.

Stellz! I'm gonna kill you!

Darcy glanced at me from her table and mouthed, "What the fuck?" as other teammates looked over. They were no doubt wondering why this attractive guy was socializing with me.

"I'm sorry. But did you say I smell like coconut?" Adrian asked.

"Ummm…yes. Your coconut. It smells good."

Adrian tilted his head, looking like a gentleman in a suburban hip hop sort of way. "Excuse me?"

"You smell good. Your coconut cologne smells good."

"Thank you." He looked like he was trying not to laugh. "Thank you for liking the smell of my coconut."

After he said the word coconut, I panicked inside, wanting to clarify that I didn't like *his* coconut, which insinuated much more, even if my nerves told a different story. "Oh shit. That's not what I meant. I meant your smell. It's a good smell."

"Dorothy, thank you for clarifying." Adrian looked at me sideways, his eyes a distinct hue between almond and dark chocolate. He responded in an even tone, the words rolling off his tongue like the clearest water running downstream.

"You're welcome, Adrian," I replied, wondering

if he had a nickname.

"Stella's boyfriend is protective of you," Adrian said.

"He's like that with all of Stella's friends," I lied. The truth is Eric always flirted with me, but never crossed the line. I made sure of that. When I told Stella he had held his hand against the small of my back one time in the hallway, she wasn't upset. She said she accepted that he was a natural flirt. I had agreed to tell her if he ever did anything to make me feel uncomfortable. Luckily, I hadn't had to talk to her about her flirty boyfriend getting too close.

"Seems like a swell guy."

"He takes care of Stella. And she's completely into him. They're a match made in heaven."

"If you say so," Adrian replied before he tilted his bottled water to take a sip.

"What do your tattoos mean?" I asked. One of his tattoos twisted into his shirt from his lower neck with one symbol having intricate curves that looked like a heart.

"Which one?"

"The one that looks like an upside-down heart."

"This one?" He pointed to it. "It represents the sound *Ba*." He pointed to the wavy symbol. "This sounds like *Ta*." He pointed at the last one. "And this sounds like *La*. In English, it spells *Bathala**."

ᜊᜆᜎ

The shrill of the school bell broke through the air. Voices murmured and food trays slammed against metal containers around us. A strong pull of gravity kept me from standing up.

Adrian squinted. "What class do you have next?"

A sweet scent of coconut lingered around us. Hell yeah. He definitely smelled like coconut. "I have science after lunch."

With the full intention of walking away, I picked up my tray and moved my feet underneath the table. I fell backwards, sending my food tray flying. I was ready to absorb my fall with my butt, just as I had learned from years of basketball training, but a strong hand held me parallel to the floor while catching the tray in mid-air. I was jolted upright, the tray back in my hands.

Adrian chuckled. "Don't lose your balance." His laughter evaporated as he gently let go of me.

"Thanks," I said, my mind spinning. "You have frickin' quick reflexes!"

Adrian smiled as he backpedaled. "It was nothing."

"That was incredible. That had to be a half-second reaction at the most."

"Like you said, frickin' quick reflexes." He waved as he slid through the cafeteria door, not giving me a chance to reply.

My mind slowly regained its balance as Miss Watson, a food server, lifted one bushy eyebrow at me. She snatched the tray out of my hand when the second bell rang.

Shit. Late for science class.

I ran out of the cafeteria, the swirling motion in my head gradually replaced by a skittish feeling that forced me to take deeper breaths. I sprinted like

I did in basketball practices, thankful I had decided to wear leggings instead of the black Luluemons play off the pleats skirt I had deliberated over wearing this morning.

Mr. Cotton's voice echoed from the half-open door to his classroom, the beginning of a lecture on the functional mysteries of the human appendix. Oh great. Why would anyone lecture about the useless appendix? It was science not biology.

I stopped a few steps from the door, ran my hands through my hair and adjusted the buttons of my cream tunic. I walked into class, hoping everyone assumed I was apathetic as ever, even if Adrian's glorious, bronze face floated in my mind.

CHAPTER 8: ADRIAN

ꦏꦭꦏ

Kenneth's laughter had me smoldering. "How are you, brother?"

"Shut up, *kuya**."

My brother was having a good old time at my expense. I punched the empty air wishing Kenneth's face was within arms' length.

"Easy there, kiddo," Kenneth said, his laughter dissipating. "You would do the same thing if I were in your place."

If the roles were reversed, I would be more diplomatic, more understanding. Definitely empathetic. "Kenneth, you'd be frustrated if you were babysitting, just…like…me. We both know Kaptan would never send you to protect a human girl from Sitan."

"Never predict the future. Live in the moment like me! I sit comfortably in Mandalagan as you mope in Vegas wishing you were back home. Now that's real."

"Don't remind me."

Kenneth laughed. "You punched the air like a madman!"

"Okay, okay. You've had your fun. What's so important that you had to contact me?"

"Kaptan wanted to see how things were going."

That was it. Kaptan couldn't tap into my thoughts. He had Kenneth—my one *kindred*†—

| * | A term of endearment that means "older brother." |
| † | Describes Adrian's special connection with Kenneth. |

check in with me.

"Is he worried?"

"The girl is important. He's worried Sitan is closer than we know."

"I've been lectured on the importance of this girl." Kaptan had spent hours with me discussing how she might have the abilities of an Urduja descendant. In a way, I knew her better than I should. "So far it's more exciting than the last Mandalagan Council. Can't you tell?"

"I can tell you're enjoying yourself."

Dorothy's round face popped in my mind, her light brown eyes and artificially brown streaks meshed with her wavy hair that complemented her golden skin. Today in the cafeteria, she looked feeble, insecure and unable to speak. She was overwhelmed by my presence. Again.

"There are entertaining moments," I said before realizing I had *drifted*[*], giving Kenneth the chance to see my thoughts.

Kenneth's crackly voice rose. "Too late! Now I know what she looks like. And based on what I see, she must intrigue you!"

She did not intrigue me. She amused me, especially when she looked confused the first time she saw me. "She's...entertaining. But if you're implying anything more, you know it's impossible for me to brand with her."

Kenneth snorted on the other end. "Yes, I

*

(cont from page 41) Within Adrian and Kenneth's Danag culture, each being has five kindreds in a lifetime.

Term #17 in Terms of Consequence. Only kindreds can visually "drift" into each other's thoughts in Adrian and Kenneth's Danag culture.

42

know. Such things are impossible." He agreed with me, which meant he thought I was wrong. I hated my brother's damn reverse psychology.

"You still think the teachings aren't true?" I asked.

"The teachings never state it's impossible to brand with royalty."

"But it doesn't say it can happen."

Kenneth sighed. "It's a matter of interpretation."

We'd always disagreed, ever since we were kids. No matter the topic, Kenneth was the devil's advocate. Somehow, our bipolar opinions bonded us as lifelong kindreds. It was explained to us that we balanced each other, allowing all sides of a situation to be considered. Yin. Yang.

"Can we drop the subject? The fact I haven't branded is not worth the time at the moment."

"I agree. Your love life is truly sad. How is her friend, Stella?"

"There's a distinct difference between her and Stella."

"How so?"

"I can tell Dorothy is a descendant of Bathala, while Stella's only worry is to look gorgeous to keep her boyfriend from looking at other girls."

"Sounds like Stella is in a bad relationship and oblivious to her best friend's potential. Are you sure Dorothy isn't aware?"

"She interprets her intuitions as human."

"Such as?" The doubt in my brother's voice was obvious.

"Besides defending herself at a nightclub?"

"Yes, besides that."

"*Kuya*. She smelled me."

"She smelled you?"

"Yes, she smelled me."

"She smelled your scent?"

"I was caught off guard when she said I smelled like coconuts."

"If she can smell you now, imagine what she'll be like down the road. I'm glad Kaptan sent his most trusted Timawa to babysit."

The tone of Kenneth's voice emoted sincerity. My brother was a pain in the ass most of the time, but he was my kindred, someone I'd die for without a second thought. "Tell sister, mother and father I miss them."

"I will. Call me soon, brother. And remember, it's not impossible."

"I'll believe it when I feel it."

The odds of branding with Mandalagan royalty was like finding a tiny needle in the middle of a rocky haystack. It would never happen. I was a mere Timawa warrior sent to protect Bathala's bloodline, not mate with it.

"You think I'm crazy," Kenneth insisted. "But you'll see."

"No use debating over something inconsequential."

Kenneth chuckled. "Inconsequential? Far from it. Let's resume this conversation another time. Shall we?"

Kenneth knew his laugh bothered me, but that's why he ended our communication with his laughter dissolving on the other end. What were brothers for?

I folded my arms above my head and stared at the ceiling. Yes. Dorothy was attractive with her flat nose and shiny cheeks, her eyes slanted downward at each end. She moved effortlessly, which made her pleasant to stare at when she walked. She was athletically fit, accentuating her curvy figure. But no, I didn't think of her sexually. She was an attractive girl who had smelled me, an instinct attributed to her potential. She was simply an attractive mortal girl I would never brand with.

As if to remind myself of this reality, I opened my drawer and took out the Holy Bible, turning to the important Leviticus passage Danags memorized, a subtle reference to our ancestors and how we became a secret society, and why Dorothy Dizon had to be protected.

Leviticus 17:11[*]

For the life of the flesh [is] in the blood:
and I have given it to you upon the altar
to make an atonement for your souls:
for it [is] the blood [that] maketh
an atonement for the soul.

Atonement.[†] Frustration surfaced inside me at the misuse of the word in modern times. My people knew the true meaning. Yet humans would never understand that this passage was an obscure mention of the Danag people, feared and admired by Spanish conquistadors for God-like abilities centuries ago. *For the life of the flesh is in the blood,* I repeated. *For it is the blood that maketh an atonement for the soul.*

Blood.

My people held the truth about world history and protected this truth with charades of lies and

---

[*]   *The third book of the Pentateuch, Old Testament of the Holy Bible.*

[†]   **Atonement** *has theological meaning that's been lost in modern-day usage.*

misconception because, as Kaptan reminded me, humans had to evolve naturally. If they reached *enlightenment*, they would embrace our abilities and traditions, not imprison or kill us, and perhaps help fight our biggest enemy, Sitan.

Until this day arrived, we lived secretly in Mandalagan, saving mortals from Sitan's evil and selfish motivations. We were like secret ninjas who protected mortals around the world.

But humans would remain oblivious until they were ready. I prayed to Allah for Dorothy's safety, hoping she was the one the great warrior Urduja yearned for centuries ago.

---

*   *Many variations of this word used throughout history. In this novel, Enlightenment refers to the state of consciousness that allows a being to see a world hidden from human view.*

CHAPTER 9: DOROTHY

ﺑﺴﻢ

My high school days were counting down like a rocket about to blast off into space and the unknown, affectionately known as *the future*. To live in the moment, I stayed busy to not think about life after high school.

My last exams were over, but the monotonous Othello discussions in English class endured. Miss Wood's voice warped into background noise as she recited her favorite Shakespearean lines as if trying to prove her obsession with Shakespeare was a normal thing. Miss Woods enthusiastically recited the famous Act V line.

> *I kissed thee ere I killed thee, no way but this.*
> *Killing myself, to die upon a kiss.*

It was ridiculous to believe a kiss mattered when someone you loved had just died! And you were the killer! Shakespeare's fabrication of the kiss had me happy to hand in my last extra credit assignment of my high school academic life; a sarcastic eight-pager about the stupidity of Othello's possessive love over Desdemona and how jealousy was the root of all evil.

After school, Stella and I went to Fashion Show Mall to look for graduation outfits. It took over two hours until Stella yelped with joy at finding a Lulu's enlightened blush sleeveless midi-dress she couldn't live without. I ultimately decided on a glacier Rebecca Taylor stretch knit fit & flare dress that complemented my caramel skin tone when I looked at myself in the dressing room mirror. Stella and I agreed on Gucci espadrille sandal wedges that matched the color of our dresses, my foot size noticeably smaller.

We were more than pleased that our fashion choices fell below the budget our mothers had given us. We didn't have any financial guilt eating sashimi at Kona Grill and having boba at Kung Fu Tea, our conversations focused mostly on Adrian and Eric's obvious dislike for him.

"I had to calm him down after we left the cafeteria!" Stella exclaimed after dabbing her salmon sashimi in soy sauce. "He didn't want to leave you. Which led to an argument over whether or not you could handle being with a guy like Adrian."

"What am I? A child? And why did you leave me?"

"Because! You were *obviously* into him. And you *obviously* needed to find out if you could hold a conversation. I've never seen you so nervous!"

I swallowed tuna sashimi, savoring the wasabi heat percolating in my throat. "Oh my God, Stellz! I was about to kill you!"

"But you had time alone with him."

"Only to almost trip over myself. I swear he was laughing the whole time!"

Stella swiped her eye-skimming bangs from her face. "Cleng. He came over to our table to talk to you. I'm sure he was happy to have you all to himself."

"And I'm sure I made a great impression."

"Come on! This hot guy made an *obvious* attempt to hang out with you! Your social status just blew up! If you had any social media accounts, you would have a million likes! *Everyone* was staring!"

I had been shocked myself, not only at the fact he had talked to me, but at my heart's rapid palpitations throughout our conversation in the cafeteria.

⊱

After I dropped off Stella, I found mom napping in her room, giving me quiet time to focus on my last monumental high school task left to worry about— my yet-to-be-written valedictorian speech.

But three to four hours sleep a night did not help me stay focused. Any food ended up in the toilet, except for diniguan—somehow that settled in my stomach. Plus, my period hadn't arrived in weeks! I'm irregular, but this was extreme. Nausea accompanied the approach of aunt flow, so it should have arrived by now. But instead of working on my speech, I was rolled up like a ball on my bed dealing with shitty abdominal pains throughout the night.

⊱

The next morning, I somehow made it to school and hid myself in the library to write the greatest valedictorian speech ever written, except I couldn't even get it started. When I started a sentence, it was soon deleted.

I stared at my laptop, frustrated by my lack of creativity. To be remembered forever, this speech had to be organized, concise and heartfelt, but everything I wrote sounded cheesy and clichéd. I closed my eyes and fought off an incoming wave of nausea.

This frickin' speech shouldn't be this hard.

Random thoughts flooded my mind that ran the gamut of the books I'd read, my basketball games and the good times with Stella. I second-guessed my decisions to decline junior and senior prom invitations, but attending prom with boys who wanted to get lucky wasn't my idea of a good time. But I should have gone, especially when Stella offered to double date.

I definitely should have attended when my basketball sisters decided to go as a group! But I cited my mom's health as a reason to stay home. She had been diagnosed with liver cancer that week. Although she dismissed the diagnosis like it wasn't a big deal, I wanted to be with her to make sure she was okay.

A trace of regret settled inside me as I stared at my laptop, trying to find some sort of inspiration. I took out a copy of Othello, hoping Shakespeare's brilliance would stimulate eloquent prose for my speech. But reading Shakespeare made me sleepy until the most sanguine voice I'd ever known made me turn.

ය

"Hey, Dorothy. Do you mind if I sit with you?" Adrian's voice made me look up at his impeccable smile, my stomach churning with sudden turbulence.

"No," I somehow answered. "I don't mind."

Adrian sat and placed his backpack at his feet. His coconut cologne made me dizzy. It smelled exquisite, as exotic as the sound of his voice. I shifted in my seat, knowing Stella wasn't here to kick me underneath the table this time.

Adrian leaned forward. "What are you working on?"

Anxious energy had me close to gagging until air broke down my throat. In an instant, my pinched lungs felt weightless. I could breathe. Surprised at my body's sudden temperature change, I noticed Adrian's polo shirt fit effortlessly on his muscular upper body.

"My valedictorian speech. I can't put my thoughts together."

Adrian pointed at my laptop, tattoos on his arm weaving and curving into his shoulder. "You're having writer's block."

"Something like that."

"Maybe I can help."

I wondered why he would offer his assistance. I had yet to hold a non-stuttering conversation with him. "I can't even get it started."

"Since you're stuck, I have a question."

"Sure," I replied, the conviction in my voice equal to that of a fifth grader.

"How did you feel being named valedictorian?"

I slid loose hair from my forehead and looked away. The word valedictorian made me feel embarrassed. "The one thing I remember is Stella's hug after it was announced over the P.A."

"Stella." Adrian smiled. "How long have you been friends?"

"Since forever. I couldn't imagine life without her." Thoughts of Stella flooded my mind like a mirage. The late-night talks on the phone. The sleepovers where we discussed our mothers and how coincidental it was that both of our dads had disappeared.

"Is that what you'll remember about this time in your life? You and Stella?"

"Besides basketball and all the books I've read?"

"Yes," he said with a grin. "Besides Shakespeare and all the English classics you love."

I had Othello next to my laptop; he assumed I loved Shakespeare. But I read all kinds of books with my favorites ranging from *Huckleberry Finn* to *US Weekly*. Sure, I liked to read, but didn't love it. I read to take a break from basketball or homework.

"I'll remember we've been there for each other. I'm convinced Stella and I are at the beginning of a great friendship that will be remembered years after we're gone. I feel we'll rely on each other at every bend in the road."

Adrian's dimples ignited the surface of his bronze skin. "The way you talk is poetic. I think your speech will be fine. And did you say you love basketball?"

Blood rushed to my face, the blessing of extra melanin hopefully covering up my reaction. "I was the varsity starting point guard the last two years."

"For real?"

"Yup." I mimicked shooting a basketball with my solid follow-through motion. Elbow in, my palm raised and my fingers in the air. "Don't let my size fool you. No one can steal it from me and I'm a killer outside shooter."

"Damn. I had no idea. You must be fast."

"I'm not the fastest, but I know how to create space and I have excellent court vision. Ask Darcy Johnson, our starting center. She had at least ten points a game from my dimes in the paint. She credits her scholarship to Loyola Marymount to my effective guard play."

Adrian still had a surprised look on his face. "You drive to the basket at your size?"

"Heck yeah! Getting in the paint is my forte. Darcy sets the high pick and I dribble through it. She rolls to the post or pops to the three point line. I drive to the rack or dime it back to her. Bam! Buckets all day baby! Defenses knew what was coming, but couldn't stop it."

Adrian craned his neck. "What the heck? I wouldn't know you played ball if you didn't tell me. You got real basketball swagger!"

"I sure do, thank you."

"*Waysaypayan*," he answered in *Visayan**, the native language of my mother, meaning: you're welcome.

"You speak Visaya?"

"I'm fluent. My family is from the Visayan region of the Philippines."

"So is mine. My mom wants me to go this summer to visit. I've never been there."

His eyebrows perked up. "Sounds like you're not excited to go."

The Philippines was a third-world country and, according to my mother, the land my father chose over us. No. The thought of going to the Philippines did not excite me, especially with my mother being sick. I didn't want her to travel in her condition. "I'm not sure I can handle being eaten up by mosquitoes and having little lizards stare at me while I sleep."

Adrian moved his hands from his chin, as if the Philippines triggered an old memory. "Those geckos add to the beauty there. You'll love the people, so willing to make you happy. Most families are trying to feed their children more than a meal a day. Poor families live in bamboo huts with the threat of a typhoon constantly at the back of their minds. But regardless, poor people smile, even without adequate dental work. They have a belief that things will always get better."

Adrian paused, shifting in his seat before continuing with the fluidity of a seasoned storyteller. "To the trained eye, life there is anything but primitive.

---

*   *Visayan is sometimes spelled Bisayan. In this novel, we use Visayan for consistency.*

The history of the islands is fleeting, but when one remembers, it's the land of a thousand unknown tribes written out of history."

The way he spoke made my stomach knot up. "What history are you referring to?"

His eyes sparkled like stars in the sky. "Before the Spanish colonized the islands, there was a structured society in place. Timawas were warriors who protected *Tumaos**, the royalty of each tribe, made up of rajahs and their families. Timawas were raised to fight and follow the orders of rajahs."

"I've never heard of Timawas or Tumaos or the word rajah associated with anything in the Philippines," I said.

"This doesn't surprise me. The Spanish wiped out native traditions. You probably never heard the word *Uripon*† either.

"What's Uripon mean?"

"That's the Visayan word for commoners of the tribe. Timawas were above Uripons, but lived their lives serving the Tumaos."

"Filipino tribes were made up of Uripons, Timawas and Tumaos?"

"Dorothy, they weren't even called Filipinos prior to the Spanish. They were islanders later called Filipinos in tribute to *King Phillip II*‡. Before 1565,

---

*   *Tumaos are in the nobility class in the Visayan three class structure, usually blood relatives of the datu, leader of the tribe. This is a Visayan term, known as **Maginoo** in Tagalog.*

†   *Uripons are the commoners in the Visayan three class structure.*

‡   *Son of Charles V and Isabella of Portugal. Known as Philip the Prudent. King of Spain (1556-98) and King of Portugal (1581-98). The Spanish Golden Age occurred during his reign in which the arts and literature flourished.*

there were thousands of tribes on the islands. Some tribes lived in harmony while others fought over land and sea rights, even if they had Islam in common."

"Isn't the Philippines predominantly Catholic?" I asked.

Adrian's lips straightened. "This is what I meant by the island's fleeting history. Islam ruled the land, along with *Hindu*[*] and *Buddhism*[†]. By the fourteenth century, the islanders were predominantly Muslim."

I knew Filipinos to be Catholic or Iglesia Ni Cristo, not Muslim. Catholicism was my mom's sanctuary. An uncomfortable feeling ran through me. "How do you know that?"

"My family has written evidence from our ancestors. Have you heard of the *Laguna Copperplate Inscription*[‡]?"

"No, I haven't."

"It's a pre-Spanish document found in the Philippines written in *Kawi*[§], an ancient script used by the *Majapahit Empire*[¶] in the south. The Copperplate

---

	(continued from Page 54) The Philippines was named in his honor as Las Islas Filipinas.
*	*Hindu was practiced in the Majapahit Empire, overtaken by Islamic conquests in the 1400's. It's unknown how prevalent Hindu was practiced by tribes in pre-Spanish Philippines.*
†	*Buddhism heavily impacted Java and the Majahapit Empire and was well-established in China by the 14th century.*
‡	*Laguna Copperplate Inscription changed historians view on Philippines history. See Page 275.*
§	*Kawi is an ancient written language of Bali, Java and Sumatra.*
¶	*A 13th to 16th century empire in Java that controlled Bali, Madura, Malayu and Tanjungpura. Some historians argue this empire existed in modern-day Indonesia and parts of Malaysia. They expelled the Mongols from Java. It is said the spread of Islam led to the empire's demise.*

is dated 900 A.D. and describes islanders worshiping *Anito*, a spiritual term for the animals in the physical world and spirits of the afterlife. My ancestors passed on Kawi and Alibata documents through each generation. By the fourteenth century, the documents describe a Muslim life throughout the islands."

"Shouldn't you inform the Philippine authorities? This would be huge news!"

"We keep it in the family for now. But maybe one day we'll share it with the National Museum of the Philippines. The Copperplate confirmed the validity of our documents and made us realize we are true descendants of a society of Uripons, Timawas and Tumaos."

"I can't imagine the Philippines being a structured Islamic society."

"Yes, seems hard to believe. The Philippines is the one predominant Catholic country in Asia for a reason. The Spanish didn't colonize islands in the south like Indonesia or Borneo, but fortified the islands they renamed the Philippines. Islam was completely wiped out except in the southern Philippines where the mountainous terrain made it difficult to colonize."

"I've never heard about this history of the Philippines."

"Sadly, most people haven't either."

"Could I see your family's documents? Must be hard to read an ancient script."

"Very difficult to translate. That's why I have my tattoos." He pointed to his lower neck. "Remember these? I showed them to you at lunch the other day."

"Yeah, I remember."

ᜃᜒᜎᜒ

"These tattoos are *Alibata** script, the Filipino version of Kawi."

His golden neck and shoulder wasn't hard to stare at. "I've never seen tattoos like yours."

"Most people haven't, although there is a growing underground following. My tattoos connect me to my true Timawa ancestry."

"You're Timawa?"

"Yes, according to my family documents. My ancestors lived in the service of an unnamed rajah. I'll show you if you go to the Philippines this summer."

"Now I'm warming up to the idea. I have something to look forward to besides possibly finding out more about my father." My insides swarmed in a million directions. This was the first time I'd mentioned my dad to anyone besides Stella—my mom's bitter commentary didn't count.

"Ah. Your father. What do you know of him?"

"I don't know much except from what my mother tells me. And her perspective is extremely one-sided."

Adrian's face became serious. "Do you remember anything about him?"

No one had ever asked what I remembered *about* my father. Me and Stella usually talked about what

---

*   *Alibata is ancient script of the Philippines, most likely derived from Kawi in the south. This was eradicated when Spain colonized the islands. Also known as **Baybayin**.*

happened to him, not what we remembered when our dads were in our lives. There were mostly blurred memories, with his commanding voice being the only clear recollection.

A lump had formed in my throat. "His voice made me stop in my tracks, but it didn't make me afraid; it was more like I didn't want to disappoint him. He told me to stop crying once, but I'm not sure if it's real or a made-up flashback."

Adrian's eyes softened. "I can see your father being like that."

"You must think I'm crazy."

Adrian looked like he was lost in another distant thought. "Filipino fathers command respect from their children. It's a trait passed down through generations."

A surging energy made me clench my fists. "That's the one memory I really have, but it doesn't mean you know him. He's the last man to use as an example for Filipino fathers."

Adrian slumped, as if he knew he had crossed an invisible line. "No no no no…I didn't mean it that way. We're getting to know each other, and I have no right to sound like I know what you've been through. But I know you a little better now, and hopefully my perspective will help you see the world differently."

"What do you mean?"

He frowned before he answered. "What I mean is…one day you'll see things in a completely different light. When that day arrives, you can count on me."

He was being sincere, although I wasn't sure what he meant by seeing things in a completely different light. "Okaaay."

"We're still friends?"

He spoke like he knew something I didn't. "Yeah. We're friends."

Adrian picked up his backpack and stood. "I'll

stop while I'm ahead. Good luck on your speech, Dorothy."

I wanted to say, "See you later," or, "Thanks," but he had already started walking out of the library, his coconut cologne trailing him. Once he turned the corner, I stared at my laptop and closed and re-opened my eyes.

Family. Friendship. The Future.

One hour later, my valedictorian speech was complete, with revisions to get to later. By finishing earlier than expected, I considered attending Tae Kwon Do. A sharp pain jabbed my ribs, making me more determined not to let cramps prevent me from working out for the first time in months.

ᔑ

I had made it to the dojo right before class started, but my head was swirling twenty minutes into the workout.

"What's with you?" Christian asked, my usual sparring partner. "No velocity in your kicks. You're not following through at all."

"It's one of those days," I panted.

Christian swiped his spiky black hair. "Come on, Dorothy. Bring it!"

I extended my leg for a double front kick combination, but stopped in mid-motion. "I'm not feeling it today. Taking a break."

Christian shook his head and wrapped his arm around my shoulder. It was easy for him, being nearly a foot taller than me. "Don't sweat it. You're just a girl anyway."

I knew he was kidding. "The same girl who got my red belt on the first try. Unlike you."

"You'll never let me live that down." Christian playfully pushed me before retreating towards the punching bags on the other side of the dojo. "But I'm the black belt now and you aren't."

I gave him the finger before reaching for my duffel bag to wipe my face with a towel. The red belt around my waist was a reminder of how I hadn't progressed in Tae Kwon Do in the last two years. Other students punched and kicked around me as I ignored Christian's goofy smile.

My thoughts moved randomly between Adrian, my mother and my upcoming freshman year at UNLV. Soon, I would be a Valley High graduate and starting college. College! I tried to stay calm as my phone vibrated in my duffel bag. The caller ID flashed Stella's name, vibrating a second and third time.

I held the phone to my ear. "Hey, Stellz."

"What up, Cleng. Are you busy?"

"Of course. You know all about my celebrity life at the dojo."

"I should have known you were at the smelly dojo."

"Better than sitting at home wasting time on Facebook."

Stella laughed. "And since when did you get a Facebook account?"

For most of my life, social media was too exhausting. But now, maybe it wasn't such a horrible idea. My entire social life consisted of martial arts classes, basketball camps and living vicariously through Stella. "Haven't clicked on the register link yet, but I've been thinking about opening an account lately. Snapchat and Instagram too."

"About time. But to warn you, I have a lot

of Snapchat friends. Even more on Instagram and Tumblr. And only old people use Facebook."

I laughed. "And yes, I know. I need to listen to you, especially since Zac liked your IG selfie. I am soooo jelly of your social media status."

"Can you believe I have a thousand new followers since last month!"

"What does Eric think about Mr. Efron following you?"

Stella laughed. "He says if Zac's into me, then Vanessa *will* be into him!"

"That's too funny. Even if Vanessa doesn't know he exists."

"If Vanessa Hudgens does follows him, you know it's on! I still hate her for having dated Zac for over three years!"

When it came to actor Vanessa Hudgens, Stella held the *crab mentality** prevalent in the Filipino community. Whenever a Filipino rose to the top, other Filipinos trash-talked and pulled them under like crabs in a water tank.

But Stella had light brown highlights amidst her shiny, black hair, an hourglass figure, legs that shone, and looked absolutely killer in stilettos. Stella gave Vanessa Hudgens a run for her money.

"I know you didn't call to hate on your favorite Pinay celeb. What's up?"

"The bonfire is what's up! And you're totally going with me and Eric."

---

*   *Crab mentality is also noted as an issue across various cultural communities. Filipino crab mentality has been prevalent for centuries due to jealousy and envy. It is an ongoing joke in the Filipino community. As they say, every joke has some truth to it.*

Ah, the infamous Lake Las Vegas bonfires. Sandra Emerson, a varsity cheerleader, had a super-rich family who owned a mansion at Lake Las Vegas, a private resort village about twenty miles outside the strip. She threw parties at the mansion every few months when her parents were out of town on business. Sandra had become famous in school for her cheer-leading abilities and her off-the-hook parties.

"I've never gone. Why should I go now?"

"Because your special friend Adrian will be there!"

"You're kidding."

Stella responded enthusiastically, like she'd been holding in this part of the conversation for too long. "I found his Twitter profile and messaged him on how he liked our school. He DMed back that he thought the school was boring. I told him of course school was boring, but to check out the bonfire tonight. So like…he asked if you were going. Of course, you aren't supposed to know he actually asked about you! When you see him, don't tell him I spilled everything!"

"Stellz!"

"You have to go! Adrian will be there and you can take a walk around the lake with him."

Taking a walk around the lake was code word for leaving the party to make out. It was physically impossible to actually walk around Lake Las Vegas in one night since it spanned 320 acres of developed land. Stella had told me about the first time Eric took her around the lake, the first time they kissed.

"You are such an instigator!"

"I can't believe Adrian didn't ask you directly," Stella continued in a half-kidding tone. "Don't you guys talk like every day now?"

"Hardly. I held down one conversation with him in the library earlier today."

"You talked to him without fainting? What a day it's been for you!"

"Stellz. I should probably stay home tonight. My mom might need me if the meds don't help her sleep. And she's been talking about death lately like she's already a goner. She's frustrating sometimes!"

"Of course, I knew you might say that. I talked to my mom and she said she'll go to your house to hang out with Tita Meredith."

"That's sweet of Tita Yasmin."

"Us De Guzman women are super sweet. You know that!"

"I don't know what to say."

"Say you'll go."

"Okay. I guess I can't refuse."

"Will do." Stella paused before continuing. "And Cleng?"

"Yeah Stellz?"

"Does Adrian know you can literally kick his ass?"

"No, I haven't told him about Tae Kwon Do."

"Do not tell him. You'll scare him off. Wait until he's your boyfriend."

"Oh my God. Just pick me up by eight-thirty. Okay?"

෫

My side throbbed with waves of pain until I arrived home. I tried to focus on an outfit for tonight's party, but my itchy skin looked dry, especially my cheeks and forehead. My cheekbones didn't shine like Stella's, except of course when my sweat glands excreted moisture around my armpits and forehead (which it did after basketball and martial arts workouts). It was some sort of genetic defect blamed on the person who couldn't defend himself—my father.

Two outfits from my closet looked the cutest: a purple halter top with blue jeans and a white long-sleeved camisole with a beige skirt. After sizing myself up in the mirror, my arms looked big in a halter top and a skirt looked too hoochie for a bonfire. I decided on my favorite beige ventana short-sleeved camisole and black pima cotton manta yoke skirt, an outfit that didn't reveal my physical imperfections.

With my outfit determined and my stomach somewhat settled, I helped my mom cook *apritada*[*] while she was on the phone with her brother in the Philippines speaking Visayan at a hundred miles per hour. The ebb and flow of the native language felt soothing, even if it was hard for me to understand. I heard her say "cancer" multiple times, yet still sounding cheery. She didn't want to worry her brother and said so right before she hung up the phone.

I considered ditching the bonfire, thinking it was a bad idea to be away from mom, but before I could change my mind, Stella had pulled up to the front of the house with Tita Yasmin. I helped with the grocery bags as Tita hugged my mom.

"We're having a girls night in like the old days!" Tita Yasmin proclaimed.

"Yasmin, you *buang*![†] We're too old to be acting like teenagers!"

Tita Yasmin revealed a bottle of white wine. "And of course we'll have drinks!"

I tried to grab the bottle, but Tita Yasmin had

---

[*]   *Term #6 in Terms of Consequence. A favorite dish of many Filipino families, including mine!*
[†]   *A Visayan term translated into English as "crazy".*

already moved to the other side of the kitchen island. I turned to mom. "The doctor said no alcohol."

"Okay, *iha**!" She answered with a wide grin before giggling with Tita Yasmin.

Stella tugged on my arm. "Let's go, Cleng. Your mom is a grown woman. And you know my mother will take care of her."

I waved bye to mom while gesturing for her *not* to have a glass of wine. She waved back holding up the wine bottle as I retreated to the front door. "Bye! Have fun! Say hi to all the boys at your party!"

"Mom!" I yelled. "No alcohol!"

By the time I squeezed in the backseat of Eric's Honda Civic, I had already texted mom twice to follow doctor's orders. Throughout the ride, Stella and Eric told me to stop worrying, even as I texted mom three more times not to drink.

༄

Stella played Julie Plug's "Devoted," one of my favorite 90's alternative songs, in a blatant attempt to calm me down with the song's dreamy chords. After the song ended, Stella turned up the bass on Pinay's "Is It Real," egging me on to sing with her.

It frickin' worked. I was harmonizing the chorus by the time we merged onto the freeway.

Luckily, highway patrol was nowhere to be seen, which was always the case when Eric drove. As long as

---

*   *A common Filipino term of endearment used parent-to-child.*

I had known him, Eric drove like a madman and never got pulled over. He said he was dope like that, but us girls chalked it up to pure luck.

As the burnt-orange sky canvas became the backdrop for the setting sun and rising moon, Eric turned left onto Lake Las Vegas Parkway and made a right onto Grand Mediterra Boulevard. We approached a driveway crowded with parked cars in front of a Spanish style mansion.

"Are you sure there's enough parking Eric? Looks completely full."

"Trust me, there's more than enough parking on this property."

We drove past the black iron gate and curved left alongside the house into a yard as big as half a football field overlooking Lake Las Vegas, the growing moonlight shimmering off the calm waters.

"This is their backyard?" I asked.

Stella pulled my arm as Eric raised the parking brake. "It's disgustingly beautiful isn't it? Sandra is so set for life."

Teenagers congregated at picnic tables next to a flickering fire. Another group stood on the rear porch of the mansion holding red plastic cups in their hands. Club music thumped from inside the house with the familiar melody of "Back To You" by Selena Gomez kicking in.

Stella looped my arm through hers and pointed towards the house. "Cleng. With this being your first real party outside of your basketball banquets, don't get drunk and jump off the balcony. Okay?"

"You know the smell of alcohol makes me gag," I replied. "I'll try not to jump off the balcony. Sober."

"I know you too well." Stella laughed.

We approached the bonfire, the crackle of twigs and the smell of burnt wood filling the space around us. Eric handed us two cans of Sprite from an open cooler near the picnic table. "Here's to the fresh taste of lemon-lime. Especially for you, Dorothy."

"Thanks!" I pulled the tab and took a sip.

Eric smiled before acknowledging the baseball players who held up beer cans in his direction, motioning him to join them.

"Be back," he murmured. "Don't get too crazy, kids."

"More like you! Don't drink too much!" Stella said.

Eric nodded and retreated towards the house.

"Why does it feel like we're the parents?" I said. It wasn't a question.

"Because." Stella pulled me to the picnic table. "We know better, as always." She popped off the top of a Seabreeze wine cooler and laughed.

"We are obviously too smart for anyone to listen to," I said.

"Obviously!" Stella started to dance when Michael Jackson's "Billie Jean" started up from the house.

Her dancing predictably attracted a group of guys wearing baseball caps, t-shirts celebrating their favorite sports teams and khaki shorts. They were from Centennial High in Summerlin and were obviously mesmerized by Stella dressed in a pima cotton blend tank and a ponte scallop hem skirt. Stella had dressed down from her usual couture self, yet still rocked her outfit better than a Kardashian. Each guy took turns complimenting her on how she moved.

When Stella told them I was a star basketball player and valedictorian of Valley High, one of the guys challenged me to a game of one-on-one basketball before he fell on his ass imitating a crossover dribble. After getting clowned by his friends, their female friends joined in their drinking games until Taylor Swift's "Gorgeous" made the girls yell and go in the house to dance. The guys continued to chug drinks at each other's urging, making me wonder how long they could go before they puked.

With more alcohol in their systems, the guys blatantly flirted with us. One guy tried to hold Stella's arm, but she effortlessly got out of it by circling her hand away from his. When their female friends returned, we politely left, a reminder to never have our guard down around drunk guys.

We walked in and out of the crowded house, waving marijuana clouds from our face. We finally found Eric dry-heaving by the kitchen.

"Eric! How many drinks did you have!" Stella scolded.

"I don't know," he answered. "I lost count! Can you just chill!"

They were quickly in an argument on their search for a bathroom. I went outside where my small frame wouldn't get swallowed up by the crowd. Teenagers walked by me at the perimeter of the bonfire. The guys from Centennial had paired off with random girls in the backyard.

There was literally no one at this party to hang out with besides Stella and Eric. Darcy had ditched, but she wasn't into partying since basketball was her life. She was probably at home breaking down game film in preparation for college summer ball.

Eventually, I sat at one of the picnic tables, grabbed another Sprite from a cooler and watched the full moon shine above Lake Las Vegas. One sip of Sprite made a cramp in my stomach flare out. Once the cramping stopped, I pulled out my phone to pass the time.

CHAPTER 10: ADRIAN

ကြဲကြဲကြဲ

D orothy was in the vicinity, but she wasn't in the house. Stella and Eric were arguing in the far corner, the marijuana haze shrouding their animated exchange.

Stella said she would make sure Dorothy attended, but she was in the middle of an argument with her beloved Eric. He was obviously too immature for her, but who was I say anything. Stella was a fool for thinking he was the one.

I was suprised she had found me online on my burner Twitter profile. I used twitter to stay up on news and never added friends. How Stella found my profile is a mystery I hoped she would shed light on.

Our DM conversation made me realize that Stella's glamorous looks disguised a simple, down-to-earth girl who happened to like makeup and fashion. She had asked a lot of questions about where I grew up and how I liked Valley High. As usual, I deflected my answers and didn't give up details on Mandalagan or my family. But I happily expressed how much Valley High sucked.

It was nice to DM without being distracted by her physical form. Stella was physically stunning and reminded me of the alluring beauty of warrior Urduja, her amulets and bracelets blending in with her burnished skin. If Stella went to the Philippines, Danags would think she was the prophesied female.

But Dorothy was no doubt the girl who had tapped into her ancestry. She had defended herself at the club and had smelled my scent. She possessed a special aura with her polished, mahogany skin, her intelligence and athleticism. No doubt Danags would be impressed she played basketball.

I walked into the backyard where Dorothy's mortal scent sprung to life. Near the bonfire, Dorothy's silhouette emerged by the lake, illuminated by the full moon shining in the sky. Months from now when the reality of her ancestry took hold, she might be a completely different person. But tonight, she looked mysterious against the backdrop of the moonlight shimmering off the lake. I hesitated the moment she looked up from her phone. And when she smiled, my heartbeat quickened.

CHAPTER 11: DOROTHY

Adrian's smooth voice made me catch my breath. "Pretty night, isn't it?"

"Hasn't anyone told you sneaking up on someone is bad manners?"

He gazed at the moon. "I didn't know you were fragile. Are you sure you're a basketball player?"

The carbonated fizz from my Sprite tickled my nose. "Fragile? Don't let my size fool you."

"I plan not to, thank you very much."

"You're very welcome."

Adrian took a step on the wooden deck. "I take it this is the first time you've been to the lake?"

"Did Stella tell you?"

"I won't reveal my source, so I'll just say I figured it out on my own."

"You're a bad liar."

"I don't lie. *And* I can read people."

"You think you can read me?"

"Maybe," he answered. "We've only had a few conversations together."

"I only remember one real convo in the library when you schooled me on Philippines history."

"That's right! The valedictorian of the school admits she got schooled!"

"I'm a victim of public school curriculum."

"Now I feel bad. It isn't your fault American school districts don't teach the Philippines' true history."

Laughter erupted from the direction of the house, the distant thumping of EDM beats ricocheting into the night. Adrian gazed at the moon while standing on the wooden deck that extended over the lake. The deck creaked beneath us, the club music dissipating into the distance. Adrian found a pebble and threw it in the lake.

He held another pebble and flipped it in his hand. "Why are you by yourself? You don't like being around drunk teenagers?"

"Stella's mad at Eric. That's my signal to leave."

"I saw them talking in the house. Eric looked like he was sobering up."

"He doesn't want to get her in a bad mood. She'll ignore him for days."

"She's like a sister to you, huh?"

"We don't have siblings and we grew up like sisters."

"You're closer than a lot of siblings. I'm close to my brother, but my sister and I aren't at all."

This was the first time he mentioned his family to me. "I didn't know you had a brother and sister."

"They're in the Philippines. Have you heard of an island called *Negros*?"

"I'm seen it on a map. It's close to *Cebu*† right?"

"Yeah, it's next to Cebu. People speak Visayan on both islands."

"I wish I was fluent in Visayan."

"Your mom didn't teach you?"

"I grew up in the States with a mom who wanted me to assimilate. I understand some of it, but I sound

---

*   *Before Spanish colonization, this island was called Buglas by natives. Centuries later, it is called Negros, the name given by the Spanish in 1565 due to the dark-skinned natives they observed. I wish they kept Buglas, which means "cut off" since this island was separated from a larger landmass during the Ice Age.*

†   *Humabon ruled Cebu when Magellan arrived in 1521.*

72

so American when I speak it."

"Some first-generation Filipinos wanted their kids assimilated and didn't pass down the language. And some look down on *Fil-Ams** who don't speak the native dialect. It's an impossible double standard."

I sat at the edge of the deck, my hands pinched underneath my thighs. "Double standard is right. I get that funny look sometimes from Filipinos who don't know me when they ask if I speak. I feel bad when I say English please. Whatever. I shrug it off."

Adrian rested his feet, his biceps brushing against my arm. "Good for you. And it's never too late to learn, but it's hard if no one talks to you in Visayan every day."

"My mom speaks to me in English," I said. "I guess it's a habit that's hard to break. It was me and her growing up. She's stuck in her ways."

"Your family is small! My large, extended family in the Philippines is always in my business! It was a big adjustment to come to the States on my own."

"Well, if it means anything, I'm glad you're in Vegas."

"Me too. Otherwise, I wouldn't be here with you."

I nudged him. "Wow! Nice line! You must say that to all the girls!"

"I hardly engage in conversation with anyone. I'm a private person."

I slid closer to him. "I don't know about that. You've opened up to me."

"I guess I have." Adrian's baritone-sounding laugh gave me goosebumps. He looked up at the

---

*   *Shortened slang for Filipino Americans.*

moon. "As a kid in the Philippines, I stared at the moon all the time."

"What would you think of while moon gazing?"

He paused before answering. "In my family, my dad retold *Filipino folklore** stories about the moon's powers."

"What powers?"

"In Filipino folklore, the moonlight illuminates things certain people can see."

I gazed up at the moon. "Certain people? Like who?"

"Like our Lolos and Lolas. They can see *Duwendes†*."

"Duwendes?"

"Think of them like Irish elves, but instead of being green, they're deadly white and resemble dwarves or goblins. And instead of a pot of gold at the end of a rainbow, they're running around causing havoc."

"What kind of havoc?"

"Things like glass falling from a cupboard, or a car breaking down. Things that happen for no particular reason."

"Elders see duwendes?"

Adrian smiled. "Ask our Lolos and Lolas about duwendes and see their reaction, especially during a full moon."

"Like tonight?"

---

*   *Filipino folklore is from pre-Spanish times that were passed down to generations orally with very little written accounts.*

†   *Goblins/dwarves in Filipino folklore. This term is prevalent in various cultures around the world to describe mystic goblin-like beings who are either evil or mischievous. The way Adrian describes them is related to their depiction in Filipino culture.*

He crossed his dangling feet. "Yeah, exactly like tonight."

"I didn't even know Filipino folklore existed. *That* in itself is pretty cool."

Adrian's eyes twinkled in sync with the moon. "Filipino myth says *vampires** called *Danags†* lived in the Philippines. They fed off islanders and formed close bonds with those they used for daily blood. And since mortals are their food supply, they protected them at all costs."

"I've never heard of vampires being in the Philippines."

"Most of the world talks about the European and Greek influences on the world. My family taught me an alternate perspective: Greek mythology was completely borrowed from Polynesian and Pacific Island folklore."

"There is no way that's true!"

"You share the opinion of the entire civilized world. But my father says Zeus is Bathala, the supreme god of the Philippines and Poseidon is Amanikable, the Filipino god of the sea."

"I've never heard of the existence of *Filipino gods.‡*" AP Greek mythology was a requirement my junior year, but Bathala and Amanikable were from my own culture and I had never heard of them.

---

*   *The word "vampire" reflects traditional vampire lore, but with the perspective it was influenced by Southeast Asian folklore permeating from Indonesia, Polynesia, Japan, China and the Philippines.*

†   *Term #15 in Terms of Consequence. In Filipino folklore, Danags are said to have lived in harmony with humans.*

‡   *This novel focuses on Bathala and his daughters, but there are many more gods in Filipino folklore not mentioned worthy of a novel of their own. The stories of Filipino gods were eradicated by Spanish colonialism.*

"When Ferdinand Magellan landed in Cebu in 1521, he befriended and converted tribal leader *Humabon** to Catholicism. This started the eradication of these ancient stories, while some historians believe the Spanish planted these stories to control the islanders when they returned in 1565. However it happened, the ancestral history was lost. Even *Alibata†* script was replaced by Spanish and Latin writing systems."

"What's Alibata again?"

"Alibata was the native writing system prior to the Spanish. It's like the Kawi script I showed you in the library the other day. It has Indian and Arabic roots."

"Indian and Arabic?"

"Yes, there was heavy Indian and Arab influences on the islands before the Spanish." Adrian leaned in closer. "Tell me, what's the Visayan word for thank you?"

The answer was obvious, even if I wasn't fluent. "Salamat."

"*Salam* is an Arabic salutation meaning peace. The suffix -at is Tagalog for the English word *and*."

---

*   *Humabon is known for converting to Christianity when Magellan landed. Some believe Lapu-Lapu was the king who ruled over Humabon, which Magellan misunderstood when he ordered Lapu-Lapu to convert. Others say Lapu-Lapu ruled Mactan island and a Humabon rival. Although there are historical question marks, Humabon's place in Philippine history is set as the first to convert to Christianity. Lapu-Lapu is a Filipino national hero for killing Magellan in 1521, which is interesting since some believe he was a Muslim man. This is an animated topic of discussion in historically conscious Filipino households!*

†   *The writing system in ancient times. Also known as Baybayin. Today, you may see Filipinos with Alibata tattoos in tribute to their homeland, the Philippines.*

"And peace."

"And peace. Salamat." Adrian said.

"Indians and Arabs traveled all the way to the Philippines?"

"Since before the days of Christ. Only the sun and moon know the exact truth. One traveler, *Ibn Mattuta** traveled all over the islands in the fourteenth century. Look him up when you have a chance."

"I will for sure." I shifted my leg up and leaned my chin on my knee. "One of your tattoos says Bathala right?"

Adrian nodded. "Yeah! You remember!"

"You showed it to me twice already! Who is Bathala?"

"Filipino folklore names Bathala as the Supreme Being of the islands. He had three beautiful daughters named *Mayari, Hana* and *Tala.†* Mayari controlled moonlight, Hana the morning light and Tala the light emitted from stars. Duwendes, vampires and gods become mesmerized by the allure of Mayari's moonlight, like Bathala himself with his fatherly love for his daughters. Together, Bathala and his daughters bring focus back on the main objective of all deities."

The way Adrian spoke impressed me. It would be a miracle if these stories would be remembered a hundred years from now. "And what was that main objective?"

"To always protect humans."

A shiver spiraled up my spine. "And why would

---

*   *A Moroccan world traveler who has the only written account of Urduja and Tawalisi.*

†   *In FIlipino folklore, these three daughters influence others with their beauty. Mayari is the focal point of this novel, although Hana and Tala's influence shouldn't be disregarded.*

humans need to be protected?"

"Humans hold the key to progress in the physical world. Duwendes, vampires and gods are in another dimension, so to speak. Without mankind's ambition, the physical world would stop its progress. Only mortals expand boundaries."

Frogs croaked around the lake as the thumping music from the house suddenly stopped. The chanting of *chug! chug! chug!* in the distance grew in volume until an excited yell made it obvious someone had given in to peer pressure. The music started up again and drowned out the drunken soliloquies in the Emerson mansion. It would be a pain to search for Stella in a crowd of inebriated people, but Adrian's stories about Filipino duwendes, vampires and gods had me transfixed on the moon.

"Mayari is the name of the moon goddess?" I asked, a part of me wondering if the moon really had mystical powers.

"In Tagalog myth, Mayari is the most beautiful goddess."

"Mayari." I repeated as I accidentally skidded my hand against his.

The wooden deck creaked as I pulled myself up, pretending our hands hadn't touched. "We better head back. From the sounds of the party, I'm driving home."

"I'll help you find Stella and Eric. There's a lot of drunk people in the house."

"I appreciate that. Being around inebriated teenagers isn't my cup of tea. And by the way. Thanks for the history lesson. Again."

"*Waysaypayan*, Dorothy. You are more than welcome."

↰

The music became louder as we approached the grassy edge of the bonfire. Once we entered the house, the smell of marijuana surrounded us. We slithered our way through the kitchen and into a room where a crowd was huddled around an orange bong. The cannabis made me gag until Adrian's familiar coconut smell helped me find a breath. Adrian offered his hand and I accepted it, the touch of his hand making me blush.

He led me into an open area where people sang along to Drake's "God's Plan." We became wedged between girls who'd taken permanent residence on the dance floor. Trapped by the human wall, we danced until we found a crack to slide through.

Once Beyoncé's "Single Ladies" started up, the crowd stonewalled us, but I spotted Stella and Eric on the other side of the room. I pulled Adrian through an opening in the crowd and stepped in front of Stella who excitedly grabbed my arm. For the next three minutes, we teased Eric and Adrian with our finger-wagging and impressive amateur lip-syncing abilities. The guys played along without giving up their cool demeanor.

Once the song ended, we left the house with Stella pointing her ring finger at Eric while shouting in her high-pitched voice how great it was to be a single lady. Everyone laughed along, until it came time to decide who would drive. Eric didn't look like he was sober enough to drive as he slipped behind the wheel.

"Are you sure?" I asked him. "Weren't you throwing up earlier?"

Eric started the ignition. "I'm fine. It's been over two hours. I'm good!"

"Eric! Don't be a chauvinistic fool. Let Stella drive."

"Chauva-what? Dorothy, you're using big words again."

"She's making sure you can drive," Stella said. "Can you?"

"Yes! I'm fine! He place his hand on his heart. "Scouts honor."

"I don't think so." I turned to Adrian. "Can you give me a ride home?"

"Okay," Adrian replied. "But to warn you. I like to drive fast."

Eric slowly reversed the car and slowly moved the car through the driveway to sarcastically prove he was sober. Stella crossed her arms and waved at us until Eric stopped the car abruptly. The guys from Centennial High had blocked the driveway.

"Yo! Get out of the way!" Eric yelled.

The guy who boldly flirted with Stella earlier approached the driver's side. I ran up and intercepted him a few feet from the car. I smelled alcohol on his breath.

"Hey there," I tried. I had forgotten his name. "What's up dude."

"Dorothy right?" His speech was slurred. "I just want to talk to Stella. That's all. I swear."

"But you see...It's a bad idea because the guy driving is her boyfriend."

"It doesn't matter if she has a boyfriend. She's my girl."

"Oh my God. No she's not your girl."

His boys a few feet away had started laughing.

"What is this. A dare?" I asked.

His eyes were glassy. Yup. An obvious drinking game dare.

"What the fuck!" Eric yelled. A car door slammed and footsteps approached. "Dude. We're trying to leave!" Eric craned his neck.

"That my girl," the drunk guy slurred.

Eric looked back at Stella. "She's your girl? I think you're my bitch!"

The drunk guy swung his arm wildly, which I guess was supposed to be a punch. Eric blocked it and cocked his fists back just as Adrian came out of nowhere.

"Eric, my friend," Adrian said, holding Eric's arm. "Go home. And you." He head-nodded at the drunk guy. "It's time for you to leave."

The Centennial boys had yelled at their boy to follow them back in the house. He retreated, catching up to his friends who teased him on how much he sucked.

Stella looked annoyed when Eric climbed back in the car. She half-waved at me before Eric peeled off.

"That was stupid," I said as Adrian and I walked around the corner of the mansion.

"It's boys being boys," Adrian replied. "Boys do stupid things."

"Eric would have punched him and who knows what would have happened."

Adrian pointed his keys at a row of parked cars. There were two loud beeps and a flash of red from a silver sports car with a thick blue stripe running down the middle. It was the newest model of the Ford Shelby.

"This is your car?" I asked.

"This is my dad's influence. He has a weakness for sports cars and I'm a direct beneficiary."

"Apparently."

Adrian opened the passenger-side door for me, the new car smell and the soft, leather seats looking luxurious. After he sat in the driver's seat, my phone vibrated with a blue text message from Stella.

Stella: Tita Meredith is asleep, so picking
up my mom at your house.
Me: Is Eric okay?
Stella: Still pissed at that guy. But nothing a
rub on the thigh won't fix.
Me: TMI!
Stella: Near your house.
Me: Okay. I should be home soon.
Stella: See ya! And I want details on your walk
around the lake with Adrian!
Me: Nothing happened! TTYL!

Tension rose in my chest knowing mom was about to be home alone.

"Everything alright?" Adrian asked.

"Yeah. Just need to get home."

"Not a problem. You'll be home before you know it."

We sped away from the Emerson mansion. On the main road, Adrian drove fluidly, every turn and lane change as smooth as his sanguine voice. I held on tightly to my seat, amazed I didn't rock left or right at the high rate of speed we were traveling. We pulled up to my house in no time.

"Thanks for driving me home," I said once Adrian skidded to a stop. "And thanks for stopping Eric from punching the stupid drunk guy."

"Not a big deal." He held a mischievous smile. "Can I open the door for you." Without waiting for an answer, he pressed a button and the passenger-side door opened.

"Are you trying to impress me?"

"Is it working?"

I stepped out of the car, closed the door and leaned into the open window. "I'm not the kind of girl impressed by a fancy car."

Adrian looked past my shoulders. "Are you sure it's just you and your mom? Your house is gigantic!"

I looked back at my house. "It's a bit much, I agree."

"How big is it inside?"

"It's over four-thousand square feet with five bedrooms and four baths." I had heard my mom say this proudly to visitors through the years.

"Holy crap! That's huge for two people! No wonder you're not impressed with my fancy car."

I tried to hold my smile. "Your car is completely overrated."

"Overrated or not, it's a fun drive." He revved up the engine. "Have a good night. I'll see you at graduation tomorrow." He drove away, the sounds of his tires squealing on the left turn out of the subdivision.

I went upstairs and checked on mom—her bedroom light was out, which meant she was asleep. I opened the door slowly and hovered over her. She was snoring like a banshee. Two wine glasses were on the dresser, which meant she hadn't listened to me about not drinking alcohol. But her relaxed face made me smile.

I knelt by her bed and prayed for mom's health. I thanked God for my blessings and pleaded with Him to keep mom's cancer from becoming more serious. After I said Amen, I kissed her on the forehead, my heart aching that she hadn't noticed I was in the room in the first place.

CHAPTER 12: ADRIAN

ॐॐॐ

My conversation with Dorothy at the lake was exhausting. She deserved to express herself around me, so I had summoned everything I had to keep her emotions balanced.

Admittedly, it took more out of me than I had anticipated, especially with the stupid fight that was about to go down. If it wasn't for my influence over human emotions, there would have been a major throw down. One of the guys had reached for his pistol, but instead, he felt a sudden need to sleep off his alcohol. All of them did.

A ravenous hunger had now overtaken me.

I parked the Ford Shelby in the self-parking garage of The Venetian casino. The suffocating Vegas air felt like warm rain against my skin. I slid through the automatic doors of the casino, the blast of air conditioning making me shiver. I hurried to the elevator of the Venezia Tower and stepped out on the tenth floor, the smell of fresh tropical plants flooding my senses. Splashing water from the pool area sounded inviting, but Bouchon's Restaurant was in the opposite direction.

The attractive Filipina hostess adjusted her ponytail and maroon button-down uniform when I approached. She led me to a table in the courtyard that allowed my body to seep in the dry, Nevada air. She handed me a menu and said the waitress would be with me in a minute. I imagined the meal I was about to have. My impatience grew until a gorgeous blonde came by to take my order.

"Good day, sir. How are you?" She placed a glass of water on the table.

"I'm famished." I suppressed a flame of hunger in my throat when blue veins emerged from her pale neckline.

"What would you like to order?"

"Diniguan," I said.

"Diniguan," the waitress repeated, her smile fading. "Anything else?"

"Yes, please tell the chef I only write in Alibata."

"What do you mean, sir?"

I replied slowly. "I only…write…in Alibata."

The waitress moved from the table, her curvy figure retreating to the kitchen of the restaurant. Once she returned, her scent made me woozy. "The chef will see you now," she said without making eye contact.

I followed her through the kitchen where she stepped into an obscure door near the walk-in freezer. We were engulfed in darkness, but the blonde didn't slow her pace. She moved quickly and opened another door. My eyes adjusted to see a candle on a table in the middle of a large, hollow chamber.

The waitress led me to the table and motioned me to sit. "Please wait here. If you want anything, ring the bell." She pointed to a French bell on the table. She began to retreat, but I placed my hand on hers.

"I'm sorry. What was your name?" I asked.

"Janna," the waitress answered.

"Thank you so much, Janna."

When I released her hand, she moved quickly, the slamming of the door echoing throughout the chamber.

ॐ

Danags tried to avoid being seen in public, but we patronized restaurants worth our time. Bouchons was one of these restaurants, a unique place, even for my people. There was absolutely no other place outside Mandalagan that presented food like this fine establishment.

A door creaked open in the darkness and slammed as footsteps approached the table. The face of the person was indistinguishable, but I had a suspicion who it was by the sound of the heavy footsteps.

"You're here," a baritone voice echoed through the dark.

"It didn't hit me until today," I replied.

The voice took a step forward, the candle illuminating his face. "Good to see you again, my friend."

"A pleasure, Harvey."

Harvey's bald head held a faint radiance from the candlelight. "I was starting to feel offended you hadn't visited the nightclub or Bouchons."

"I was trying to hold off. I can go months without eating in the field."

"Yes, a test of your will. Sometimes, it's best to give in to cravings."

"I usually don't feel hungry until I return to Mandalagan. But something in the Vegas air has me craving sooner than I expected."

Harvey smiled. "You Timawa are trained to withstand hunger under all circumstances. But there's something in Vegas that hits your weak spot. Must be the mix of desert air and man-made air conditioning. How is your family?"

"They're fine."

"And Abigail?"

"She's doing well."

"I'm glad," he said with a distinct sadness in his voice. He moved towards the table. "Let me help you satisfy your craving."

"For the record, you've already helped me. You watched Dorothy and Stella until I got here. We are grateful you saved her from the situation at the club."

"If that guido was more than human, I probably wouldn't be here today."

"And that's why I'm here," I replied. "You have backup now."

"Finally," Harvey murmured.

I chose to ignore Harvey's ingratitude. "I met your waitress, Janna. She's beautiful."

"She's been with us since she graduated college. An innocent girl."

"Who escorts Timawas to secret chambers?"

"She knows to be courteous. Ask Dorothy and Stella. They've enjoyed her company at the club."

"I don't doubt you," I said. "I know how hard it is to find good help."

Harvey's lips straightened. "Just as I know how hard it is to protect a man and his dead wife."

"Do not insinuate your loyalty has swayed, or I'll end you now!"

"Threats do me no harm!" Harvey yelled. "Remember what I've sacrificed! Isn't that enough?"

"It's best you move on."

"I have moved on! Stop with the innuendos about Janna!"

"Does Janna know about your wife?" I asked.

"She knows my wife is dead."

"Do you love her?"

"Yes. I love Janna." Harvey paused. "She has

given me a reason to live."

I tried to stay composed hearing he had found someone to love. "I'm happy to hear it."

"I'm still processing the idea of loving again. But Janna is a special girl. I can't think of a life without her."

"I hope it works out. You deserve all the happiness in the world."

"As you do. Have you found someone in Mandalagan?"

"No. I am still riding solo," I said. "But I don't want to bore you about my love life. Right now I need to eat."

"Well then. Let's get to it." Harvey clapped his hands loudly, triggering overhead lights to turn on. A white flash blinded me until various animals appeared on the other side of thick glass panels. There were wild pigs, a goat and a horse. My hunger was now at the tip of my mouth. "I hope this is to your liking."

"Nice," I said. "I'm impressed as always."

"We take pride in our cuisine. What would you like to start with?"

"The horse."

"I'll release the animals one by one, starting with the horse." Harvey retreated from the table. "And I have a surprise after your animal entrées."

Harvey retreated through a door in the chamber's dark perimeter. Seconds later, the horse's whinnies became louder as the glass panel slowly slid to the ceiling. The horse, adorned with white spots across its brown body, stepped out of its prison, the sound of its hooves muffled by the red carpet of the chamber. I sensed fear instantly.

To prevent the animal from suffering, I bit the horse's throat and drained the blood, its eyes still open. The glass panels slid up for the pigs, their high-pitched squeals silenced when I snapped their necks, sucking the blood from their bodies. The goat's panel slid open next. I tackled it and sucked its body dry.

A satisfying swarm of blood settled in my system. There was one thing that would completely satisfy me, but I never gave in to the desire for mortal blood. But today, a surging hunger pang made me lick my chops.

"And now a surprise." Harvey's muffled voice came from an intercom somewhere in the room.

The wall panels turned one-hundred-and-eighty degrees, revealing a glass panel with a man's arms and legs chained to metal hooks. I leapt forward at the fear and confusion in the man's eyes.

"Harvey. A surprise, indeed! Why are you tempting me with this mortal?"

"He's the guido who hurt Dorothy in the club. Turns out he has a history of abusing young girls, arrested seven times for attempted kidnapping of a minor, arrested five times for spousal abuse. His wife disappeared years ago, but the police couldn't pin him to the crime. I thought he may be an exception to the *Danag law** regarding the treatment of humans."

The fact that this guy even touched Dorothy made me hate him. He was evil, and my rage burned at the thought of him putting a finger on her. The pathetic look on the man's face—his eyes bulging in fear and his screams stifled by the glass—made me think of one of Sitan's soldiers in Europe from years ago, who went on a killing spree simply for pleasure.

---

*   *Danag law is to protect humans, a law Adrian abides by as a Timawa warrior. But this shows how a Danag can make an exception for humans they despise.*

I remembered the honor of turning his body to ash.

"Release him!" I yelled, my mouth salivating.

The glass panel slid up, the chains releasing the man's arms and legs. He fell to the ground, his graveled screams ricocheting through the chamber. He scrambled away until I grabbed his foot and dragged him across the floor, his yells piercing the air.

Without hesitation, I snapped his body in half, his blood-curdling screams a catalyst to drain him slowly; I wanted him to feel pain. When his last scream ended with his eyes open, I had sucked all his blood and turned him over so I wouldn't see his face.

As I sat at the table and rang the French bell, a sudden calm came over me. My insides churned in bloody satisfaction, the mortal blood sweeter with animal blood already in my system.

A door slammed and heavy footsteps approached. Harvey emerged out of the darkness. "Is that enough for you?"

"More than enough. Thank you."

"You're welcome, Timawa."

I offered to help clean up, but Harvey insisted he would take care of it, insisting there would be less suspicion if he worked solo. I thanked him again and he walked with me out of the chamber.

He said Janna had changed him for the better and he was on his way to a new life. I worried he might be influenced, but Janna was a nice girl who would keep him in line. I sensed it when I touched her hand.

But it was obvious he still missed his wife.

Harvey had sacrificed years ago when his wife had died. The fact he still accepted us amazed me; he had been given the raw end of the deal.

By the time I left Bouchons, I felt better about Harvey's loyalty. Yet, there was a part of me that didn't completely trust his human tendencies. But he had proven himself time and time again, so I gave him the benefit of the doubt.

Harvey deserved the benefit of the doubt.

He had given me a meal that would keep me focused solely on Dorothy's well-being, the threat of Sitan always lingering. Sitan hadn't been seen yet, but history had proven he struck when we least expected. My Timawa instincts had been spiking lately, a sign that something was on the horizon. I didn't like being paranoid, but Sitan was unpredictable, even when we expected him.

Once I arrived home, I prayed to Allah that Sitan would leave tomorrow's graduation alone. Like Kaptan warned, he was probably a step ahead of us.

CHAPTER 13: DOROTHY

꽃꽃

The families of graduates packed the Orleans Arena, a casino on Tropicana Boulevard with a bowling alley and a movie theater built around the main floor.

A butterfly feeling in my stomach had me biting my lip. Some classmates had large families, but Stella and I only had our mothers. Pining for things I didn't have was childish, but today, something was missing.

"Cleng," Stella whispered, reaching for my hand. "This is it. We're like, graduating high school." Stella's eyes had watered below her long lashes.

"I know Stellz. I guess we're officially grown-ups."

"I guess! Whatever that means. I'm still clueless what to do after high school."

"Just like me. Remember I have no clue either!"

"Yeah, I know," Stella relented. "But still…"

I wrapped her in a hug. "Let's enjoy this moment. High school graduation comes once in a lifetime, unless you want to take AP calculus again."

Stella laughed over my shoulder. "Definitely not! I wouldn't have passed that class without you!"

"And I wouldn't have survived without you," I replied, my throat constricted.

We separated and laughed at ourselves with tears running down our cheeks.

"You two better not get me emotional!" It was Darcy and two of my basketball teammates, Tanya and Melanie.

I swiped my eyes and cheeks with a tissue. "Oh my God! I already miss playing ball with you guys!"

Darcy fanned her face with her hands. "Don't get me started, little Dor! Do not get me started!" We collapsed into a group hug.

Eric's familiar voice interrupted us from the side. "I see there isn't a dry eye in the room already." He grabbed Stella and gave her a kiss.

The voice of Miss Munashi, our school principal, boomed through the P.A. system. "Family and friends, please enter the auditorium. The ceremony will begin soon. Valley high graduates, please take your places for the procession. Thank you."

Principal Munashi's announcement didn't prevent Stella and Eric from being preoccupied with each other's lips. Stella had her arms around his neck, and Eric caressed her waist. Darcy and my teammates were quickly in conversations with another group I didn't know that well. I sidestepped out of the circle and scanned the sea of red graduation gowns.

A guy about Adrian's height and skin tone in jeans and a green polo turned in my direction. I waved, expecting to see Adrian's chiseled face, but Edgar Llantos, a junior I knew in passing, waved at me, surprised I greeted him. I had never waved at Edgar Llantos in my life! Heat rose to my face, but there wasn't time to dwell on my embarrassment too long. Adrian was staring at me a few feet away.

*Glowing** like the sun.

My contacts weren't dry, but there was gold light bordering the edge of his body like a halo, the sight

---

*   ***Bioluminescence*** *is the ability of organisms to omit light by chemical reaction and is one of the world's oldest fields of study. In Filipino folklore, there are legends of* ***bioluminescenct*** *beings. An interesting tidbit: the vampire squid in the ocean depths uses* ***bioluminescence*** *as protection. They light up when predators approach!*

93

of his beautiful splendor making everyone else look insignificant and obscure.

"They say you see the world differently when you're on the brink of something amazing," Adrian said. "I'm excited to hear your amazing speech, valedictorian."

"Y-y-you're glowing," I whispered.

Adrian's eyebrows darted down. "I'm glowing?"

"Yes!"

He stepped towards me and lowered his voice. "You see me glowing?"

"Yes, I think!" I wondered why no one else noticed Adrian's golden splendor. "You look... magnificent."

"You see me glowing?" Adrian repeated. "Are you sure?"

"Yes! You're glowing. Are you sick?"

"No, I'm not sick," Adrian whispered, his bronze face and neck sparkling with silver, glittered dots.

"You look...magnificent," I heard myself say again before the sound of Principal Munashi's voice broke me out of my trance.

"Now introducing, your Valley High seniors!"

The band started playing the traditional graduation song and the procession starting ahead of me. Adrian had somehow positioned himself between me, Stella and Darcy's circle.

"Listen," Adrian said softly. "Don't let this be a distraction, you understand? I'm here for you."

"What are you talking about?"

"Remember it's imperative not to let anyone know what you see."

"And what am I seeing? Are you sick? And why can I see you like this?" Our hands were suddenly enveloped in a radiance that triggered a sharp shiver through me.

"Dorothy. I promise I won't let anything happen to you." He pulled me into a hug and another magnificent glow. The bright light blinded my view of the procession. And then he was gone.

In a daze, I stumbled in my place in line, looking for Adrian's dazzling face. How did he disappear so quickly? I moved next to Stella who had a funny grin on her face.

"What?" I asked defensively.

"I saw that," Stella replied, her grin widening.

"You saw that too?" A slight tension in my chest made me hold my breath. Did Stella see Adrian glow like I did?

"Of course I saw you and Adrian hugging! It's official, that boy is completely into you," Stella teased.

I exhaled and tried to process everything. I was about to give my valedictorian speech and Adrian was glowing.

Glowing!

I looked for Adrian to confirm that he had actually been there. Maybe I imagined the whole thing? But it seemed real, even with the strange way he acted, as if he was confused and surprised to be radiant. But how could I *not* see it? How could everyone else *not* see it?

"Stella, Dorothy. It's your turn." Mr. Cotton's urgent whisper snapped me back to the present.

Stella clasped my hand and we entered the auditorium. Camera flashes blinded us on our way to our assigned seating near the front of the stage. Stella tugged at my arm and pointed to where our mothers stood. Mom wiped her eyes and Tita Yasmin waved frantically at us. We waved in their direction, trying to suppress an onslaught of emotions within the confines of my stomach. Mom mouthed the words, "I love you" as I entered my row. Stella squeezed my hand.

This was it; our final moment as high school seniors.

↜

There were over a thousand students in my senior class, so the procession took a while. After what seemed like forever, Principal Munashi stepped forward with her big hoop earrings and trendy outfit. "Thank you all for coming to the Valley High graduation ceremony," she said.

A loud applause as she continued. "I will remember this particular senior class for its dedication and commitment to excellence. Don't you agree?"

Another loud applause. "Okay," Principal Munashi said after the applause died down. "And who more to exemplify this commitment to excellence than the valedictorian of this year's senior class!"

I clutched the paper in my hand as she continued. "A person I've seen grow from a wide-eyed freshman into the young woman she is today...your valedictorian, Miss Dorothy Claire Dizon!"

Without making eye contact with anyone, I consciously made an effort not to trip on the steps of the stage. Principal Munashi hugged me once I reached her.

"They're all yours," she whispered in my ear. I placed my paper on the podium, trying not to panic at the thousands of eyes looking at me. I read the first line of my speech to myself, a memory cue I learned from my mom. My mouth felt dry. I swallowed and took a breath, rubbing my clammy hands together.

"Hello," I began, my voice cracking above a whisper. I wiped my sweaty hands against my graduation gown nervously.

From a distance, I heard someone yell "Dorothy! We love you!"

Stella was standing, her face wide with encouragement. Darcy, Tanya and Melanie stood up and yelled my name. I took another breath and assessed the crowd, a sweeping strength overtaking me like a sudden gust during the calmest summer day.

"Hello everyone. I'm Dorothy Dizon, your valedictorian, a title I wouldn't hold without the support of my mother."

A light applause from the audience. "Without Meredith Dizon, I don't know where I would be. She showed me how to cook Filipino food like *tocino, pansit and lumpia*[*]. She emphasized the importance of good hygiene. She taught me to live proudly as a Filipino and American. She showed me the importance of commitment and hard work as a single mother and all-star realtor. And lately, her fighting spirit against insurmountable odds. I know I'm loved by the most unbelievable mother and I stand before you because of her example. Mom, thank you for believing in me, even during those days I swore I hated you. I love you."

I clapped in her direction and applause started. It grew louder, and when I extended my arm to my right, mom swiped the edges of her watery eyes. Tita Yasmin placed her arm around her as I segued to the next part of my speech.

"When we moved here, my mom bonded with another mother – Miss Yasmin De Guzman – sitting next to her today. She has been a second mother to me, and happens to be the mother of my best friend

---

[*]   *Popular Filipino food cooked in various styles in Filipino households.*

in the world, Stella De Guzman."

A loud, exuberant low voice yelled "Yeah, Stella! We love you too!" Other students chimed in. I glanced at Stella. She had both hands lightly pressed against her lips, her eyes watering as soon as she met my gaze.

"Starting in third grade, we talked on the phone for hours, a habit that got worse when we were given mobile phones, for safety reasons of course. Growing up, she was at most of my basketball tournaments, even though she hates basketball! She welcomed my basketball sisters into her life, even introducing us to the intricacies of makeup and fashion. She is what every friend should be. I know for the rest of my life, regardless of what may come, we will always be there for each other."

Not willing to chance an emotional breakdown, I continued. "I also want to give a shout to my basketball sisters! It was fun schooling you in practice every day. And breaking your ankles during one-on-one drills."

The audience broke into a friendly laugh.

"But seriously...regardless if we won or lost, we had each other's backs and we represented our school with pride and class. League champs the last two years baby! Thank you basketball sisters for memories to last a lifetime."

Darcy stood, flexed her muscles and yelled "lady ballers baby!" Tanya and Melanie replied with yells of their own that were soon dissolved by a friendly ovation.

"Now if you look at the meaning of the word valedictorian, it is a derivative of the Latin phrase *vale dicere*, which means to "say farewell". In one respect, I agree we are saying farewell to our days at Valley, but we are also saying thank you to our family, friends and the faculty of our school, and hello to an unknown future! Even if only some of us reminisce with fond memories, our high school experience undoubtedly influences us and serves as the foundation for whatever we do next. Recently, I was reminded by a new friend that some people aren't as fortunate. Many people have bigger concerns, such as how to feed their children or how to survive through the night. As future leaders, we can use what we learned to give back to the less fortunate and make our time worth remembering."

People were quiet, smiling, and supportive. At the far right, light grew in intensity. Inside its perimeter, Adrian looked determined and focused, his teeth clenched. The glow around Adrian retreated, and another glow near the front of the stage emerged like a beautiful apparition.

A light around Stella!

Each blink of my eyes reconfirmed it; Stella had a faint golden light running along the edges of her white graduation gown, a radiance so faint it looked as if she needed an electrical charge. But undoubtedly, she was ablaze in golden effulgence.

There was only one way to stay composed. Keep speaking. "Today will be a day I will remember forever. It is the start of an existence with no certainties. But instead of letting uncertainty cloud our paths, let the unknown guide us to fulfill our destinies, whatever that will be."

My eyes darted between Adrian and Stella. "Valley High seniors! May God bless us all. Here's to the class of 2018!"

Faculty behind me shook my hand as Adrian and Stella's splendor made me anxious to return to my seat. Somehow, I reached Stella, her light beams a breathtaking vision. Stella stretched for a hug, enveloping me in her aura.

"Stellz, you're radiant," I whispered.

"You are too," Stella replied. "What a beautiful speech. I'm so proud of you."

↶

Principal Munashi had started motioning students in the first row to approach the stage. Light applause accompanied each student's name. My view of Adrian was blocked by thirty rows of students between us. I remembered Adrian's urgent plea.

Remember it's imperative not to let anyone know what you see.

He was caught off guard that he glowed. He was surprised. And like a revelation, his words from the library echoed louder in my mind.

One day you'll see things in a completely different light. When that day arrives, you can count on me.

I half-expected someone to strap me in a gurney for psychiatric evaluation. Who in their right mind sees people glowing? I had to be going insane. But why did I feel overwhelmingly normal? Do crazy people recognize they're insane?

Stella tugged on my arm, her body still ablaze. "It's our turn, Cleng."

Stella's name was announced and I yelled as loud as I could as Stella accepted her diploma. A nice ovation followed when my name was announced, my basketball teammates yelling my name the loudest.

When Darcy strutted on stage, I yelled as she broke out into a dance before walking off. I cheered on Melanie and Tanya, the last two senior basketball sisters, the realization of not playing another high school basketball game hitting home.

Stella clapped and yelled when Eric accepted his diploma. It was cute to see him blow kisses at her, but I pretend-gagged when she caught his phantom kisses with her hand. I gagged even more when Eric pointed at her and clasped his hands to his chest, signaling she was his heart.

And then a beaming white light blinded me. After my eyes adjusted, there was Adrian illuminated as he effortlessly moved through the crowd. When he locked eyes with me, a searing pain resonated through my body. He immediately unlocked his gaze and slipped through the crowd. The rolling ache subsided when Adrian disappeared, giving me a chance to catch my breath.

↜

We threw our graduation caps in the air and Kool and the Gang's "Celebration" boomed over the speakers. Our mothers came down from the stands holding bouquets of roses. Mom told me how proud she was. My reply was a long hug.

Darcy, Tanya, Melanie and my junior basketball teammates came out of nowhere and almost tackled me. We took our last team photo with Darcy cradling me like a baby, one of our signature poses. I slapped high-fives with each teammate, becoming emotional that our basketball season had ended with a loss in the playoffs. Darcy squeezed me, thanking me for the years we played together, yelling in my ear that whatever happened down the road, she would be there, no matter what. We were Vikings for life and she was only a text message away.

Out of the sea of people, Christian from Tae Kwon Do emerged with an attractive Filipino girl next to him. He looked clean in a collared-shirt and khaki pants.

"Christian? Is that you?"

"Hey!" Christian approached. "Happy graduation, valedictorian!"

"I didn't know you would be here."

"I'm full of surprises." He turned to the girl. "This is my cousin, Giselle."

"Hi," Giselle said, waving. "Nice to meet you. And I love your Rebecca Taylor dress underneath your graduation gown!"

I gave her a peck on the cheek and a semi-hug. "I like you already for noticing!" Giselle rocked a turquoise mini-dress, giving her an attractive style of her own. "And thanks for coming. You shouldn't have."

"Christian wanted to hear your speech," Giselle said. "It was really great."

"Thanks." I felt blood rush to my face as Christian looked at me.

I heard mom's voice. "Cleng, who is this?"

"Mom, this is Christian. Christian, my mom, Tita Yasmin and you know my best friend Stella."

Christian placed the back of his hand on Tita Yasmin and mom's foreheads, offering the traditional Filipino sign of respect. Giselle did the same. Christian joked with Stella about joining us for workouts at the dojo. By the googly eyes Stella gave me, Christian was making a good first impression.

"Let's go to lunch!" Mom proclaimed.

Mom and Tita Yasmin had already reserved lunch at a restaurant at the Bellagio. Stella told Eric to meet us there, which made me think of Adrian. Where was he? The red and white graduation gowns scattered across the auditorium didn't make it easy to find him.

"Do you need help looking for someone?" Christian asked, probably noting how difficult it was for my vertically challenged self to see anyone in the crowd.

"No," I answered. Then a thought. "Do you and Giselle want to go to lunch with us?"

"Sure! If it's no trouble."

"No trouble at all!" Mom replied with way too much enthusiasm. I guess she liked Christian. "It's settled. We'll meet at Bellagio."

Christian and Giselle walked with us out of the arena. Once we entered the main casino floor, a faint coconut smell intensified a swarm inside of me. I wanted to see Adrian and find out why he glowed. Why Stella glowed. And what he meant when he said he would be there for me if I wanted him to be.

↜

By the time we were seated at one of the high-end restaurants in the Bellagio, I was famished. I ordered a medium rare T-bone steak with baked potato, salivating at the thought of eating meat. It took forever for our food to arrive, the pleasant conversation with Christian and Giselle making the wait bearable.

They were like brother and sister, having grown up practically down the street from each other.

Christian reminisced how Giselle scolded him for not attending a four-year college. He was in his second year of junior college and Giselle wanted him to join her at Arizona. Christian said he had options, with UNLV being one of them. Giselle joked about me and him attending UNLV together next fall, which made Stella join in on the teasing.

When Christian laughed, his dimples were hard to ignore, his collared shirt and khaki pants an obvious change from his usual sweaty self at the dojo. I tried to not stare at him, but we locked eyes a couple times in the middle of our group conversations. I smiled and looked away each time, hoping I played it off casually. Once the food arrived, Christian noted how fast I ate for a girl. I replied my small frame was not a pre-requisite for how I ate food. Everyone agreed that my size didn't reflect my huge appetite.

After dessert, Christian and Giselle said they had to get going to a family thing. As we said our goodbyes, Christian gave me a soft hug that brought me to his chest, making me feel lightheaded. He reminded me about workouts and I promised I would make it to a few this summer. He said he looked forward to seeing me kick ass.

I appreciated him for hanging out for my graduation, so I gave him a friendly peck on the cheek. It was nothing, but Giselle fake coughed and Stella's eyes widened as if I had swapped spit with Zac Efron. Mom didn't seem to notice, engrossed in her conversation with Tita Yasmin. Christian and Giselle waved and walked out of the restaurant, Giselle nudging him a few times before they disappeared from view.

After Stella and Tita Yasmin declared the rest of the day their mother-daughter time, mom decided to run a few errands. I reminded her to take her meds, but she ignored my reminder, emphasizing she was meeting up with a new friend after she was finished with her errands. After prodding her for more details, she admitted it was a male friend she had met during an open house. I teased her about going on a date even though she wasn't calling it a date, happy she didn't let cancer keep her from living the life she wanted to live.

With my mom out on the town, I couldn't ignore that Adrian had lingered in my mind throughout the entire lunch. With impatience brewing, I backed out the Mercedes and started driving, motivated to find him, wherever he might be.

CHAPTER 14: ADRIAN

ကာၣ်ကာ

My Timawa frustration was building. "How am I supposed to explain this?"

Kenneth's silence didn't help me answer my own rhetorical question, but this wasn't new; Kenneth became a quiet listener when I was emotional. Yin. Yang.

"How do I explain glowing like a frickin' light bulb? And are you going to say anything?"

"I've never heard you use that word before."

"What word?"

"Frickin'," Kenneth said. "She's rubbing off on you."

"Shut up, *kuya*."

"Perhaps he sensed something between you and her."

Kaptan's instinct of sensing branding partners was as useful as my talent for predicting probability. He knew when beings had a connection with each other, which came in handy in diplomatic situations with the Filipino people. But this was Dorothy! Potentially the most important Danag female since Urduja of Tawalisi!

"I'm not sure what to think anymore. This girl's ability is—"

"Special," Kenneth interjected. "But she's the one who saw you glow. She's probably confused and scared."

"And I'm supposed to help her make sense of it? I can't even understand it myself. I'm only here to protect her."

My rising voice echoed against the walls of my

bedroom. Kenneth's sunken eyes and hollow cheeks showed concern. He was the one person in the world I spoke to freely and the one person I listened to, even with his contrarian perspective. This was the curse of being kindreds.

Kenneth broke the silence. "You *are* there to protect her, and that includes protecting her from herself. I'm sure her human instincts are trying to rationalize what she saw."

I hated it when Kenneth made sense. "Do I pretend it didn't happen?"

"Just talk to her, but reveal only what her human heart can handle. When she goes to the Philippines, she'll see for herself."

I nodded, privately thankful he was my kindred, but doing everything not to show my appreciation. "I guess that's all I can do."

"I'll check on you later," Kenneth said, a sympathetic look on his face. "And make sure not to overwhelm her the next time."

"I'll try. Say hi to mother and father. And, of course, sister."

The connection blurred with Abigail, Kenneth's wife, sneaking up behind him and waving goodbye. It ended with darkness and a zap of white light.

ॐ

My host family had me stay in a room at the rear of a house built like most Vegas tract homes: a sandy-colored wood structure covered in stucco built on a five-thousand square foot lot. They were out of town for the weekend on a trip to San Francisco, so the house was eerily quiet, which suited me fine.

I liked quiet.

But when I heard tapping on my bedroom window and saw Dorothy looking gorgeous in her white dress, I froze, not sure what to do. Her expression was caught between fear and surprise until she smiled. After realizing I was staring at her, I slid my feet underneath me.

Dorothy moved to the side to give me room to step in the backyard. Her smile had disappeared. She was cautious. Tense. I gritted my teeth, trying to lower my body temperature. Within seconds, Dorothy's shoulders sank in a way that told me I wasn't giving off too much energy. I led her to a wooden bench where we stared at the kidney-shaped swimming pool and the splashing water of the man-made waterfall my host family had installed. How symbolic that we sat in front of a waterfall, even if it was fake one.

I was trying to gather my thoughts when Dorothy crossed her golden legs, making it impossible to concentrate. It didn't help that she was next to me in a white dress that hugged her hourglass body. Her straightened hair was styled with barrel curls falling gently on her neck and shoulders, her forehead with extra shine from the sun. And when she craned her neck, blue veins rubbed underneath her skin. I pushed away my instinct to get closer. She was possibly royalty and I was merely a Timawa grunt. If anything happened to her while she was vulnerable, Kaptan wouldn't let me live another day. I would always be an insignificant grunt, even if I defended her from Sitan and his army.

Dorothy adjusted her dress and kept her legs crossed. I stared in the direction of the waterfall, trying to formulate words to explain what had happened today. But how could I explain I wasn't mortal? How she was more than she ever imagined? I remembered my brother's words.

Reveal only what her human heart can handle.

చ

"Dorothy. How did you find me?"

She sat with her raised eyebrows locked in position before relaxing when she looked at me. "I don't know. I guess you could say I followed your scent."

"Ah." I tried to hide the surprise in my voice. "Interesting you had no idea where I lived but still found me."

Dorothy inched closer to me. "Adrian. What's up with the light surrounding you at graduation? You were glowing, right? Or am I crazy?"

Here was my chance to deny everything, to sway her thoughts to a safer place. It would be easy to say it was her imagination; humans were easily overwhelmed by frivolous things like high school graduations or valedictorian speeches. But how could I close the door on her? I had been sent to protect her, to guide her as she discovered her ancestry. Although it would intrigue me see her reaction, it would be counterproductive to tell her she was crazy.

"Dorothy. I don't see the world through your eyes, but maybe I can help dissect the meaning of what you thought you saw."

She put her hand on my arm as I tried to keep my temperature low enough for her to function. Her soft skin didn't make it easy to stay composed.

"You're talking so general and you're hiding something. Who are you trying to protect?"

You. I'm protecting you.

"I promise I will do everything I can to show you the truth."

"If you want to show me the truth, why don't you talk freely?"

She had a point, but this had to be delicately explained. "I am speaking freely, within the guidelines I'm forced to follow."

Dorothy leaned in and locked her brown eyes on mine. "Adrian, there was light around you like a halo. I've never seen anything like it in my life."

There was no doubt my non-answers contributed to her confusion. "Please. Give me a moment."

"Fine." She tipped her head to one side, revealing beautiful veins on her neck.

Oh my. She was becoming irresistible. "What you saw is relevant, but I don't understand it either. You aren't supposed to see me like that. You're supposed to see me as a teenage guy who likes fast cars and hip hop music."

She reached for my hand. "But you're not *just* those things, are you?"

"That's up to you to decide. Am I like any other guy you've ever known?"

"Adrian, you're anything but a typical guy."

"I guess I'll take that as a compliment."

A warm desert breeze swept up her hair and exposed veins disappearing in her shoulder blade. Her scent, a smell somewhere between the sweetness of mango fruit and mortal blood made me inch closer. She crossed her legs. Again.

Focus! Focus dammit!

"I even saw Stella glow. Is that crazy or what?"

"You might have to accept the fact there is no way to understand it yet," I said in a low voice, trying not to let her mesmerizing scent distract me.

"And why not?"

"Because you're not supposed to see anyone glow until you understand who *you* are."

"You're saying I don't know who I am?"

How could I explain that there's a secret world distinctly *nonhuman*, a world utterly different than what she understood? "Dorothy. You know who you are to a certain extent. You're eighteen years old and you graduated high school. You're Filipino and American. But what if everything you know is predicated on assumptions about the world that are misleading and false? What if what you know isn't *you*? How would you react to that?"

She answered without hesitation. "I guess amazed and scared at the same time. Like how I feel now. But I need to know what it was and understand *why* I saw it. The best I can get from you is that there's more to life than I ever imagined."

She held the palm of my hand with her thumb, her soft hand distracting me. "But it's something you feel inside. Right?"

Her thumb started to circle my palm. "If it's a part of me, I should see you glow all the time. Shouldn't I?"

"Dorothy, it's best you don't see me that way all the time. At least until you fully understand. I'm hoping you can trust me."

She stopped circling her thumb, giving me a momentary reprieve. She was lost in a distant thought and loosened her hold. "You're asking me to trust you? Even if you won't tell me implicitly what's going on?"

The mesmerizing mango smell of her skin forced me to clench my free hand. I shook off a mental image of licking her skin. "Undoubtedly yes, but it has to be your own choice. Trust cannot be coerced."

She stretched out her shoulders and legs, crossing her feet underneath the bench. "And what if you betray my trust?"

"Dorothy, it's not in my best interest to betray you."

"Then that's what I'll do," she said in a resolute tone. "I haven't been myself ever since I met you. And there has to be a reason besides the obvious conclusion."

Her intuition surprised me. "What's the obvious conclusion?"

"Stella thinks my pathetic love life led to this big moment with you. And a part of me believes it too."

I frowned at how weak humans were for assuming love was always the answer. "What does the other part of you conclude?"

She ran her finger through loose hair behind her ear. "That this isn't love, but something else that will reveal itself in time."

My jaw hung open. Mortals always felt entitled to an explanation, one of their biggest faults, but also their greatest strength. This is why the deities needed them; humans searched for more. But Dorothy was willing to dismiss the notion of falling in love, even if it meant giving up the right to know. She was willing to trust me without any plausible reason to support her decision.

"You have no idea how mature this is of you."

Dorothy straightened her lips. "I'll go along, but I have one request."

"And that is?"

"Don't make me look like a fool."

"I'll do everything in my power not to, as long as you do the same for me." I grabbed hold of the bench, fighting every instinct to taste her skin. Another breeze had brought her mango scent streaming through my nostrils.

"Now what?" She asked.

"I guess to start, go with me to the mosque this weekend."

"Mosque?"

"Yes, my mosque. I'm *Muslim**, you know."

"Where's your mosque?"

"It's towards Henderson. It's called Masjid-e-Taweed."

"What's it like?"

"The best way to find out is to visit with me. What do you say?"

"I'd love to. As a Catholic girl, this will be new for me."

I touched her hand. "I promise I'm not trying to convert you to Islam or anything. But I want you to understand me better. Religion isn't supposed to be divisive. The Philippines has been ground zero of this religious debate. I'm glad you're visiting this summer."

"I haven't actually agreed to visit. I'm supposed to talk to my mom about it."

I had a glimpse of her mother, Meredith Dizon, at the graduation ceremony. She could pass

---

*   *Most historians agree that Islam was the dominant religion on the islands now known as the Philippines during the 13th-14th centuries. Today, Islam has a presence in southern Philippines, particularly in Mindanao.*

for a former pageant queen. Dorothy resembled a younger version of Meredith, except Dorothy had softer cheekbones, a stronger golden hue and was obviously more athletic. I thought of the changes she would experience once she made it to Mandalagan. It would be amazing to see.

"It'll be amusing to see you get bitten by mosquitoes in the province. Negros is best experienced outside the city."

"My uncle lives in the province. That's where my mom said we would stay."

"I see." Her hypnotizing mango scent was continuing to tempt me.

"Adrian. Why are you looking at me like that?"

I averted my eyes. "No reason. Just trying to make sense of this."

"Me too," Dorothy said as she leaned closer to me.

Another desert breeze whipped through the yard as an abrupt surge of energy twisted through me. I wondered what would happen if I surrendered to my intimate desires as our conversation became light, talking about our favorite songs and movies and what to expect if she went to the Philippines. I was impressed with her knowledge of music, downloading the songs of Ruby Ibarra onto my mobile device based on her recommendation.

As day turned into dusk, I resisted the urge to rub the small of her back when we hugged good night. She had to get going to see if her mom needed anything. I told her I admired her close bond with her mother. She held my neck until letting go and circling the car to the driver's side.

It was more clear that it was a matter of time until she proved herself to be a descendant of Bathala and Urduja. She was royalty. *Tumao.* I could not break the Timawa pledge of never crossing my people's social boundaries, even if her soft skin and hourglass figure tempted me. I had an urge to hug her again, but I somehow resisted.

I waved when she drove off in her Mercedes, the exhaustion from holding myself back surfacing like a tsunami wave about to flood the shore. And once I was back in my bedroom, I prayed to Allah for more willpower and unyielding control the next time I saw her.

CHAPTER 15: DOROTHY

ﺶﺶ

I tried to read the blurry digital clock on my dresser, not sure if it was morning or night or how I ended up in my bedroom. I stumbled into the bathroom and rinsed my face, scraping muta from the corners of my eyes. My hair was scattered in various directions as an abdominal shift made me run to the toilet, eventually vomiting water and air.

Thinking a hot shower would relax me, I took off my pajamas and underwear and threw them to the side. The full-length mirror flashed my naked body as the water turned from cold to hot, sending a soothing shiver up my spine.

Thank God for hot showers.

I closed my eyes and relaxed my shoulders, letting the hot water open up the pores of my skin, until I remembered what happened with Adrian yesterday. I opened my eyes, the hot water mixing with sweat on my brow.

Had I really agreed to trust him?

I turned off the water and swung a towel around me from armpit to knee. At the vanity, I wiped the mirror in circles, my face surrounded by shower steam, the dark brown hue of my eyes staring back at me, the heaviness in my arms and legs returning.

I was going against my better judgement to implicitly trust Adrian, the kind of Filipino guy my mother warned me about. A guy with tattoo-filled arms! A guy who loved sports cars! And how would I bring up the fact Adrian *and* Stella were glowing at graduation? There was no way anyone would believe me.

A knock on the door interrupted my panic. My mom's familiar voice was muffled on the other side of the door. "Wake up now, iha. It's time to eat."

The 'it's time to eat' reminder made me cringe. Even at eighteen years old, I couldn't shake years of programming by my Filipino mom. After throwing on a UNLV t-shirt and sweatpants, I went downstairs hoping to explain my sudden desire to travel to the Philippines.

ↄ

Mom stood over the oven wearing an apron and a spatula in her hand. The perspiration on her skin made her face glow like it always did when she cooked. For me, cooking was assiduous. But mom spent hours on new recipes and religiously watched cooking shows on the Food Network. The egg and cheese omelette and pancakes on the table looked immaculate. And she looked healthy.

"Good morning, *anak*!" She wiped her forehead with a towel, removed her apron and sat across from me. "Our valedictorian deserves the best breakfast after the beautiful speech yesterday."

I took a small bite, glad to hear her call me *anak*. She only called me *anak* when she was in a good mood. "Thanks, mom. Food looks delicious." The tangy taste had somehow formed bile in my throat. I forced myself to swallow her food.

"So what's on the agenda today?"

"I'm not sure."

"Your Tita Yasmin is taking Stella to Fashion Show Mall, so maybe we can meet them. Buy a couple new outfits from Dillards to start off your summer. Whatever you want, it's on me."

"That sounds good. I totally need to add to my wardrobe."

"And afterwards, we can hang out. Before I know it, your freshman year at UNLV will start."

I placed my fork on the table, my hands sweaty. "I've been meaning to talk to you about our summer. Is that offer to visit the Philippines still on the table?"

"Of course it is! You know I wanted to buy tickets months ago!" Mom clasped her hands together. "I'll see if Tita Yasmin and Stella want to go. Imagine you two girls shopping together at SM Mall!"

"Mom—"

"We've never been on a trip together! I'm curious. What changed your mind?"

"Mom, you don't understand."

"What's not to understand? Your last summer vacation before college, something you won't forget. And you deserve it, *anak*. Especially after your speech."

"MOM! Please listen for a minute!"

I yelled, something I never did, and it grabbed her attention. "I know you want to go. But are you healthy enough to travel?"

She started to reply, but instead, she gasped and struggled to take a breath. I jumped to her side. "Mom, are you all right? Mom. Say something! Mom!"

She turned towards me, but didn't have enough air to reply. I did the only thing I could think of; I gently placed my arms around her stomach, avoiding pressure on her side. I clasped both of my hands together and pressed against her navel. Once a slug of omelette flew from mom's mouth onto the counter, I released my hold. She inhaled, followed by a series of short breaths.

I couldn't believe it. I had almost killed my mom.

I handed her a glass of water. "Mom! Are you okay?"

She inhaled a glass of water and wiped her mouth with her sleeve. "I'll be fine."

"Are you sure? You choked!"

"But I'm fine, thanks to you." She leaned on the granite counter, taking breaths.

"Did you take your meds?"

"*Susmaryosep,* Cleng! I always do!"

"Okay, I'm just making sure."

She had looked energetic moments ago, but now she held her hand to the side of her body. "If you go to the Philippines. I go to the Philippines. I don't care I'm sick."

"Mom. If you have to stay, I won't go either."

She shook her head. "No. We're going. You haven't been back to the homeland. And it's time I told you everything. I don't know how much time I have left. So as long as I can walk...it's my responsibility to help you."

"Mom. You've helped me all my life."

"I've put a roof over your head and provided meals everyday. But there's more...and you need to go to the Philippines to see it."

"What are you talking about?"

Her facial expression was blank. "It's about your father."

"What about him?"

She sat down at the table, fidgeting with her hands. "Cleng. Your father. He's alive."

ᔕ

I sat down, her words hitting me all at once. My father was alive? "Mom. What are you talking about?"

"He left us, but he didn't disappear like the authorities think."

"Didn't Vegas detectives say he's missing because of some psychopath?"

"Yes. But...he's probably in the Philippines."

"Why would you think that?"

"Cleng. We've received remittance for years. That's how we've been able to afford this house. Our cars. Our lifestyle."

"Are you frickin' serious!"

Mom's breathing became heavy as if she was running out of oxygen. "He had been acting strange and suddenly he said he had to go. That it was life or death."

"This has got to be a practical joke!"

"Cleng. When I think back, it's still confusing to me. But...he sent you a card."

"A card?"

Mom revealed a brown envelope in her hand. "I think it's him. There's no return address."

I took the envelope and rubbed my fingers across the stationery. He had missed my birthdays and abandoned us without a trace, but decides to send a card for my high school graduation. This made no logical sense.

"There's no return address," I repeated.

"I'm sorry, Cleng. This has to be overwhelming. But maybe this card will help us understand why he left. Do you want to open it? Or shall I?"

I studied the envelope, it's tan parchment vibrant and crisp. "Can I wait?"

"Of course, Cleng. Let's wait. Only when you're ready," mom replied right before she nearly collapsed.

~

"Mom!"

I ran to her side and held her gently around the waist.

"I'm dizzy," she said weakly. "Can you get me another glass of water?"

She sat on a stool as I quickly grabbed a glass and filled it with water from the refrigerator filter. After a few sips, I helped her upstairs and into bed for a nap. She had become exhausted in a matter of minutes and the pain on her side made her yell out until the painkillers responded.

I was reeling from the news about my father, but still kissed her forehead and meticulously tucked the blanket under her chin once she fell asleep. Seeing how weak she looked tempered my frustration of her not telling me about my father all these years. I held her hand and the card in the other while praying a silent Hail Mary. My insides squirmed at saying just one Hail Mary, so I held her rosary and knelt at her bedside. I started with the first bead, holding mom's hand.

Hail Mary. full of grace...the Lord is with thee... Blessed are thou among women and blessed is the fruit of thy womb Jesus.

Halfway through, my phone vibrated with a blue text message.

> **Adrian:** *Having a barbecue at my place Please join me for a late lunch at 1:00 pm. After, I want to take you to Masjid-Tawheed, my mosque. Hope to see you.*

My stomach nearly jumped into my brain. I texted Adrian I would love to go. He replied he would pick me up in an hour. I texted him back with a smiley face emoji, just as a new green text notification popped up on my screen.

> **Christian:** *Busy today? Let me know if you can hang out away from the dojo. I'm free this evening.*

I replied I had a barbecue to go to but could possibly meet up later. I didn't mention it was a barbecue with Adrian. I reminded myself Christian was a friend who didn't need to know about Adrian. But inside, I felt guilty for holding information from him. I promised myself to tell him face-to-face the next time I went to the dojo.

ഗ

After the last Hail Mary, Our Father and Glory To Be, I called Tita Yasmin to stay with mom while I went out. She agreed as long as *Hawaii Five-O* episodes were still on our DVR. Tita Yasmin had a crush on Daniel Dae Kim. I assured her all the episodes were there.

I put on Maroon 5's "Girls Like You" and changed into a black haute hippie broken wings silk halter top and my favorite Patagonia tech fishing skort. I played with different hairstyles, deciding on wispy side-bangs and barrel curly hair, knowing it was more important to *not* worry about my bangs getting in my face instead of worrying *if* my hair stayed in place. I looked cute, even if I cringed at the baby fat hanging below my arms; I definitely wanted to tone up again with more workouts.

After I finished with dabs of eyeliner, I stared at the graduation card from my father in my drawer. I rubbed the envelope, listening to Ruby Ibarra's "Us" in my earbuds, trying to muster enough Pinay strength to open a card from my father, but put the card back in the drawer when Tita Yasmin arrived at the house. I had so many questions, but mom was asleep. My questions would have to wait until she was ready to answer them.

Tita Yasmin said Stella was still asleep at home, and if I wanted, to go over and beat her with a pillow to wake her up. She always spoke in an animated way that put me in a good mood. I was about to ask her about my dad, but held my tongue. Mom would have to be the one to answer my questions.

When Adrian blue texted me he was outside, I kissed mom on the forehead and waved bye to *Tita**. I grabbed my Givenchy logo embroidered track jacket and opened the front door. Adrian was leaning against his Ford Shelby, his arms folded across his chest and a smirk on his face. I quickly closed the door behind me.

"You take forever to get ready," he said.

"How long have you been waiting?"

"Not too long. I would have arrived earlier, but I figured you might take a while."

---

*   A Filipino term of endearment used for aunties (blood related or not). **Tito** for men.

I crossed my arms, trying to keep the blood from rushing to my face. I was hoping the Vegas sun made my skin shine. "What makes you think that?"

Adrian looked me up and down. "You're a girl, so in my experience, girls take forever to get ready. You look great by the way." He opened the passenger-side door and waved his hand inside. "Today, I have a chance to show you I'm a gentleman."

I slid into the car's front passenger seat. "As opposed to?"

"The glowing weirdo from yesterday who you now implicitly trust for no good reason." He shut the door and hurried to the other side of the car. He jumped into the driver's seat and turned the ignition.

"Yes. It would be nice to see you act like a gentleman for a change," I teased.

Adrian revved up the motor. "And now she has jokes." He smiled before he squealed the tires and sped out of my subdivision.

꙳

Like the other night, Adrian's fluid driving avoided all red lights and highway patrol. Eventually, we skidded to a stop in front of a house in a subdivision near our high school.

"Sorry it took so long to get here. I'm more cautious when you're in the car."

I opened my door. "You drive like a calm maniac, so I know you're being sarcastic. I'd hate to see when you drive alone."

He laughed. "Better if you didn't. Trust me."

Adrian rushed to my side of the car. He held my

hand before quickly letting go. I leaned against the car, surprised by the rolling force below my abdomen. I wanted to touch his hand again but resisted the urge to reach out to him.

I turned towards the sandy-colored house. "So who am I meeting again?"

Adrian answered as we strolled up the driveway. "People very important to me. So please try to be on your best behavior."

"Well, considering how you looked at my graduation, I make no promises."

"Duly noted, Dorothy. Duly noted."

The house had sand-colored stucco and a burnt-orange tiled roof, the turquoise shutters and wide windows giving making the house look gigantic from the outside. Wide windows brought in more light, giving any house more appeal. Mom had taught me to never judge a house from the outside, even how nice wide windows made the house look.

We entered a side gate that opened into a backyard. A man and woman sat in lawn chairs and three children were in the rectangle swimming pool. An older Filipino couple in matching red and white Hawaiian shirts stood by the barbecue grill. The smell of chicken and steak made me salivate.

The woman near the pool took off her sunglasses. "You're here!"

"Hola!" The older gentlemen held up a piece of uncooked steak from the grill. The sight of the juicy steak looked soooo good.

"And as you can see, I brought my friend," Adrian said. "Everyone, this is Dorothy, the girl I've been telling you about."

The man by the pool reached out to shake my hand. He wasn't more than thirty years old. "Hi, Dorothy. I'm Gus."

"And I'm Anna," said the woman next to him. She had short black hair and wore a yellow two-piece bikini that showed off her dark skin and slim figure.

I smiled, noting how friendly they were. "Nice to meet you."

Anna grinned and turned towards the older couple. "And these crazy old people are my parents."

"Dorothy!" Anna's father pulled me into a hug. "Call me Tito Frank!" He put his arm around the older woman next to him. "And this hundred-year-old lady over here is my wife, Lilia."

Lilia shot Frank a playful look before elbowing him in the ribs. I turned and gave her a cheek-to-cheek kiss and hug. "Dorothy, by the time you're married as long as us, everything gets old, especially unflattering jokes about a woman's age."

I laughed. "I'm glad to meet all of you."

"Good!" Frank said. "Now come on over and get some grub!"

The three children in the pool were yelling at each other in the water, diverting Anna and Gus's attention. I followed Tito Frank to a table set up with paper plates, cups and utensils. Four steaks sizzled on the grill.

"How do you like your steak?"

"Medium rare sounds great, Tito Frank. Thank you."

He chuckled, his brown wrinkled skin jiggling below his neck. "Ah, Adrian. She's polite too."

"Tito, thanks for the unnecessary commentary."

"You're welcome, my boy." Frank flipped the steaks with steel tongs as Lilia motioned me to sit with her at the patio table. I obliged, hoping it wouldn't take long for Tito Frank to cook a medium rare steak. I was starved for meat.

"I'm so glad to finally meet you," Lilia said,

patting my knee.

"I didn't know I was the topic of conversation."

"Adrian doesn't say much, but he mentioned you a few times. That's more than enough for us to know you're someone special."

"That's news to me. He's not that easy to read."

Lilia raised an eyebrow. "I'm guessing he talks more about the Philippines."

"Yes, exactly! He's told me a lot about Philippine history. More than I ever expected to know."

"Doesn't surprise me. He's in love with our homeland's history."

"He sure is."

"Take it from me. He'll open up. Men start talking if you don't push them." She shot a glance at Frank. "And trust me, I know from first-hand experience."

I laughed. "I'll take your word for it."

"Your steak is ready!" Tito Frank proclaimed. He had snuck up with the steak on a plate and placed it in front of me.

"Thank you," I replied. The burn below my ribcage had me salivating at the sight of blood oozing from the medium rare meat. Frank smiled and returned to the grill where he and Adrian began speaking in hushed tones.

Lilia looked at them suspiciously. "Now what are those two up to? Excuse me Dorothy, but let me make sure my husband isn't giving Adrian more bad advice."

Once Lilia was a safe distance away, I literally devoured four slices, the burn for meat slowly eased with each bite. By the time I had eaten half the steak, Gus had one of the boys on his shoulders while Anna pushed her two daughters in a purple floating tube, the girls screaming in delight when Anna picked up speed. Gus bobbed up and down in the water, his son holding on for dear life.

Lilia returned to the table holding a drink with an umbrella in the glass. "They are adorable. Aren't they?"

I nodded diffidently. A part of me wondered if kids were in my future.

Lilia continued. "Anna married Gus way too young, but she swore she was in love with him. Although we objected, they married anyway." She pointed to the boy playing with Gus. "Abraham came along seven months after they married, and the twins, Abby and Alana, four years later."

"How old was Anna when she married Gus?"

"The ripe age of eighteen. But they've proven us wrong, having been married for seven years. It seems like yesterday when Anna was a wide-eyed girl following her older sister around."

"You have another daughter? Is she here?"

Lilia's smile disappeared. "No, she's not here anymore."

I sensed I had hit a sensitive subject. "I'm sorry, Tita Lilia. My mom always says I ask too many questions."

"It's okay. The reason you ask questions is the reason you're valedictorian of your class."

"I don't know. It could just be a bad habit."

"I don't think it's that, so I apologize for my reaction. It's difficult to re-visit painful memories." Lilia tilted her glass. "Anna is all we have now. Her sister died a few years ago."

"Oh. I'm *so* sorry."

"It's okay. Death happens. We're coping as best we can and we're finding a new normal. Anna took it hard; she looked up to her sister her entire life."

I didn't know what to say. Lilia was mourning

and I didn't want to press any further, even as questions popped up in my mind. How did she die? And when?

Lilia sat back and had another sip from her drink. "But that's a conversation for another day. Today, I want to get to know you. Adrian won't admit it, but he has taken a liking to you."

Adrian approached and pushed a tropical-looking drink in front of me. "Looks like I got here just in time. My auntie loves to analyze people, and she thinks she has me figured out."

Lilia smiled. "My nephew thinks he can outwit me. But he doesn't know I'm always a step ahead of him."

"Or so you think," Adrian replied. "Or maybe, I'm a step ahead of you, but I let you think you're ahead of me."

"Ah ha!" Lilia slapped her thigh. "Perhaps it is I who is the fool?"

Adrian laughed lightly. "I would never call you a fool. That's bad manners."

"So, we're back at the beginning. Your auntie is always a step ahead of you."

They shared a laugh. I held the drink Adrian had given me that smelled like coconut, mangoes and strawberries mixed together. I had a sip as Anna dried off the kids with oversized beach towels. Tita Lilia and Tito Frank brought food into the house while Gus motioned his kids to plates filled with steak, potato salad and beans. Abraham, Abby and Alana ate ravenously once they sat down, making Gus and Anna laugh.

"They're eating like they've never seen food before!" Anna exclaimed as she affectionately sat on her husband's lap.

The two little girls had cute dimples and adorable flowing black hair that settled above their shoulders. On the other hand, Abraham had a serious expression until one of his sisters needed help to cut her steak. Although he was only seven years old, he carried himself much older.

Adrian returned with s re-filled glass with the same fruity drink. "This should quench your thirst for good, but let me know if you need another one."

"Aren't you too young to be an amateur bartender?" I teased.

"I blame Gus. He's an admitted alcoholic." Adrian laughed, the smile on his face making me glad I accepted his invitation today.

Anna pulled up a chair, the scent of swimming pool chlorine in the air. "Hey, Dorothy. Wanted to apologize for Adrian. I'm sure he did something that got you mad."

I laughed at Anna's animated way of talking. "Did he admit as much?"

"He never admits to anything, but he does, however, give me a guilt trip for having rowdy kids!"

I glanced at Abraham, Abby and Alana eating at the neighboring table. They looked like angels. "Your kids aren't rowdy at all."

"Don't let their current demeanor fool you," Anna said. "They are monsters, but good kids overall, even if they drive me crazy sometimes."

"I don't know how you do it," I said. "I'd never guess you gave birth to three kids. You look great."

Anna waved off my compliment. "Once you have kids, remember one thing."

"What's that?"

"Body wrap. It's a girl's best friend."

Tita Yasmin had a body wrap treatment at Spa Bellagio a couple years ago. At the time, I didn't think algae, seaweed, and mud was the answer to healthy weight loss, but seeing how great Anna looked made me a believer.

"So, I hear you might go to the Philippines," Anna continued, changing the subject.

"My mom and I talked about it literally this morning."

"You'll have fun. Maybe you'll experience first-hand some of the crazy things that happen there."

"Crazy things?"

"Adrian's told you the stories. Right?"

The night of the bonfire flashed in my mind, the made-up images of vampires, ghosts and duwendes. "He's brushed the surface with me."

"Well…we believe the old stories aren't just myths."

"Who? You and Gus?"

Anna shifted in her seat. "You just met me and my family. I don't want you to think we're lunatics."

I leaned in. "Now you have me curious."

Anna smiled. "You sure you want to hear this? It sounds so far-fetched."

"Please," I insisted.

"Okay. But don't say I didn't warn you," Anna said, hesitating. She took a sip from her drink. "My parents think there's some truth to Filipino folklore and actually believe vampires settled in the Philippines. That's why we were in California yesterday. A woman in San Francisco thought she had evidence."

"Evidence of Filipino vampires?"

Anna smiled. "See. I told you it sounds crazy."

"I definitely didn't expect you to say that." I adjusted my position in my chair. "What evidence did the lady have?"

"Evidence that went nowhere. But even if it was a dead end, this is all a jigsaw puzzle my parents are determined to piece together. But what they have so far makes you wonder." Anna leaned in closer, lowering her voice to a whisper. "All I can say is that it has to do with physiology and DNA. My father doesn't look like it, but he's a brilliant physician who fell into this when he noticed the *appendix** of one his patients."

"Appendix?"

"Yes. When he showed me the details, it made me a believer."

"What did you see?"

"Let me leave it at that for now. It's hard to get into details with the kids around. Let me get your number and we can communicate that way."

"Sure!" I took out my phone. "Now you have me curious."

Once we exchanged numbers, Anna took the kids in the house to wash off the swimming pool chlorine. I helped put away left-over food in the fridge. By the time we cleaned up, I was getting anxious to get home to check on mom. I said goodbye and promised everyone to see them soon. I meant it too. They were nice people who didn't treat me like a high school kid.

In the car, Adrian looked at me, his face serious. "Ready to visit Masjid-e-Tawheed?"

I had forgotten that he wanted to take me to his mosque. I hesitated thinking about mom. "I wouldn't miss this for the world," I replied.

༄

I had been raised *Roman Catholic*†.

---

*	*Important to note the appendix's function in the human body is still a mystery.*
†	*The Philippines became a majority Catholic country with Spanish colonization.*

I had been baptized as an infant, had my first communion in the second grade and was confirmed in the eighth grade. Sitting in the wooden pews at Saint Joan of Arc on Sundays was a prominent part of my childhood. I say *was* because I hardly went to church anymore. As a kid, I stared at the image of Jesus nailed to the cross and wondered how people could be so cruel.

Mom had always answered my questions patiently, referring to the Blessed Virgin Mary and God's miracles. She pointed to Mother Theresa and other modern-day saints. She spoke of Jesus and the sacrifice he made by dying on the cross for mankind. She quoted Bible verses and reminded me God was always watching.

Mom's strategic use of Catholic guilt worked until eighth grade when I openly debated with her about everything with the Catholic Church. Why were priests and clergy arrested for molesting children? Was Jesus really the son of God? Does the Holy Spirit really exist? She stopped forcing me to go to Sunday mass by sophomore year and I became a Catholic who went to church only on Easter and Christmas.

But as we pulled into the parking lot of Adrian's mosque, Masjid-e-Tawheed, I held on to my Catholic faith for dear life. I had to be violating an unwritten code between Christians and Muslims to never cross into each other's territory.

Adrian patted me on the leg once we parked. "You'll be fine, Cleng. I promise you will."

"I guess I'm nervous. I've never visited a mosque before."

"I can tell. But hopefully you'll find this to be a good experience."

We entered a wide concourse with a wooden, oval-shaped ceiling. Adrian beckoned me to take off my shoes and he did the same. Books were on low tables leading into a prayer hall. A man was kneeling at the front of the hall next to an open book I assumed was the Quran.

"I must wash myself," Adrian whispered. "Wait here." He motioned me to a bench outside the prayer hall.

He walked into a courtyard on the side where he began washing his ears, face and arms from a water fountain. He patted himself with a towel and stepped in front of the prayer hall entrance. "Oh Allah, open the door of mercy for me," he whispered.

He entered the prayer hall and he fell to his knees and closed his eyes in front of the Quran. He bowed and clasped his hands together. He stood, kneeled and bowed with his arms extended on the ground multiples times with his eyes closed. I recognized him saying "Allah" more than once, but the rest I didn't understand. When he stood up for the final time, I followed him into the concourse garden.

"I'm done with the Asr," he said in a low voice. "My midday prayer."

"You pray every day?" I asked.

"Yes. Five times a day."

"I'm lucky if I remember to pray once a day."

"Everyone prays in their own time."

"Do you pray here at the mosque five times a day?"

"Schedule permitting. If not, I pray at home. The important thing is to take time out of the day to surrender to Allah. Islam means surrender."

"I didn't know that."

"Yes, we surrender time to Allah in exchange for safety and peace."

"I see," I said, not sure what else to say.

"The Tagalog word *salamat* originates from

Arabic and means *and peace*. Islam is a religion of peace."

"Are there a lot of Muslims in Vegas?"

"It's a growing community. There are four mosques in Vegas that pretty much stay under the radar. Each mosque is open for us to pray, read the Quran and socialize. We caught Masjid-e-Tawheed on a calm day."

"It's nice here. So quiet."

"It is peaceful. I wish the mainstream recognized the majority of Muslims are good people. Muslims are not terrorists, just as not all Christians are mass shooters. But historically speaking, this has been going on for centuries. Christians versus Muslims. Muslims versus Christians." Adrian searched for my eyes. "But I don't want to bore you with my biased perspective. I'm just happy you came today. This was out of your comfort zone, so it means a lot you saw what's important to me."

Dry, desert wind hit our faces when Adrian opened the door of the mosque. The wind was swirling, so we rushed to the car. Once we buckled our seat belts, I leaned over and kissed him on the cheek. "Thank you for inviting me."

Adrian smiled. "*Waysaypayan*, Cleng. Now let's get you home. I don't want your mother upset with me before she meets me."

He reversed out of the parking lot and got back on the freeway. I didn't look at the speedometer. He was driving way too fast! In record time, he skidded the Ford Shelby to a stop in front of my house.

"Good night, Dorothy."

"Good night, Adrian." I kissed him again on the cheek before stepping out of the car, my insides squirming at kissing Adrian on the cheek twice in one day.

꒦

Once in the house, my mom was staring at a *balikbayan box** in the kitchen.

"Mom! Where's Tita Yasmin?"

"*Sus*, Cleng! I told her to go home. I woke up and haven't stopped! I'm crushing it! I'm slaying! Isn't that what you millennials say?"

"Oh my God, mom. You need to rest."

"Cleng! I'm fine!" She motioned towards me. "So Tita Yasmin and I got lucky and found affordable flights to Negros. We leave in three days."

"Are you frickin' serious?"

"Serious as a heart attack."

"What about your chemo sessions?"

Mom placed canned spaghetti in the box. "My doctor said I don't need them anymore. I'm healed!"

"Mom! Stop joking!"

"Cleng. Don't you know life is a comedy? I will never stop joking."

"Mom!"

"Okay, fine. My doctor says a trip to the Philippines won't kill me as long as I'm back for my July sessions."

"He did?"

"Yes. He did."

"Then I need to pack!"

"Yes you do, *iha*. But *after* you help me pack this

---

*   Describes a Filipino returning to the Philippines after an extended period living in another part of the world. "Balik" means "to return" and "Bayan" means "home" in Tagalog. The box is an actual cardboard box sold in three standard sizes by various Filipino vendors for travelers to pack items for loved ones in the Philippines.

balikbayan box."

Since she called me *iha*, she wasn't asking. My need to pack became irrelevant to her strategic use of the guilt trip. I began squeezing t-shirts, pants, sandwich crème cookies, boxes of See's Candies, Kit Kats, Hershey's and Baby Ruth candy bars, shampoo, perfume, hair conditioner, soap, toothpaste, toothbrushes, towels, toilet paper, canned peaches and oranges, canned spaghetti and beans, packaged cough drops, and of course, I stuffed the Filipino *pasalubong*[*] staple known as Spam, into the balikbayan box. Once we tied the rope around the box, we pushed it against the wall next to another balikbayan box she packed while I was at the barbecue.

Mom insisted we clean the house on account of her being in a OCD cleaning mood. As long as she was active, she had energy. And if she had energy, she didn't feel sick. And if she felt healthy, life was normal and mom's liver cancer was an afterthought. I welcomed her energy and scrubbed the kitchen sink while she vacuumed.

We engaged in small talk while we cleaned, but avoided talking about my father, the gravity of the unopened graduation card too much for either of us to start the conversation. I told her about meeting Adrian's Vegas family, but didn't mention visiting his mosque. I wasn't sure how she would feel about that.

By midnight, mom's medication had kicked in and she was snoring as soon as she laid down. After tucking the blanket under her chin and placing her meds on her dresser, I took out my DKNY purple

---

[*]   *The Filipino term to describe the practice of travelers bringing items back home from the place they visited.*

luggage bag for the trip. I had my closet open, trying to decide what outfits to pack. As the full moon filtered in through my bedroom window, I thought of the Filipino legends of duwendes, vampires and deities. Mayari was shining bright tonight.

The story of Bathala and his daughters influence in aligning the three deities of the Philippines sounded like fiction, just like the stories of mischievous duwendes. But then I remembered what Anna had said earlier. *My parents believe vampires settled in the Philippines.*

For argument's sake, say they weren't crazy. Adrian's Vegas family were nice people and Anna's excitement over her father's research was genuine. Even though she didn't go into detail, she believed her father was onto something.

This brought me to two conclusions.

Anna's parents were insane. Or they truly believed in what they were doing. This left a nagging question in my mind as I gazed at Mayari through my bedroom window.

What else did this research reveal?

CHAPTER 16: ADRIAN

ॐ ॐ ॐ

I had completed a set of a hundred chest presses and high-fived strangers who watched me lift four-hundred-pound weights. It would be entertaining to start one-arm presses, but dismissed the notion knowing it would cause unnecessary stir. I pretended to struggle around rep fifty, yet pressed forward as my mind wandered into *Dorothy land*.

Frank and Lilia had loved meeting her and had teased me repeatedly after I took her to the mosque. I didn't mind them thinking I had interest in a girl; it made me seem like a typical hormonal teenager. I needed them to think I was a typical teenager. Frank and Lilia had questioned me lately about my knowledge of Philippines history. Their research had somehow led them to a connection between the appendix and Filipino folklore. I wished I could tell them everything.

Of all people, they deserved the truth.

At thirty reps, a small crowd of human fitness freaks had circled around me. I heard cheers as I hit rep number ninety. Shit. I'd let my mind wander. I had done something amazing in human terms, which meant I was being noticed. I absolutely did not want to be noticed.

Sweat dripped from my neck and forehead. I took off my shirt and looked at myself in the full-length mirrors. The Baybayin scripted tattoos spiraled around my neck and down my shoulders and chest. My biceps and triceps bulged against my skin, my six-pack more defined since I'd arrived in

Vegas. I lifted a 150-pound barbell and held it above my head and slowly lowered it behind my neck. I repeated the movements thirty times before the burn in my muscles became consistent. The three tattoos on my chest that humans wouldn't understand had me homesick for Mandalagan, but kept me focused on why I was in Vegas in the first place.

ᜱᜋᜀ

I finished my set and high-fived a few more admirers. It was approaching midnight and I wanted to get back to the house. Harvey was silently watching my host family and he had green texted me he was bored out of his mind.

I got a drink of water and walked into a fitness room to punch at an empty bag. A Filipino guy was working on his roundhouse and kicked a bag on the other side of the workout room. He impressed me with a swift roundhouse to side-kick combination, looking like a seasoned fighter.

The kid head-nodded at me. "Hey bro. You wanna spar?" He asked.

"Sure. I need to work on a few things and looks like you can defend yourself."

"You sure?"

"Absolutely."

The kid thinks he can take me. Adrenaline rushed through me, but I held it back with long breaths. There was nothing to prove here. Just have fun. "Before we start, I should know the name of my opponent."

"Christian," he answered. "Christian Lumaga.

And you?"

"Adrian."

"Cool. Nice to meet you." Christian put his right foot in front and raised his fists to his face. "All right then. Ready to spar?"

"Bring it," I answered.

He attacked with a series of kicks I blocked easily with my forearms. He swept low for a spin kick, but I jumped over it and saw an opening. I threw a right hook, connecting with his cheekbone. Christian went down on impact.

"You okay?" I asked, kneeling next to him.

He was on his back and tried to gather himself. He didn't answer right away. "Yeah, I think so. You got a wicked right hand."

"Thanks."

Christian stood and bent over. "We have Tae Kwon Do workouts on Tuesdays, Wednesdays and Thursdays. Come by if you can."

"Thanks for the invite, but I don't train in Tae Kwon Do."

"What do you train in?"

I considered the question for a moment, preparing for the odd look I always received when I said it. *"Eskrima.*"

Christian nodded thoughtfully. "I've heard of Eskrima. It's Filipino stick fighting, right?"

"On the surface. But there's definitely more than that."

"You got me pretty good. Didn't even see the punch coming. You're fast."

---

*   *Eskrima is Filipino martial art that goes back centuries.*
      Also known as Kaliradman, or "Kali" for short.

I tried to change the subject. "I'll try to stop by your workouts when I have time." I retreated towards the door and zipped up my duffel bag. "I'll see you around, kid."

"Sure, man." Christian answered. "See you next time, Adrian."

It was one in the morning by the time I returned to the house. Harvey waved at me from his car as he drove off. His last text was one of assurance that all was well. I thanked Allah once again for Harvey still being on our side.

Back in the house, I showered and prayed the Isha'a before double-checking Frank and Lilia were sleeping okay, as well as Eric, Anna and the kids. Relief swept through me hearing them snore.

Once in my room, I stared out the window at Mayari, thanking her for my blessings as I emoted my love for the earth. My light had intensified as I connected with my *Anito*. I reeled myself back by thinking about Dorothy and wondering why I hadn't branded with another.

No doubt, I wanted her as my own. I realized this when she found me at the house after graduation. Somehow, I resisted, but now I couldn't stop thinking that she was the female I was destined to love.

---

*   *Ancestral and natural spirits in pre-colonial Philippines.*

CHAPTER 17: DOROTHY

ﻢﻌﻟﺍ

The morning after the barbecue, Stella was sulking on the phone instead of embracing the idea of traveling to the Philippines. "I don't want to go to the Philippines!" She exclaimed.

"And why not? And you know you sound like a bratty second grader, don't you?"

"Cleng! It's my last summer with Eric before he heads to UC Irvine, and who knows what'll happen. I want to spend as much time with him as I can."

"Stellz, I know you and Eric will be going strong after high school. Irvine isn't far and you can Facetime or Snapchat the days you're apart."

"I hope you're right, but there aren't any guarantees. He'll get lots of play out there. You know he's a flirt. And have you seen how gorgeous California girls are?"

"But he loves a Vegas girl. Don't doubt it or you might as well break up with him now."

"I *was* thinking of breaking up with him. To let him sow his wild oats without feeling guilty about cheating on me. I don't want to hold him back."

"Stellz. Are you serious?"

"Yes, I'm serious. I'm going to community college while he'll be surrounded by intelligent and gorgeous women at Irvine!"

"Oh my God, Stella! If you love him, let his actions do the talking. Or at least talk to him. Have you done that yet?"

"No. Not yet."

"Stellz! What am I going to do with you?"

She was completely in love with Eric, but she

assumed he didn't love her the same way she did. I didn't know if Eric completely loved Stella, especially the times I caught him looking at me in *that* way.

"I'm sorry," Stella said, her voice cracking. "I've been so emotional lately. Everything's been overwhelming. I break out crying at anything these days. You know it's bad when you bawl during a Justin Bieber song you've heard for the millionth time."

"Justin Bieber!"

"I know! I don't get it. What's wrong with me? It's not like I'm PMSing. I have two weeks until my period, and you know how regular I am."

"An emotional month for sure," I said, hoping I made Stella feel better, yet sensing I was doing a poor job of consoling.

My menstrual cycle was sporadic and unpredictable, but Stella's was like clockwork. I thought of her radiance at graduation. Did *that* have anything to do with how she was feeling now?

"I wish he wasn't such a flirt. I know he looks at you and other girls. But that's just him."

"He is a flirt. But in his defense, I haven't felt uncomfortable around him the last few months. He's trying to change."

"Maybe I should should just talk him."

"That's all I'm frickin' saying. And anyways, it's too late to back out of going on this trip. My mom said your tickets have been purchased."

"Yeah, for a flight that leaves in three days! I'm completely not ready to leave Eric for three weeks!"

"Call him. As in *now*. He might actually be an understanding guy."

"But what if he agrees to break up? That would kill me."

"Just give him a chance. Okay?"

"I have no choice. I'm just so...scared. But I'll

see how it goes when I call him. Here goes nothing."

"Call me after. Love ya, Stellz." I ended the call and placed my phone on the dresser, hoping Eric would reassure Stella that *everything* would be okay.

ᔦ

I was going crazy waiting for Stella's callback, so I decided to head out to a nearby coffee shop. Time always seemed to go by faster in coffee shops.

I grabbed my keys and waved to mom who was completely engrossed in a soap opera on The Filipino Channel. I was about to ask if she took her meds, but her animated reactions to the soap opera was a sure sign she was having a healthy day.

At the coffee shop, I found a vacant table in the corner. I listened to Bazzi's "Mine" while browsing the Internet on my phone. The online news articles were too depressing, so I caught up on sports, specifically noting Cleveland and Houston fans hating my Warriors for being the best NBA team on the planet. Golden State haters amused me; how in the world could anyone dislike Stephen Curry or Klay Thompson?

A distant "hey there" made me take off my earbuds. It was Anna waving as she nibbled on the straw of her Frappuccino.

"Oh my God, Anna!" I circled the table and hugged her.

"I would have ordered you something if I knew you'd be here. Can I get you anything?"

"Oh no, thank you. I've been lactose intolerant since forever. And I try not to drink coffee. Caffeine gets me all jittery."

"Well high school kid, that's good to know." Anna said. "Can I join you? I have some time to kill before I have to pick up the kids from school."

"Absolutely!" I motioned her to sit. "I wasn't doing anything important."

She smiled as she sat. "I hope you had a good time at our family barbecue."

"Yes! Of course I did!" I circled back to my seat. "Adrian wanted me to meet all of you that morning. It was a nice surprise."

"So, are you and Adrian serious?" Anna laughed. "You'll find I'm a direct person. It's on my mind, so I'm asking."

"I'm not sure. I guess we're still figuring out what we are to each other."

"I'm only seven years older than you, so I still remember what it was like being young. With me and Gus, we just knew. We couldn't keep our hands off each other. Such innocent times. And before I know it, I'm a mom of three, changing diapers and wiping snot from my kid's nose."

I laughed. "I can already tell you're a great mom."

"I do the best I can. I'm a work in progress." She glanced at her phone. "I have a little time before I have to pick up the kids from school. The chaos begins with after-school snacks and helping Abraham with first-grade homework. You'll be surprised at how complicated it is to match triangles with rectangles!"

"I noticed how protective he was of Abby and Alanna at the barbecue," I said. "He's a good *kuya*."

"Yes, he is," Anna agreed. "He carries himself older than his age. I want him to enjoy being a kid, but he remembers my sister and how we were devastated by her death. And now he hears us talk about my dad's research. He's so observant."

I wanted to ask Anna about her sister, but something tugged inside to leave it alone. "Your dad's research is a major subject over the dinner table?"

"It's probably all we talk about besides the kids," Anna said. "We want to visit the Philippines again, particularly Cebu and Negros."

"I'll be in Negros, so if there's anything I can do to help while I'm there, let me know."

Anna took a sip from her frap. "I might take you up on that offer. Especially since the Visayas is a major area of vampire activity."

"It is?"

"My dad believes so and has compelling evidence like stolen blood from hospitals. Dead caribou. And the stories of locals being saved by lightning-quick beings who come out of nowhere."

"Aren't those stories from any third-world country? And besides, don't vampires kill humans for their blood?"

Anna paused. "Yes, if you believe American and European folklore. But when my parents are on their medical missions, they encounter locals who tell stories of beings who stay out of sight. One time my parents were in Northern Negros and a kid needed his appendix removed. He was accompanied by his mother and all seemed normal until my dad removed his appendix and the boy's skin illuminated. When my dad said something about his skin, the mom quickly covered him and left towards the village."

I thought of Adrian and Stella glowing at graduation. "He was glowing?"

"Like the sun," Ann said. "But that's not the strangest part. The boy growled when he saw blood from another patient. His mom said that the boy was scared, but my dad saw it differently. The kid looked infatuated with the wound."

"Maybe he was still reacting to the anesthetic?"

"That was a possibility. But they didn't stick around for dad to find out. He tried to find them in the village, but no one knew who he was talking about. Locals said they must have been from the mountain."

"Were they from the mountain?"

"When my parents hiked a couple kilometers up, no one knew them."

"That's strange."

"But even more strange was when my dad analyzed the kid's appendix. It was filled with blood."

"Blood? Is that normal?"

"No, it's absolutely not normal. Especially since it was animal blood. He could tell by the blood's consistency and texture. It definitely wasn't human."

"Animal blood in his appendix?" I remembered my science teacher's banal lecture on the unknown purpose of the human appendix. There were many working theories, with one being that the appendix processed bacteria to help with digestion. But even with today's medical advances, there wasn't a clear understanding of the human appendix's true purpose.

"The appendix was storing blood," Anna said. "My dad thinks the appendix is sort of a storage tank to help digest and distribute blood to the body."

"Was there anything else?"

Anna laughed. "No, only the blood-filled appendix and a mother and son vanishing into thin air. My dad jokes about it in light-hearted moments, but he believes there are people in *secret societies** who consume blood to function."

---

*   *The topic of secret societies inspire curiosity and
        fascination among us all. It is said secret societies have
        founded the fabric of many governments and religions.*

"Secret societies?"

"Yes. Secret societies like *Freemasons** and *Shriners†*, except my dad thinks they live separate from civilization on purpose. And you know, he's a smart man and a brilliant doctor. One reason they go on these missions every year is to hopefully come across another patient like that boy."

"At the barbecue, you said you went to San Francisco because of your dad's research. What did you find there?"

"We met a white woman who swears her Filipino husband wasn't human. He had died a few years ago, so she agreed to exhume the body for analysis."

"Did you find anything?"

Anna shook her head. "Not much. My dad extracted the appendix, but it looked like a normal human appendix. But the stories the woman told were interesting. Like how her husband ate raw meat and salivated at the sight of blood. And that he never slept. He always asked her to not say anything to anyone about his insomnia, so she didn't until recently. And have we been talking for this long?"

"I looked at my phone and saw the time. "I guess so." I hadn't noticed how quickly the time had passed.

"Which means I have to go. But before I do, I wanted to give you a friendly warning about Adrian. Don't get me wrong. I love him like a brother. But sometimes, I wonder. He hardly sleeps and he's always thinking. From female to female, be careful. Okay?"

"Thanks for the warning. But I'm confused.

Aren't you close with him?"

"We are close, but it's complicated. If I had more time I would elaborate." She stood up. "But I do have to go. I don't want Abraham to be the kid to be picked up last."

"It was awesome to see you."

"Likewise. Even if it's confirmed my family is indeed crazy. Next time, I want to find out more about you. No more talk about appendixes and blood." She waved as she opened the door and waved again as she reversed out of the parking lot.

I stayed at the table biting my lip, Anna's warning about Adrian and the explanation of her dad's research taking hold.

CHAPTER 18: ADRIAN

꽁ᄂ꽁

"For the millionth time: Yes! I agreed!"

Kenneth's laugh on the other end was beyond irritating, like fingernails scratching against a chalkboard. "Congratulations! You have such an uncanny ability to make human girls fall for you."

I rolled to one side of the bed, covering my ears with my pillow. "Yes, quite an un-monumental feat. Except this girl isn't mortal."

"Technically she is human. And she's absolutely crazy about you."

"Kenneth, she's not crazy about me. She *thinks* she is. And she already said she's not sure what to believe."

Kenneth laughed again. "Although it's entertaining when you're frustrated, let's not dismiss the fact she agreed to trust you. I commend you for convincing her."

He wasn't being completely honest, but I sensed partial sincerity. "Does Kaptan know what will happen next?"

"It's unpredictable, but she already saw you glowing."

"That was unexpected. But she seems to have adjusted well, even if her human instincts can't rationalize her implicit trust in me. I admire her resolve."

Another laugh from Kenneth forced me to tighten the squeeze on my ears, even though it was no use. Kindred conversations were spoken silently in our thoughts, one of our most convenient communication methods. "Adrian, I think there are other things you admire about her, but you're too stubborn to admit it."

"Stop. I would have branded with her by now."

"Unless you connected and you don't know it."

"That's impossible. I'm only Timawa. And besides, the teachings say that you know when you brand."

"True," Kenneth replied. "Abigail and I knew instantly. But remember, the instance is in the moment of the realization."

"As usual, you are speaking nonsense!"

"Listen. I connected with Abigail after I brought her past the waterfall, and not a moment before."

"You never told me that. You always said you knew instantly."

"And as usual, you misunderstand me. it was the moment we passed the waterfall. She knew when she met me. It's different for everyone, as it is for humans."

"Our diet and lifespan makes us completely different from mortals."

"At the core," Kenneth replied, "we are all the same."

I heard Kenneth suddenly grunt and laugh. I recognized the playful growl of his son Noah and Abigail's high-pitched voice scolding the young boy for interrupting Kenneth. I admired my brother's ability to keep the kindred connection intact as his four-year-old son pounced on his back.

"Ah, my nephew! I take it little Noah is becoming quite a handful?"

"Yes, of course!" Kenneth replied. "I'm afraid he's taken to our more ravenous joys, but luckily he has Abigail's good looks."

"You are lucky to have Abigail. She balances you."

"As you do. She sends her regards by the way."

"Please send her mine." The connection cut off and I opened my eyes.

Moonlight streamed through the uncovered bedroom window, reflecting off the glass and touching my legs. My skin emitted a caramel radiance. I absorbed the warmth and privately thanked Bathala and my ancestors for their guidance. I freely expressed my love for the trees, the water, and the earth. I thought of Dorothy and her beautiful face, her curvy figure and the inherent goodness in her heart. I also thought of Stella's radiant physical charm, her maternal sensibility towards Dorothy a virtue I admired. I opened my eyes, surprised by how bright I was glowing. I flexed my muscles and shortened my breath. My radiance dissipated, leaving Mayari's moonlight to illuminate my room.

Mayari. Please help me guide Dorothy to Mandalgan safely. Please.

I opened up my browser, hoping the Internet would distract me enough to forget what Kenneth said.

Unless you have already branded and you just don't know it.

Branding happens once in a Danag's lifetime. It's a bond so powerful that every emotion and desire is felt by both. The two beings are essentially connected, their minds and bodies forever intertwined. Whoever branded with me would have precedent over the other kindreds in my life. And when one of the branded couple dies, the other dies quickly thereafter. This phenomenon was evident with Danag elders who left the physical world.

I imagined what it would be like to taste Dorothy's skin and feel her breath in my mouth, only to dismiss the thought. She was possibly royalty. As in Urduja royalty! The teachings prohibited a Timawa scrub like me from branding with anyone in the royal class. I accepted this as an absolute truth never to be questioned.

Before my conversation with Kenneth, I had felt refreshed after praying the Isha'a, the Muslim prayer after dusk. But now, I was heavy and lethargic. I wanted to sleep. All Timawas slept two hours a night, and within these two hours, there was only darkness. Kindreds were the only beings who penetrated this dark sleep. I found it sad I had never been interrupted. I closed my eyes, the last image in my mind being Dorothy's beautiful smile.

And then…complete darkness.

CHAPTER 19: DOROTHY

ﮚﮚ

W hen I returned home after having coffee with Anna, my mom was napping peacefully upstairs. She looked tired when I checked on her, so I tip-toed out of her room trying not to wake her up. She needed her rest.

I paced back and forth in my bedroom before taking out the card from my father. I just stared at it, coming to terms with the fact my father was alive. I should have been angry with mom, but she was... mom. The woman who gave me everything. The woman who was battling the early stages of liver cancer. Although it didn't make sense why she kept the truth from me, I wasn't angry at her. I wasn't angry at anyone. I was numb.

I put the card away and turned up the volume of my favorite 90's dance song, "Do You Miss Me" by Jocelyn Enriquez, trying not to think about anything. But the song's chorus made me think of Adrian!

I hadn't spoken to him since our epic day at the barbecue and mosque. The time apart was probably good for me; I needed time to digest everything happening between us. I was going against my better judgment to trust him, even without an explanation on the whole glowing thing. But as I thought about it more, I absolutely deserved an explanation. But everything he said made sense, even if it didn't. When he spoke to me, my heartbeat triple-timed and, without question, I sensed he had good intentions.

For now, good intentions were enough.

At the bonfire, Adrian talked about the Philippines running amuck with duwendes that older

Filipinos saw through the moonlight. Undoubtedly, these were exaggerated stories from one generation to the next. But meeting his Vegas family made me wonder where these folktales originated. Anna was a completely normal young parent. Same with Gus. In fact, they all seemed normal, except for the blood in the appendix research obsession.

To keep myself from going insane, I played with apps on my phone, settling on TMZ to catch up on celebrity gossip. After reading about the latest exploits of the Kardashians, I typed "Filipino mythology" in the Google search engine, thinking there was no harm in Philippine folklore research of my own. I took a breath before pressing the enter key. Within seconds, the page filled with search results.

I clicked on the first link, a Wikipedia page that listed various influences of Filipino folklore. Wikipedia stated the Philippines had unique folklore stories geographically separated by thousands of islands. Even with this separation, each shared the common elements of heaven, hell and the human soul.

Mythical creatures were listed, notably duwendes, the dwarves or goblins that Adrian had mentioned at the bonfire. There were also other creatures: *aswangs*, *diwata* (fairies), *ekek* (bird-like humans) and *wakwak* (a bird belonging to a witch). I scrolled further down the page to find a list of ancient Tagalog deities with the first deity named Bathala, the name I'd first heard from Adrian.

Bathala was the Supreme Being and creator and also known as *Maykapal** (Meicapal-Creator) or

---

*   *Another name for Bathala, mostly used by Tagalog Filipinos.*

Bathalang Maykapal. Some experts claim the name originated from the Sanskrit word bhatarra which means noble or great. I read the description of Bathala repeatedly, making sure I understood it all. Bathala was the supreme god of the Philippines before the Spanish arrived in the Philippines, just as Adrian said.

Bathala.

Anyone could post on Wikipedia, so I clicked on other links, with each one supporting Adrian's perspective on Filipino history. All the websites reiterated how the Spanish replaced native Filipino beliefs with Christian teachings. More search results confirmed Filipino folklore stories had Hindu and Arab origins with references to the beautiful moonlight that guided the gods around the earth.

Mayari. Hanna. Tala.

I remembered what Adrian had said at the bonfire. When we see Mayari's moonlight, jealousy and envy of each deity is replaced by a profound contentment for the world.

I typed "Mayari" into the search engine. The top results were for a Birkenstock sandal called Mayari. I retyped "Mayari Filipino" and found the Filipino references to Mayari and her sisters Hana and Tala. Mayari was described as the Filipino goddess of the moon, Hana of the morning and Tala the goddess of stars. The sisters were born from a human mother who died after their birth, and were raised by their father Bathala. Historians labeled the sisters as demigods; half human, half god.

I didn't see anything about vampires until I came across a *Filipinas Magazine* article that argued Filipino vampires, ghosts and witches were an extension of the beliefs of the neighboring countries of Malaysia, Indonesia and Japan. A blog by an American expatriate believed the Philippines was the epicenter for supernatural activity. The Philippines? The epicenter for supernatural activity?

I read more slowly when I found a website about vampire sightings in the Philippines. The term *mandurugo* described Filipino beings in the Capiz region who appeared as beautiful women during the day to attract men for blood. If I were a vampire, a mandurugo sounded intriguing. Reading on, there was another word. *Danag*.

I sat back, as something inside me stirred. *Danag*.

I buried my face in my hands, trying to think why this word, Danag, looked so familiar. According to the website, Danags were the oldest vampires in the Philippines who planted taro alongside humans until a Danag sucked the blood from a woman who accidentally cut her finger. Locals said the Danag moved faster than the blink of an eye and had superhuman powers. An entry by an anonymous commenter described Danag as a Visayan term that meant image/silhouette in the dark. Here one second, gone the next. I remembered Adrian mentioning Danags when we spoke at Lake Las Vegas. I closed my eyes, trying to remember what he had said.

Filipino myth says vampires called Danags lived in the Philippines. They fed off humans and formed close bonds with the islanders they used for their daily blood.

A shiver shot up my spine, making me jump out of my chair and open my closet door. Once I got past my clothes and the boxes at the back of my closet, I stared at the three symbols carved on the back wall, symbols that had no meaning until now.

ᜆᜈᜄ

Da naG

I repeated the English word out loud. "Danag."

Why was the word *Danag* carved on my closet wall? And what were the symbols above it? I always thought "Da naG" etched in my closet was child's play nonsense from the previous owners of the house. Now an Internet search revealed that all five letters, D-A-N-A-G, described ancient vampires of the Philippines.

Vampires. In the Philippines.

This had to be a simple coincidence. Maybe the previous owners were Filipino historians? Or perhaps it meant something completely unrelated to Filipino folklore. There couldn't be any relation between Filipino vampires and the writing in my closet. There couldn't be.

I examined the writing on the wall. "Da naG" was slanted on one line written in a style I didn't recognize with the "D" and "G" capitalized. The strange symbols were even more compelling. They looked like primitive Asian script. Both the symbols and words weren't written, but carved into the wall. I touched the symbols' lines, convinced this was Alibata script.

I backed out of the closet and minimized the web browser. I hugged a pillow to my chest. Someone had educated Adrian about Bathala and Mayari and Filipino folklore. He retold the stories with a passion that I admired. But this was the first time I'd ever heard of any of it and now the word Danag was carved in the back wall of my closet. The same term Adrian mentioned at the lake. And the symbols? What did they represent?

I closed my eyes, my mind ricocheting between reason and confusion until the vibration of my phone broke me out of overanalyzing everything. Stella's name flashed on the display.

"Stellz!"

She laughed on the other end. "And what have you been doing?"

"I was on the Internet. And no, I didn't sign up for social media accounts."

"And I wouldn't expect you to." Stella laughed again. "Anyway, did you know I have the best boyfriend in the world?"

I sat up. "So you two are okay?"

"More than okay. He came over and we talked on the couch."

"On the couch?"

"We only talked. I swear! We usually get distracted with, you know, but it was nice to talk without hormones getting in the way. He told me he wants to stay together." The bubbly tone in Stella's voice made me smile. "And get this. Eric's visiting the Philippines in a couple weeks, a last-minute family vacay as a graduation gift from his parents."

"Are you frickin' serious?"

"Totally serious. So I'm going to Negros, and Eric will meet up when we're over there. How coincidental is that?"

I pressed my hand to my cheek. "Did he mention where he's staying?"

"I'm not sure. I'm just super-excited about our talk. I love him even more."

I wondered if my feelings for Adrian were love, or a version of love that would make me look like a fool. "So you're going to the Philippines!"

"Yup. But, I have to get off the phone. Eric is still here! I snuck in the call when he went to the bathroom."

"Stellz! Is he sleeping over?"

"I don't know. Sometimes I fall asleep before he leaves the house. And my mom has no idea. But I can't tell if she's playing me. She probably knows, but doesn't say anything on purpose. Some kind of reverse psychology."

"She has got to be playing you."

"Right? Anyway, gotta go. Love ya."

I slumped in my bed, relief sweeping through me. I took out the envelope from my dad and held it, ready to open it until a sweeping exhaustion took over. I held the graduation card, imagining it had the answers to my questions about his disappearance, about his life.

And before I dozed off, I repeated the word that, for the first time in my life, now had mysterious significance.

Danag.

CHAPTER 20: ADRIAN

ॐ ॐ ॐ

I woke up sweating. By the position of the sun rays spiraling between the window blinds, it was 5:00 am, one hour before the usual time I woke up. I closed my eyes to go back to sleep, but zaps of white light blinded me as Kenneth's bony face emerged in my thoughts. My brother, my only kindred, had interrupted my sleep. This meant one thing—something was up.

"Adrian!" Kenneth said in an urgent tone. "Patrick sent a message through his kindred sister, Hertriel."

"Patrick?" I sat up. Why would Patrick force Kenneth to interrupt my sleep?

"Yes, Patrick, our favorite Timawa warrior in Canada," Kenneth replied. "He encountered a being in Toronto who attacked a fashion model."

"And?"

"Long story short, the visitor killed this Filipina model because a European cluster offered human blood if he killed her. They told him she killed for pleasure."

Adrian tensed up. "It has to be Sitan and his crew."

"Yes, the one and only. After tasting her blood, the vampire knew the girl hadn't killed anyone."

"What did Patrick do with him?"

"He did what Timawas are trained to do."

I was now convinced Patrick deserved a promotion. "I'm glad he was ready."

"He did well," Kenneth replied. "But there's more. The model's name was Dorothy. The guy was told to kill a Filipina model named Dorothy. Patrick sent me her Instagram handle, and she kind of looks like your Dorothy!"

"Sitan knows about Dorothy, my Dorothy."

"Apparently," Kenneth replied. "But a crossover within the royal class hasn't happened in any of our lifetimes, so I think her signals are throwing him off."

It made sense. Her bloodline had special protection during crossovers, according to the teachings. But even Kaptan hadn't lived long enough to know if this was true. Now, I had a front row seat; Dorothy's royal blood was indeed sending signals outside of Mandalagan.

"I have to go," I said.

"Yes, you do," Kenneth agreed. "Stay in touch."

I ended communication by blinking in rapid, spasmatic succession and scrambled out of bed. I quickly dressed and left the house, my mind racing a million miles per hour as I drove to the Vegas Strip to find Harvey, texting him I was on my way.

༃

As I turned into The Venetian casino parking garage and parked near the back of the first level, I clenched my fists on the steering wheel, frustrated Harvey hadn't picked up his phone or responded to my text messages.

I accidentally ran into a casino security guy when I walked through the automatic doors. I apologized and took the elevator to the third floor. Once the doors opened, I went straight to room 333. I knocked on the door with the rhythm that only protectors recognized.

Immediately, the door opened. I slipped through and closed the door behind me. The room was covered in a hazy cloud. I waved air from my face, grimacing through Harvey's nicotine addiction. At the far end of the suite, Harvey was staring out the window and puffing on a cigar.

"Must be important to pay me a visit with the sun rising."

I approached slowly. "Harvey. You need to respond when I text you."

"Sorry. I just woke up."

"Harvey. Please..." I stopped myself from mentioning Abigail's name. "Has there been any abnormal activity lately?"

Harvey laughed. "Besides you being in town?"

"This is important, Harvey."

"I'm sure it is." Harvey took a few puffs and turned to me. "Abigail was important to me, but I guess that didn't matter."

"She made her choice," I replied, not knowing what else to say.

"And I have to live with it," Harvey murmured.

"We're forever grateful for your—"

"I'm loyal to you because of her." Harvey smashed his cigar in an ashtray. "As long as she's happy and safe, that's all I care about."

"I know. And we're grateful."

Harvey leaned against the window. "So, you're asking a human if there's been unusual activity. I thought you sensed this stuff?"

"I usually can, but haven't sensed anything lately."

"Interesting." Harvey rubbed his face. "There hasn't been anything out of the ordinary, except for a couple of club girls from Canada. They said they were on vacation and needed a meal to hold them over for a few days."

"When was this?"

"Two days ago, late afternoon."

"Did they leave their phone numbers? Or tell you where they were staying?"

"They wanted to do what locals did. I gave them VIP passes to the club, so they might stop by Lavo one of these nights."

"What do they look like?"

"Young and attractive. One blonde, the other brunette. They looked harmless." Harvey frowned. "Why do you look stressed? What's really going on?"

"I didn't tell you the significance of the girl in the club. She's in imminent danger."

Harvey leaned back. "From who?"

"I can't go into that. We just need to protect this girl."

"Of course you can't tell me everything." He stood and walked to the window. "Why are they coming after her? For ransom?"

"You already know that the first generation of Danags lived in harmony with humans."

"Yes. I know. Cut to the chase, my friend."

I paused, trying to think where to continue. "As more generations passed, there was one ability, one sense, some Danags did not inherit."

Harvey leaned forward. "And that is?"

"The ability to be *undetected* by other Danags outside of Mandalagan. The original Danags born in Mandalagan are protected from detection in the outside world. But if Dorothy stays in Vegas, she'll be detected outside Mandalagan forever."

"Who is detecting her?"

I hesitated. Harvey should know the name of our enemy. He deserved to know. "A Danag named

Sitan left Mandalagan centuries ago and settled in Europe. It's been so long, we don't know what he looks like anymore. His army, if you can call them that, killed my grandfather and my youngest brother." I paused to hold the anger shooting through me. "They only emerge when it's worth their time, so it's more imperative to bring Dorothy to Mandalagan. She's in danger in Vegas."

"So, what do you need from me?"

"Call me once you get them to the club." I flashed my mobile device in front of him. "You know my number. So answer my texts and phone calls!"

"That's all?"

"Get those girls to the club. If I can't detect them, they're hiding something. I won't let them keep us from bringing Dorothy to the front of the Mandalagan gateway. And even then, who knows if she'll enter."

"Why is that again?"

"All beings enter Mandalagan on their own free will, escorted by Timawa warriors."

"That's right. I've heard it before," Harvey said, heartbreak bubbling in his voice.

I stepped towards the door. Harvey's voice stopped me from opening it. "Is there any way I can see her again?"

I didn't turn back. "Harvey. Even if you turned from the only world you know, I'm not sure you'll find a Timawa warrior to escort you. She already made her choice, and you'll have to live with it."

I walked out of the room, knowing that Harvey would never stop loving his dead wife.

ॐ

I left The Venetian and drove back to the house,

trying to detect the Canadian girls with the tricks that usually worked. I sniffed the air, but mortal blood mingled in with the desert. I turned the radio dial to local news, but no reports of unusual deaths in the area. I tried to intercept the thoughts of any connected beings in the area, but…nothing.

If they were indeed part of Sitan's crew, I should sense them. I was Timawa, the strongest of the Danag warriors! Did a new, stronger species of Mandalagan defectors exist?

All vampires in Europe had come from the Danags, regardless if they knew it or not. Those who honored Mandalagan's traditions retained the honor of protecting mortals, the beings that gave birth to blood-eating beings. Without humans, Danags would not exist and the Mandalagan Council decided centuries ago that mankind should be respected.

A seventeenth-century rebellion led by Sitan almost overthrew the Mandalagan Council. But the Timawas pushed Sitan and his followers out of Mandalagan and into the human world. We thought they would migrate to Hinatuan in Mindanao, but we soon discovered they were heading for Europe. As time passed, their skin had turned pale with the European climate. Through adaptation, these Danags learned human blood kept their bodies warm and they killed mortals with reckless abandon. Timawas tried to hunt them, but Sitan and his followers hid deep in the cold European terrain, only coming out at night when it was hardest to find them.

Were these Canadians working with Sitan? And were Sitan and his people now as strong as Timawas? This couldn't be. Timawas were blessed by Bathala, the Supreme Being. His blessings would always be stronger, according to the teachings. But what if the teachings were wrong?

I needed to calm my nerves, so I took out my Bible and turned to the Book of Leviticus.

Leviticus 17:11
For the life of the flesh [is] in the blood:
and I have given it to you upon the altar
to make an atonement for your souls:
for it [is] the blood [that] maketh
an atonement for the soul.

Human theologians translated Leviticus as a book of sacrifices performed prior to the death of Christ. Yes. This was true to a point, but if it wasn't for this Leviticus passage, my people's presence would be completely omitted from history. I blamed linguists for inaccurate Bible translations throughout the centuries. I thought of when people spoke Aramaic—the first language of the world— and how badly Aramaic words were translated into Hebrew and Latin and eventually English. I shut the Bible in frustration and placed it next to my Quran.

I went out to the yard to play with Eric and Anna's kids, my frustration with human linguists an afterthought once the kids jumped on my back for piggyback rides. The two girls and their older brother reminded me of the Danag children in Mandalagan, innocent and full of hope. Homesickness nestled in my stomach, a burn that came with the Timawa territory.

All the while, I kept tabs on Dorothy through the energy of her thoughts. It was difficult to read her mind, but sensed her mood and presence. And from what I gathered, Dorothy was doing some major thinking.

A buzz from my cell phone snapped me back.

"Harvey!" I answered. "Heard from them?"

"One of the Canadians texted me. They're going to the club tonight."

"Keep them occupied until I arrive." I ended the call, knowing tonight it would go down.

ॐ

I drove to the Palazzo as soon as Harvey texted me that the Canadians had arrived at Club Lavo.

At the club entrance, I was stuck behind a group of girls at the front of the VIP line gripping strawberry daiquiris in Eiffel Tower glasses. I stared at my phone waiting for Harvey's text. I tried to mentally prepare being inside an annoying nightclub. The thumping bass hurt my ears and crowds were claustrophobic. But I was the exception. Most Danags loved loud music.

"Do I really have to go in line?" I murmured to myself, my voice low enough for no one to hear.

The ladies giggled loudly in front of me, their over-exaggerated drunken exchanges a sure sign they were trying to attract attention. I crossed my arms when two of the girls smiled at me, hoping my body language was enough of a hint that I wasn't in the mood.

My phone vibrated with a green text message from Harvey.

> **Harvey:** *We're at the main bar.*
> **Me:** *Keep them occupied.*
> **Harvey:** *They drink a lot of Malibu Rums and Amaretto sours!*
> **Me:** *I'll see you in a minute.*

༃

A bouncer nodded precipitously in my direction and motioned to cut in front of the drunken ladies. I flashed my ID and disappeared into the darkness of the club stairway, immediately sensing the Canadians through the mixed smell of human flesh, alcohol and sweat. I zeroed in on the bar near the dance floor where Harvey's distinguished bald head nodded buoyantly between a blonde and brunette. The women's sparkly dresses, silver stilettos and shiny, long legs had men at the bar leering at them lasciviously. I stepped towards them and smelled alcohol. They were drunk.

"Harvey!" I yelled over the music.

He turned, a big smile on his face. "Hey, bro!"

Harvey whispered in the blonde's ear and did the same to the brunette. Both ladies turned and smiled. "A friend of Harvey is a friend of mine," said the blonde as she held out her hand. "Nice to meet you, handsome."

I took the blonde's hand and kissed the top of it. "A pleasure to meet you."

She pulled me in with surprising strength, forcing my waist against hers. She had blazing blue eyes and her skin felt smooth, but she was weak for letting alcohol overtake her. "You're cute," she whispered into my ear. "Let's play."

"Sure," I replied. "What game are we playing?"

"Anything you want." She leaned in to kiss me, but I turned my face, letting her slobber my cheek. "I like you," she said, playfully slapping my shoulders.

I smiled. "So what's your name?"

"Aria," the blonde replied. "Like the casino."

"Aria. Can I talk with you and your friend in private?"

Her eyebrows perked up. "You play that way, huh?"

I swiveled towards Harvey. "My friend has a private room here."

Harvey took the brunette's hand. "Follow me."

The brunette waved at me as she passed, her brown eyes glazed over. I took the blonde's hand and followed Harvey through the line of clubbers congregating at the bar. Harvey pushed past the dance floor and slipped through a doorway near the bathrooms.

I followed until a group of guys blocked us, forcing us to veer left as Harvey and the brunette stopped to talk to two girls leaving the bathroom. The two girls were attractive Filipino girls, their smiles disappearing as soon as they recognized me.

"Adrian! Is that you?"

"Dorothy?"

"Adrian?"

"Dorothy. What are you doing here?"

"We decided to go out last minute."

And Harvey didn't tell me.

Stella crossed her arms. "Who's your friend?"

The blonde leaned against me, our fingers intertwined. I let go of her hand. "Aria," I said in an accentive tone. "This is Aria."

Aria waved as she clasped her hands around my neck.

"Aria," Dorothy repeated.

Aria stepped towards them. "So you're Dorothy and Stella! Oh my God. I've heard so much about you!"

Dorothy stepped back. "You have?"

"Yes! Adrian was telling me how hot you are in bed!"

"He what?"

"I have to say, Dorothy. I would have no idea how much of a freak you are by looking at you."

"What!" Stella exclaimed.

"Stella, don't," I tried, but Aria already had her arms around Dorothy and Stella's waists.

"We're from Toronto and Adrian was showing us a good time. But after seeing the looks on your faces, he's obviously one of those guys who brags about his conquests." She looked back at me. "Asshole."

Dorothy glared at me. "I had no idea."

"He's so not worth it," Aria said as she pulled Dorothy's arm. The girls walked in the opposite direction, forcing an ache in my stomach. I truly felt like vomiting. Once I regained my balance, the girls had disappeared around the corner.

I looked at Harvey. "What just happened!"

Harvey shrugged his shoulders. "The Canadians found Dorothy and Stella. That's not what we wanted. Right?"

I had to hold myself back from grabbing Harvey by the neck. We had let Aria and Dala escape with Dorothy and Stella! I scrambled to the dance floor and saw the girls dancing. Aria and Dala gave Dorothy sympathetic pats on the shoulder.

They had found the girl they wanted to kill.

"We need to kill them," I growled.

"And we will," Harvey said. "But look at them. They're trying to be friends with Dorothy and Stella."

I watched them from the perimeter, noting my Timawa instincts didn't sense any danger. If I hadn't known better, they looked like four girlfriends out at the club having a good time. Aria and Dala had taken sips from their drinks and were dancing alongside Dorothy and Stella. They kept dancing and shouting into each other's ears. They hugged and took out their cell phones, apparently exchanging numbers. Why did Aria and Dala want to be friends? And why did Dorothy and Stella believe them so easily?

The girls stepped off the dance floor and headed to the exit. I moved towards them when bouncers surrounded me on all sides. I sensed a change in their intentions. I glared at Harvey, my arms pulled by two of his men.

"Harvey! What is this?"

"It's time I stood up for myself!" Harvey yelled. "All these years. And I've had enough!"

Harvey's eyes were aimless, like he was in some sort of trance.

"Harvey! Aria and Dala did something to you. Don't give in!"

"Again! Ordering me to act a certain way! I've had enough!"

There was no time and the girls were getting away. Using my Timawa speed and agility, I kicked the bouncers and pushed them to the ground. Another bouncer charged at me, but I sidestepped and shoved him into Harvey. They fell on top of each other, Harvey now pinned to the ground, his eyes raging with anger. I got out of the club, not waiting to see if they got back up, making sure they wouldn't chase after me by influencing two drunk guys to fight. The bouncers would be busy for a while breaking up the melee.

I chased the girls by trailing Dorothy's mango scent, but I didn't see them in the casino. Her scent lingered in a courtyard with a fountain, but I lost the trail by the roulette tables. I searched everywhere on the main floor, slamming my hand against a slot machine after it was apparent I wouldn't find them. I was about to go back in the club to knock some sense into Harvey, until my phone vibrated and Dorothy's name popped up on the screen.

"Dorothy! Where are you?"

Aria laughed on the other end. "Oh, Adrian. It's for me to know."

"What have you done to her?"

"She's fine, for now. But I know who she is."

"How do you know who she is?"

"Again, for me to know and you to find out."

"What do you want?"

"You leave us alone and she lives."

"What do you want with her? You want her alive. Don't you?"

"Don't start overanalyzing things," Aria said. "But you're right. We need Dorothy alive, but it's not as simple as you think. And we know how important Anna, Gus and the kids are to you. And Frank and Lilia."

My heart sank. "Who are they? I don't know anyone by those names."

"Good try, Timawa. If you don't follow what we want, they all die. Simple. As. That."

"You dare not threaten me!" I yelled into the phone.

"Whoops. I think I just did."

The line went dead. I shouted expletives into the phone, calling back three times, only to reach voicemail. I texted, but no replies. I paced the casino floor, trying to track where they went, utterly confused why Aria and Dala hadn't killed Dorothy the moment they saw her.

CHAPTER 21: DOROTHY

‎ﺑﺴﻢ‎

I took long breaths in the secluded gazebo of the Bellagio Conservatory and Botanical Gardens. Water trickled from a nearby fountain, and tourists walked the aisles of well-gardened plants and trees. I loved the abundant multi-colored flora and cherry blossoms adorned next to the beautiful water features and enchanted talking tree, the one place Stella knew would calm me down.

"What was I thinking?" I asked out loud. "He played me."

Stella had her arm around my shoulders. "Did you see how surprised he was? What a liar!"

I leaned my head on Stella's shoulder, an ache fluttering between my chest and stomach. "Maybe my mom was right. Filipino guys are dogs."

"Please don't say that. I would die if Eric turns out to be one."

I wished that I hadn't met Adrian at all. "What do I do now, Stellz?"

"I'm sure he'll apologize and give you an excuse, but it was plain as day. What Aria said was true. He's an asshole!"

"Yeah, maybe."

"Maybe! You saw how he stood there while she explained what he said to her. He couldn't say anything because it was true!"

Aria and Dala emerged from around the corner, returning from the bathroom where they had gone to freshen up. They looked stunning in their club dresses, their legs shiny and hourglass figures standing out like models. They were absolutely gorgeous.

"Adrian called," Aria said, handing me my phone. "Good thing I had it on me. He was trying to get me to go over to his place!"

"Oh my God!" Stella yelled. "The nerve!"

The Adrian I knew was sensitive and aware of his faults. He didn't seem like a player. "I don't know what to believe."

"Dorothy," Aria said. "I know we just met, but trust me. We don't make this stuff up. Girls have to stick together against playboys like him."

The murmur of tourists had died down. The sound of Frank Sinatra's baritone voice from the speakers came to the forefront. I took in the peaceful surroundings until my phone vibrated with an incoming blue text message.

Adrian: Can we talk? Tonight? Please?

I stared at Adrian's message, my hands slick at the thought of him holding hands with Aria.

Stella's voice broke my spell. "I can't believe he's trying get out of this!"

My lips straightened, not sure if I had a right to be disappointed. It's not like we were dating. But why did it feel like we were? Why was I so hurt?

The memories of Lake Las Vegas and our epic day at the barbecue and mosque flashed through my mind. Adrian seemed to be into me, but that's probably how Aria felt, like she was the only girl he wanted. And did he really brag about me in bed?

"I thought he liked me," I murmured. "I thought he respected me."

"I can't believe he's treating you like this! He's the one missing out!" Stella fumed.

"I'm replying. I want to hear his explanation."

"Don't do it!" Aria's commanding tone surprised

me.

"I need to hear his explanation. I thought I knew him."

Stella reached for my phone and somehow grabbed it. "Don't text him back! He's a good talker! Don't fall for it!"

"Dorothy. Listen to her," Aria insisted. "He's so not worth it."

But I wanted to talk to him, even as anger shot through me at the thought of him spreading lies about me. Why would he do such a thing? Adrian wasn't the guy Aria described. And suddenly, it was strange how Aria and Dala looked at me. Were they lying? And if so, why? And why would they want anything to do with me or Stella?

"Dorothy, let's have a late night breakfast at Mr. Lucky's at Hard Rock and hang out," Dala said. "By the morning, you'll have a better idea how to handle him."

I swiped my phone and started texting.

> **Me:** *At the Bellagio gardens. Meet me here. Hurry.*

I pressed send, not sure how to keep myself from caving when I saw him. The thought of saying goodbye stuck the back of my mind. At least I hadn't gotten in too deep with him. But still...it hurt. I didn't completely trust Aria and Dala, so I hoped Adrian had an explanation that made sense.

CHAPTER 22: ADRIAN

ॐॐॐ

I exited the freeway and slammed my fists against the steering wheel when I realized I didn't even have to get on the freeway. Dorothy was only at the Bellagio!

"What's wrong with me?" I yelled, turning onto Las Vegas Boulevard. I weaved through traffic and sped into the Bellagio self-parking garage. I ran into the casino and sensed Dorothy near a gazebo hidden behind the fake trees of the botanical garden. Tourists surrounded me on all sides as her scent – her sweet human mango scent – made me woozy.

I closed my eyes. Within seconds, the crowds dispersed. I wasn't using my influence over humans for evil, but Aria and Dala might hurt innocent people. At least that's how I rationalized the use of my person dispersion abilities. But when Stella, Aria and Dala approached me, I backpedaled.

A scowl crossed Stella's face. "What do you want?"

"I need to talk to her."

Stella stared with anger in her eyes, emoting a raging type of beauty. "I'm not sure that's a good idea."

"I know you don't. And with good reason, but I owe her an explanation."

Aria and Dala looked at each other. "It's okay, Stella. Let them talk. I'm sure she'll look right through him."

Dorothy emerged and looked in my direction, her eyes making my head spin until I avoided eye contact to collect my bearings. "Is what Aria said true?" she asked dolefully, her voice barely audible. "You bragged about me in bed?"

Anna, Gus and the kids flashed in my mind. Frank. Lilia. They were my Vegas family. Years ago, Danags made a pact to keep them safe. Now they were in danger.

I glanced at Aria, hating her. "Dorothy. I got a little drunk."

"Drunk!" Dorothy said incredulously. "You're using alcohol as an excuse?"

"I drank too much," I continued. "I blame Harvey."

"How do you know Harvey?" Stella asked.

Oh yeah, never explained that. "He's a family friend." I wasn't lying. Harvey was a friend of the family, my Danag family.

"How coincidental," Dorothy murmured.

"He knows my brother. I visited him for the first time at the club. I only planned to hang out a little bit."

Stella crossed her arms. "And then what happened?"

I pointed at Aria and Dala. "We bought these girls drinks at the bar."

Dorothy took a step back. "So you hit on them."

I took a few steps forward. "I know how it looks. And I'm sorry."

Aria glared at me wickedly. What was she accomplishing by letting me speak to Dorothy? I wasn't connecting something. What was it?

"Adrian, did you brag about me to Aria?" Dorothy asked wistfully.

"Like I said, I know it looks bad. I had a little too much to drink."

Stella looked like she wanted to punch me. "Adrian, being drunk is not an excuse!"

"I know, Stella!"

"And don't you dare raise your voice at me!" Stella exclaimed.

"I didn't mean to yell. I'm just embarrassed."

"As you should be," Dorothy said. "And it's obvious you're a player."

"Dorothy. Please."

"Stay away from me. Please." Her disquieted tone made me wince.

I pointed at Aria and Dala. "They're not your friends. They have an ulterior motive."

Aria started to laugh. "Okay, playboy. That's enough." She had her arm around Dorothy ominously. "Us girls stick together, even if we did just meet."

I assessed Dorothy and Stella's demeanor. Stella looked angry and had the same bewildered look in her eye that Harvey had when his men jumped me at the club. Stella was under Aria's influence. But Dorothy looked like herself. More confused and hurt, but she was alert. She was herself.

"Dorothy, don't believe her. She's not who she says she is."

"Then who am I?" Aria asked.

"Why don't you tell us who you really are? Is Aria even your real name?"

"Of course it is. I'm Aria and this is my sister Dala. You may have heard of my grandfather, Sitan. Remember him?"

"You're the granddaughters of Sitan?" I heard myself say.

Aria laughed louder. "Papa is on his way now that we've found her."

I staggered back, remembering how Sitan's army had killed my grandfather and youngest brother in Europe years ago. Anger rose inside me.

"Sitan never shows his face," I said.

Dorothy glanced between me and Aria. "Who's Sitan?"

"Dorothy," Aria said. "You seem to be in the dark about who you are."

"Aria, don't," I said sternly. "She's not ready."

"Or maybe she is?" It was Dala who spoke. "Shouldn't she know?"

"Not until she's ready!" I yelled.

"Dorothy," Dala said. "Have you noticed your appetite has changed lately?"

"Dorothy, don't listen to her," I said. "She's trying to confuse you."

"Who are you people?" Dorothy glanced between me and Aria. Stella had grabbed Dorothy's hand, still angry with the same bewildered look in her eye. Dorothy stared at her friend. "Stella, why do you look that way?"

I had to make my move before it was too late. After taking a breath, I sprinted towards Dorothy and Stella and grabbed them by the waists. Aria and Dala reacted seconds later, chasing me through the Bellagio. Dorothy and Stella screamed as I struggled to hold them in my grasp. I sprinted through the main lobby and casino floor. I lengthened my gap and ran into the self-parking garage where I quickly squeezed Dorothy and Stella in my car.

I sped out of there and saw Aria and Dala's frustrated faces in my rear-view mirror. I pressed on the gas and skidded onto Las Vegas Boulevard where I swerved through traffic. I turned onto the interstate and didn't see Aria or Dala behind me. They were fast, but not Ford Shelby fast. I pressed on the gas headed south, influencing highway patrol to ignore me. We were halfway to Primm when Dorothy screamed. Stella had a knife against Dorothy's neck.

"Stella!" I yelled. "What are you doing!"

"Shut up!" Stella seethed.

"Stella! Stop!" Dorothy yelled. "It's me! Cleng!"

I pressed the brake and pulled onto the shoulder of the freeway. It was obvious Stella was not herself. She had been hypnotized into the space between consciousness and unconsciousness the same way Harvey had been. There was only one way to break Stella out of her trance. I took one hand from the steering wheel and looked for an opening.

Stella tightened her hold around Dorothy's neck. "Don't come any closer or I'll kill her!"

"Stella. You can't hurt your best friend." In one swift motion, I snatched the knife out of Stella's hand. She was now defenseless.

I looked at Dorothy contritely. "This is not what it seems." I pulled Stella into me and kissed her, making sure our lips connected long enough to break through her trance. When her tongue explored the roof of my mouth, I held us together. When she tried to push me away, I disconnected.

Stella wiped her mouth and slapped me in the face. "Adrian!"

"Stella, I'm sorry. But I had to!" I turned to Dorothy, searching for her eyes. "I'm sorry, Dorothy. But I had no choice."

"I heard you," Dorothy replied, focusing her attention on her friend. "Stella, are you okay?"

"Your boyfriend made out with me. I am not okay!"

"I had to kiss you!"

"OMG, Adrian! You don't ever have to kiss me!"

"Stella. You kissed him back," Dorothy murmured.

"Aria and Dala somehow changed you," I said.

"Do you remember anything that happened at the Bellagio?"

"Bellagio?" Stella repeated. "The last thing I remember was dancing at the club! When were we at the Bellagio? And why are we on the freeway shoulder?"

"Stella, you don't remember anything from the Bellagio?" Dorothy asked.

"NO! I DON'T!"

"Okay, okay, okay. Let's not freak out." Dorothy said. She scooted over to her friend. "Adrian, can you take us somewhere?"

"Not a casino," I said. "Too many people. And I can't take you home until I know you're safe."

Dorothy looked at me frantically. "Where can we go?"

"The mosque. It should be safe at the mosque."

I turned off the hazards and merged onto the interstate and headed to Masjid-e-Taweed with the taste of Stella's saliva lingering in my mouth.

CHAPTER 23: DOROTHY

بِسْمِ

Stella was freaking out. She wouldn't stop shaking, so I rubbed her back and cradled her head into my shoulder. Who could blame her for her meltdown? The last moment she remembered was dancing at the club and the next thing she knows, she's making out with Adrian right in front of me!

Adrian drove with a determined look on his face, his foot heavy on the gas pedal. We didn't speak as his Shelby's motor provided relaxing white noise. What had just happened? Aria. Dala. And who was Sitan? And what did Aria mean when she said I should know? Know what? Adrian and Stella had kissed for a while, and even though they held the kiss passionately, it didn't seem as if they enjoyed it. Or did they? And why wasn't I jealous? Adrian exited the freeway and pulled into the mosque parking lot.

"We're here." He stepped out of the car and held the door open for us.

With the cold desert wind blasting in our faces, we followed Adrian inside the front entrance of the Masjid-e-Taweed mosque. After we slipped off our shoes, we settled in one of the smaller rooms adjacent to the main prayer hall. Stella had stopped shaking, but was sniffling, her arms crossed. I approached Adrian. He motioned me to follow him to the courtyard near the fountain, the trickling water offering a peaceful respite.

"I'm sorry," Adrian said. "Tonight wasn't supposed to happen like this."

"Why did you kiss Stella? And who is Sitan?"

"Sitan hurt my family years ago. I didn't know he

had granddaughters. And I kissed Stella to break the trance she was under."

"Trance? Do you know how that sounds?"

"Yes, I know. But didn't you notice how angry Stella was?"

"Even still. Was kissing her the only solution?"

"Yes, it was. Can't you see she's back to her old self?"

"Yes, her freaked out self! How will she explain this to Eric?"

"I'll talk to Eric. There's a lot to be explained."

"I hope you can explain it! First, two girls I've never met in my life tell us you're slime. They say they know who I am before you grab us and run like a bat out of hell from girls in stilettos. And to top it off, you make out with my best friend right in front of me!"

"I'm sorry about all this. If Aria and Dala are right, their grandfather, someone I despise, is on his way to Vegas to find you. And that can't happen. You'll have to trust me when I say you don't want to meet him."

"He doesn't sound like someone I want to meet." I stepped towards him. "What did he do to your family?"

"It was years ago. My grandfather..." Adrian stopped himself. "Sitan is the one person I hate in this world. I'll fill you in when the time is right."

"Adrian. Whatever it is. Tell me."

"I'll tell you soon, I promise. But you're going to have to trust me."

"I *have* trusted you! I'm still not sure what Aria said is true or not! And you kissed Stella! How can I trust you when you kissed my best friend?"

"It meant nothing. Whether you understand it or not, kissing her was the only way to bring her back."

"And why doesn't she remember anything at the

Bellagio?"

"Because of Aria and Dala. They hypnotized her."

"And your kiss broke her out of it."

"Yes," Adrian answered. "Believe me, it's you I would rather kiss."

"What? Is this another lie?" I wiped my face with my shaking hands.

Adrian reached for me, but I pushed him away before grabbing hold of his arm to keep my hands still. He didn't move, giving me the option to let go, but I held on, trying to stay composed.

"No, I'm not lying to you. I'm attached to you, Dorothy. That's why I'm so sorry about what happened tonight."

I tightened my grip. "I don't know why I believe you."

"Because you know me. I would never say boastful things to girls in a club about you. It's not my style. Aria was lying and you sensed it."

I backed off. "Why would she lie? What does she want?"

"I don't know exactly, but if you can still trust me, let's find out together."

As soon as he finished the sentence, he pulled me into his chest, his breath on my neck. I tried to hold my ground, but my mind started to swirl, and before I could resist, Adrian connected his lips to mine with a kiss I couldn't escape.

CHAPTER 24: ADRIAN

ಹ ಲ ಹ

A ria and Dala wouldn't kill Dorothy and Stella in a mosque unless they no longer respected the religion we shared. Once in the mosque, I sensed they still held Islam in high regard, even if they were pawns for Sitan to manipulate. After a few hours, I sensed Masjid-e-Taweed was the right place to keep Dorothy and Stella safe.

But I didn't take any chances. Yesterday, I had summoned Patrick to Vegas through his kindred sister Hertriel. Patrick would arrive shortly. I texted Harvey, hoping the trance he was under had already worn off. I had a bad feeling when Harvey didn't answer.

Now that I had kissed both Dorothy and Stella, I tapped into their energy more intimately than before. They were confused, not sure what to believe. I looked at Dorothy and Stella consoling each other on the other side of the room.

A knock on the door snapped me back. I opened the door to a young man wearing a gray cardigan and blue jeans while sporting a mohawk haircut. His cheeks straightened into his chin, his gray eyes a contrast to his distinct olive skin. His wide chest made his cardigan look like it was about to rip apart. He stepped inside and extended his hand.

"Patrick," I said.

He quickly bowed at my feet. "Adrian. Thank you for getting me out of Toronto."

"That exciting over there, huh?"

Patrick stood up. "You don't know how bored I

was. I worked out every day to stay sharp, knowing I would be tested at a time I least expected."

"And you did great. I'm proud of you."

Patrick walked in and closed the door. "You really think Sitan is in Vegas?"

"He's close if he's not here already."

"Who is my replacement in Toronto?"

"We summoned Sario."

"Sario?" Patrick feigned surprise. "Isn't he—how shall I say it—unpredictable?"

"He's better now. This is a chance for him to prove he's capable."

Patrick nodded intrepidly. "If he needs anything, let me know."

"As of now, your only worry is this mission in Vegas." I closed the door. Dorothy and Stella looked at Patrick, afraid and unsure.

"He's a friend," I said to them.

They didn't react, but held each other more closely.

I whispered to Patrick. "I'm sure Sitan has already heard what happened from Aria and Dala. They may hesitate at first, knowing I'm aware of them, but they'll eventually find enough courage to try something. And hopefully this one decision will be their ultimate downfall."

"It will be," Patrick replied. "But should we bring more Timawas? Are we enough?"

"Trust me. Sitan has inferior strength and speed to any Timawa warrior."

"Do you still believe that's true? You haven't seen him in years."

Patrick had a point. I wasn't sure how years of human blood affected Sitan. He was strong, but as strong as a Timawa? Maybe, but not likely. "No one is stronger than Timawas. You have to believe this,

Patrick."

"If you believe it, I do too."

"Good." I stepped toward the door. "Keep Dorothy and Stella safe. Bring them home and wipe their memory of meeting you. Stay close to them. Your mission is to always be near them."

"Yes, sir. I'll never be far."

I opened the door and turned back. "Don't forget. Wipe their memory of meeting you. And if anything goes down, I'll be there with you to protect them."

Patrick saluted me. "I will be honored to fight along side you."

I looked at Dorothy and Stella. "I'll see you soon," I said. It looked like Dorothy wanted to talk to me, but explaining the kiss with Stella had already been exhausting. So I closed the door of the prayer room, feeling better knowing Patrick was monitoring Dorothy and Stella's every move.

CHAPTER 25: DOROTHY

ﻦﻳﺮﺑ

I woke up and wondered how I ended up in my bedroom. The last thing I remembered was Adrian's kiss at the mosque. I stretched, trying to recall what happened after that.

"Cleng!" I heard from downstairs. "We have shopping to do. Wake up, *iha*!"

"Okay, mom!" I went to the bathroom as I fought through a wave of nausea. I vomited air until my system settled down. After a quick shower and outfit change, mom and I took the BMW to pick up Stella and Tita Yasmin for a Fashion Show Mall outing.

By mid-afternoon, we had four bags of new clothes from Dillards, more than happy with our new summer outfits. We went to dinner at Olive Garden and talked about Uncle Fred, my mom's brother in the Philippines, as well as the latest pop culture and fashion trends. We didn't talk about mom's health or the fact my father was alive. I was happy Mom looked completely healthy, talking about going to the Philippines. No one would have known she had liver cancer.

Throughout the day, Stella didn't bring up Adrian's kiss or the entire confusing night. And since she didn't mention it, I didn't either. For now, I was okay with burying it beneath the surface.

When Eric join us for dinner, she showed more affection than usual, which surprised me since our mothers were across the table. But Eric did a nice job of kissing our mothers' butts with compliments on their food choices and their youthful looks. Seeing Stella and Eric together made me text Adrian multiple times.

But he didn't reply to any text messages.

I stayed busy with errands that only Filipino travelers worry about. Mom and I picked up more balikbayan boxes at SBC and filled them with more shoes, t-shirts, pants and socks, on account of my mom's brother requesting more items from the States. Mom never convinced him that most everyday necessities at Target and Wal-Mart were made in China.

We spent one morning filling our shopping carts with discount shoes, camisoles and candy bars. In the afternoon, we packed another balikbayan box to the max; shoes at the bottom, trinkets in the middle and clothing at the top.

Mom didn't hear me when I asked about my dad after had gone to the bathroom. I didn't want to get her upset if she wasn't ready to talk. Her health was the priority. so I dismissed it, even though she had completely pretended not to hear me. Instead, she asked about the boy that had made me nervous at school. I told her we'd been hanging out and he was a nice person. I didn't tell her he hadn't returned my calls or text messages.

It wasn't like I had a right to be upset; he technically wasn't my boyfriend. But the longer I didn't hear from him, the more I was concerned. She told me boys would always be confusing and that if I wanted, I could stalk him through a new app she heard about from Tita Yasmin.

She made me laugh, which put me in a better mood. But I still didn't sleep the first night and I fought my drowsiness the second night.

Where the heck was Adrian?

≈

Adrian walked shirtless next to me in a forest carrying a spear, his face painted with green, yellow and red tattoos. Although he looked like a savage islander, I wasn't afraid of him. He asked if I was thirsty as a burning sensation settled in my throat. I answered yes. He laughed and kissed me, his soft lips smoldering against my cheek.

We turned a corner and saw a house surrounded by coconut trees nestled next to a river that curved alongside a mountain ridge. A chicken stall was on the left and a silo of snorting pigs on the right. It was humid, but I wasn't sweating. The sun was like a radiant shield that embraced me with its warmth and light.

I reached for Adrian's hand until I noticed his burning red eyes. I asked him what was wrong, but he didn't answer or smile. Suddenly children surrounded us. They ranged from infant to teenagers, the boys shirtless and the girls wearing simple, brown dresses. I bent down to look into the eyes of one of the younger boys. He held his stare. Once our eyes connected, an indescribable pain shot through me that made me want to die.

≈

I woke up on the verge of screaming, my

mind swirling and body shaking. I threw up in the bathroom with a burn rising inside me as I wondered where Adrian could be. I crawled back into bed, my achy body craving...something.

I was so out of it, mom checked up on me as if I was the one with liver cancer. After she promised me she had taken her meds, I was unable to eat and fell into a sleepy haze. By evening, mom had placed chicken noodle soup on a stand next to my bed that made me throw up after one spoonful.

The next morning, the weird dream and extra sleep had somehow given me an energy boost. But I still hadn't heard from Adrian. When I received a green text from Christian to meet him at the dojo, I was reminded how I had been MIA from Tae Kwon Do and had forgotten to text him after the barbecue. I responded that I would definitely go and I would see him later in the day.

ᔕ

Once I arrived at the dojo, one of the instructors teased that I was actually there in the flesh. Since Christian hadn't arrived yet, he said to use one of the punching bags while he worked on some paperwork in the back office. I thanked him and put my duffel bag to the side.

My first few punches felt good against the leather punching bag. I threw a right hook and a left jab, a roundhouse combination and another set of punches. I repeated my combination, my martial arts skills slowly coming back.

I heard Christian's voice behind me. "You must

be pissed at someone."

I turned and saw him smile, which distracted me as I attempted another roundhouse combo. "You might say that."

"You're adding to the stereotype of tiny Filipino girls having attitude."

"Ha! Me with attitude? Come on now."

"Who said I was referring to you?"

"Who else would you be referring to?"

"There's a ton of Filipino girls in Vegas. What about Stella? Or Janine?"

Janine Flores was a nine-year-old student he trained on Wednesdays. "You're comparing me to a kid half my age?"

"She's your height."

"She is not!"

"She's grown the last few months."

"Christian!"

He approached me and gently placed his hands on my hips. Surprised by his bold approach, I swiped at my bangs. He tried to connect with my eyes as he pulled me closer. "You haven't noticed because you're never at class anymore."

"Christian. Did you miss me?" I'm not sure why I asked him if he missed me except for a sudden need to know if he did.

Christian held his ground. "Yes. I have missed you. And when you ghost on my text messages I get frustrated. But now, I have to admit, I'm happy to see you. I'm all conflicted."

"You are?"

"Yes. I am." Christian's lips straightened. "Are you that oblivious?"

"Oblivious to what?"

"To the fact I've missed you? That when you ignore my messages it affects me? That perhaps I look at you as more than a sparring partner?"

My mind raced to his texts asking how I was doing. I hadn't seen him since graduation and my last text response was the day I went with Adrian to the barbecue. "I didn't know you missed me."

"It's confirmed. You are completely oblivious!"

"Christian. I had no idea."

"I know you had no idea." He let go of my hip and looked off. "It's not easy to be taken for granted."

I wanted him to feel better. "I don't know what to say."

He backpedaled. "Of course, you don't. I guess I'm the one pissed at someone."

He turned his back to me. When he started conversing with a customer who had walked in, I grabbed my bag and left, noting Christian avoiding me when I looked at him. Once I settled behind the steering wheel of my car, I took deep breaths, trying to compose myself.

What gave him the nerve to talk to me that way?

I closed my eyes, the image of Christian's face and his honest comments hitting me all at once. Why didn't I notice he wanted my attention? How could I take his friendship for granted?

I took another breath and opened my eyes, wondering if I should go back to talk to him. But what would I say? I had no idea what to say. And for no reason at all, Adrian's beautiful face floated into my mind. And then mom. I hadn't been paying close attention to her as I normally did. She was sick and I had been selfishly focused on my love life. I reversed out of the parking lot, consumed with getting home while listening to Post Malone's "Psycho" on the radio.

⇜

Mom was napping, her loud snores a welcome sound. She looked small balled up in the fetal position. She hadn't looked blatantly sick lately, but now she looked tired. She didn't wake up until late afternoon, but when she yelled at me to eat something, I smiled knowing she was feeling healthy.

By the evening, I was thinking about Adrian's face in my dream, which made me feel irritated that he hadn't contacted me in days. I turned in early when mom told me to stop moping. I was about to text Christian, but I stopped in the middle of composing a message, suddenly consumed by more details emerging in the strange dream with Adrian.

All the children were barefoot. Beautiful, yet indistinguishable women watched us from a distance and reddish-green tropical fish jumped in and out of the river. A pig (known as *lechon* by Filipinos) roasted over a fire pit, making my mouth froth. When I looked at the other pigs in the corral, a burn rose in my throat. And when I reached for Adrian's hand, he wouldn't accept it, even as pain shot through my body.

꩜

I brushed my teeth and changed into my favorite yellow and blue Warriors pajamas. I brushed my hair, a sadness overwhelming me as I thought about Adrian and Christian. I didn't want Christian to be upset, but my concern for Christian was an afterthought to my need to see Adrian.

Where was he? Did I do something to turn him off? And why did I care? I still wasn't sure if he had bragged about me in bed. I was about to call Stella to see what was up when a fluid voice I hadn't heard for days startled the shit out of me.

"You look sleepy."

I jumped back, surprised to see Adrian's dark figure next to the window. My nostrils were suddenly privy to his familiar coconut odor. "Adrian!"

He leapt towards me and covered my mouth with his hand. "Sssh. You don't want to worry your mother."

I swiped his hand away and hugged him, settling my face into his chest. I closed my eyes, lost in the moment until he broke our hug and leaned against the wall, giving me my first look at him in days. I gasped as soon as I appraised him. His face had an olive color instead of the usual pink. He did not look like the Adrian I knew.

"Adrian. What's happened to you?"

"What's happened to me? What's happened to me you ask? I'm afraid something has happened that has me...confused."

"What is it? And where have you been?"

"I've been busy."

"With what? Aria and Dala?"

"Something like that. Plus, I need to stay in control when you're around."

A burst of energy flowed through me. "And you didn't think to let me know what was going on? Did they threaten you? And what if I want you to lose control around me? What if I want you to lose total control?"

Adrian moved to the foot of the bed, his olive skin looking darker by the second. "You don't understand. I haven't been fair to you."

"What are you talking about?"

For the first time, I noticed his burning red

pupils. Like in the dream. "Aria and Dala. Sitan. They're…"

"They're what?"

He leaned against the wall, crossing his arms in obvious frustration. "They're not like anyone you know. Just like me."

"We've gone over this already."

"So why do you choose to trust me again?"

"I really don't know. I just do. Even if you did kiss Stella. Even if Aria said you boasted about me. With you gone, I realized I don't care if it doesn't make sense."

"It doesn't make sense. Right?"

"It makes completely no sense at all. None of this makes sense."

Adrian paced the room. "This has to be extremely frustrating for you."

"Of course it is! But I missed you. I want to be with you."

"Even if I'm more than you imagined."

The way he spoke made me think of the bonfire. Duwendes. Philippine gods and vampires. Mayari and her sisters Hana and Tala. How he saved me from Aria and Dala at the Bellagio. His kiss with Stella. For the first time, jealousy shot through me.

"Adrian! You're making me go crazy. You don't call or text. Then you show up in my bedroom? Of course you're more than I imagined!"

He sat between the window and my bed. "Dorothy, please keep your voice down. It wouldn't be good for your mother to see me right now."

I took a breath, trying to slow my heartbeat. "Can you tell me what's going on? Are you mad? Is that why you haven't contacted me?"

"On the contrary. Besides trying to find Aria and Dala, who have simply vanished out of thin air, I've come across a revelation that confounds me."

"And that is?"

He crouched down and covered his head before standing upright against the wall. "I've been dreaming of you."

I stepped back. "You've been dreaming of me? I've dreamt of you too."

His eyes widened. "You have?"

I stepped to him, his coconut aroma making me light-headed. "What's going on with you? With us?"

Adrian started to pace the room again. "Before I can discuss that, would you happen to have any diniguan in your kitchen?"

His blood-red eyes made me think it was best to answer honestly. Mom had left-over diniguan from the night before. "Yeah, there's some in the fridge."

"Can you get some for me?"

"Now?"

"Yes, now," he answered. He suddenly looked like he was about to faint.

"Okay. Just…stay here. I'll be right back."

&

I backed out of my room and quietly closed my bedroom door. Mom's door was shut, which meant she had already turned in for the night. Good. I didn't want to explain why I wanted to bring diniguan upstairs. I stayed on my toes to lighten the sound of my footsteps down the stairs and into the kitchen. I opened the fridge and grabbed the half-filled pot of diniguan on the second shelf. Based on how hungry Adrian looked, I thought he would eat it all, so I placed the pot on the stove, turning the burner to ten.

After what seemed like forever, the dark brown soup bubbled and the sour aroma of pig's blood made my stomach churn. I swallowed a spoonful before turning off the stove, the taste satisfying a burn below my ribcage. I hurried upstairs holding the pot with oven mitts. I entered my bedroom, making sure not to spill any of the bloody soup on the carpet. Once I closed the door, Adrian grabbed the pot out of my hands and tipped it towards his mouth.

I heard gurgling sounds as he hurled his face into the diniguan. Seconds later, Adrian swiped his mouth with his forearm and placed the pot on the floor. He sat on the edge of my bed looking more calm and relaxed after he had eaten – no, guzzled – diniguan in a matter of seconds.

"Thanks," he said. "You don't know how hungry I was." His eyes weren't red anymore, only slightly pink, my eye color when my contact lenses irritated my pupils. He walked to the window.

"So I can see you glowing and you have late night cravings for diniguan. Anything else I should know?"

"For now, that's pretty much all I can admit."

"Why do you always hold back? As if I'm too frail to handle the truth."

He frowned. "I can't say more than you can handle."

"And where have you been? No texts. No calls. You just ghosted!"

"I was busy."

"You said you were away because you can't control yourself around me."

"No, I didn't say that."

"Then what did you mean?"

Adrian leaned against the wall. "I was busy trying to find Aria and Dala. Those girls tried to hurt you and Stella, even if you weren't aware of it at the time. I've been searching all over Vegas and no one has seen them."

"So you forgot to eat while looking for them? It looked like you hadn't eaten in days, but now, you're okay after eating diniguan?"

"I'm okay for now."

I placed the oven mitts aside. "Do you want anything else from me?"

A sudden urge to hold his hand beleaguered me, but the dream rushed into my mind when he wouldn't take my hand by the river. I hesitated as my hands began to shake from all the effort. I wanted to touch him.

"Stop it," he said, his tone sharp.

"Stop what?"

"Stop thinking about things I can't answer."

"Are you talking about my dream?"

"Maybe."

"How did you know about my dream? I only told you I *had* a dream."

He turned to me, his face stoic. "Dorothy. It's getting difficult to control myself around you."

"Why are you fighting your feelings? I *know* love may not be the answer, but we already spent time together. I feel...no, I know I have feelings for you. And that's not easy for me to admit."

"Dorothy, stop. Please." He moved across the room. "I'm not good for you."

A surging, burning sensation assailed my body. I rubbed the buttons of my pajama top to fight it off. I wanted to kiss him, the thought of caressing his chest making me warm. "Adrian, I don't know what's come over me, but I've missed you."

His face became serious, his eyes darting between my face and body. For a brief moment, I welcomed his stare, his attention completely on me. I stepped towards him and reached for his hand. I caressed his arm and leaned in to his chest. But when I looked down, I saw my exposed bra and panties. Somehow, I had taken off my pajama top and bottoms!

"Dorothy, please. You don't want this." Adrian had his hands on my waist and caressed the space between my undies and bra.

I closed my eyes, the warmth of his hands making my head spin. "Adrian. What are we doing?" I whispered in his ear, my arms draped over his neck.

Adrian's breathing became heavier as he tried to break free, but the wall and my warm body had him trapped. Your skin, I heard him say. So soft...

Mom's muffled voice startled us, our hands stopping in mid-motion. "Cleng! Are you okay?"

"Mom?" I grabbed my pajamas from the floor to cover myself.

"Why do I smell diniguan? It's not good to eat so late."

"Late-night munchies. Sorry I woke you."

"Go to sleep now. We'll talk about your poor eating habits in the morning."

"Good night, mom."

Once her footsteps retreated from the door, I turned to continue where we left off, but Adrian was gone. I checked the closed windows, opened my closet and checked under the bed. Adrian had vanished.

I grabbed my phone on the dresser and dialed his number. After a few rings, his voicemail picked up. "Hi, this is Adrian. Please leave a message." Then the beep. "Where are you? It was just my mom! How did you leave my room?"

I ended the call and texted him to come back, but no dot dot dot.

I sat on my bed, not sure what to do. Should I

look for him? And how did he get in and out of my bedroom? The window was closed; there was no way he could leave without making noise. I checked my closet and under the bed again, half-expecting to see Adrian's beautiful form, but he had literally vanished into thin air.

I recapped our conversation, hoping to find a clue. He had stayed away from me on purpose because he was looking for Aria and Dala. He said he stayed away because he couldn't control himself around me, so he stayed busy so he wouldn't think about me. He looked malnourished, but after he had eaten left-over diniguan, his natural color returned to his face. He said he was no good for me, even after I had somehow stripped down to my bra and panties. Then he bolted the moment he heard mom's knock on the door. And that's when embarrassment made me hug my pillow. I had spontaneously stripped down to my bra and panties! I was all over him!

The hope of his return gradually faded as I vacillated between hot and cold. I eventually succumbed to a sudden weariness and into the same dream by the river, more details coming to light.

Adrian held an infant with the same fiery red-colored eyes. When I extended my hands, Adrian pushed me aside, his face stern and protective. Anger beset me as painful cramps rendered me to the ground. I craved something to eat. Adrian kneeled to me with a chalice that I ravagedly drank from, only to vomit when I realized what I drank. Adrian massaged my back, not letting me near the baby, his temperament calm and reassured. I stopped vomiting, but collapsed as another agonizing spasm made my body convulse.

I woke up screaming, my bed sheets drenched in perspiration with a searing pain burning in my stomach.

CHAPTER 26: ADRIAN

I had some explaining to do. I had literally disappeared from Dorothy's room once Meredith interrupted. And the fact I had stared at Dorothy when she was half-naked formed a knot in my stomach. Yes, she was the one who took off her pajamas. Yes, her body made me hold my breath, especially when she tightened her shoulders. It was impossible not to stare, so when her mom had knocked on the door, I got out of there before I did anything I would regret.

Thank you, Meredith.

Kenneth was trying to reach me through kindred thoughts, but I ignored him. I was a complete wreck. I needed time to understand why I lost self-control around Dorothy.

Once I returned to my room, I skipped over the Bible and flipped open the Quran. I read a passage that always helped me gain perspective.

> *"On those who believe and do good works there shall be no sin for what they eat, provided they fear God and believe and do good works, and again fear God and believe, yet again fear God and do good. And Allah loves those who do good."*
> *(English translation, Al Quran 5:94)*

I gradually regained my regular breathing pattern as I repeated the verse. *There shall be no sin for what they eat.* I was doing good by protecting mortals. I undoubtedly feared Allah. Even though Danags had longer lifespans than humans, we still had the same questions about the afterlife. I ate animal blood for sustenance, not pleasure.

I thought of Urduja, the woman warrior of ancient Tawalisi, a land her father ruled prior to the islands becoming the Philippines. She had sacrificed the right to defend her territory against invading Mongols to fulfill a greater purpose out of obligation to the rajah, her father. I exhaled, wondering if I would be unselfish if placed in the same situation.

The lessons of the great *Kolipulako*[*], a Muslim man accused of being the devil by the missionaries, had shaped our people's beliefs. He had literally moved mountains to protect the Danag people from Spanish rule. Spain would return after he killed Magellan, so he used his abilities to build Mandalagan, a home covered by mountains and the complicated volcanic rings of the Philippines. Mandalagan was a place humans would never find.

I placed the Quran back in the drawer next to the Bible and slammed the drawer, frustrated the ancient knowledge remained obscure. The Spanish renamed Kolipulako "Lapu-Lapu" and erased his Muslim identity. A Filipino hero, they say. But he was not only a hero. Kolipulako was the most revered King of the Danag people, an ancestor of Bathala sent to earth to save our people. And yet, here I was protecting mortals from this truth. My

---

[*]   *Possible real name of **Lapu-Lapu**, although Antoine Pigafetta records state his real name was Cilapulapu. It is said he is of Bornean descent. He ruled Mactan, an island next to Cebu. Considered a Filipino national hero for killing Magellan. Term #25 in Terms of Consequence.*

mind raced back to the present and how I had to protect my host family, Dorothy and Stella. Since the kiss, I hadn't stopped dreaming of Dorothy by the river in Mandalagan. She looked beautiful in her native land, but the dream was consuming me. I now avoided sleep like the plague.

And then there was Stella. Since we kissed, her thoughts were more prevalent in my mind, her emotions swinging from hot to cold. She had been spending time with Eric, but her thoughts were somewhere else. I sensed her fear of facing whatever it was she was thinking about.

My mentor, Bulosan, would find this amusing. He warned me about using the kiss as a tracking device. Another lesson learned. I tracked Dorothy more intimately, but I wanted to throw up when she felt nauseous and my head literally hurt from all the thinking she was doing. And now add Stella's thoughts to the mix. I remembered Bulosan's childlike excitement when he told me to never question his greatness. Never again would I ever question the great Bulosan. Never again.

ॐ

The last two days had been uneventful, a haunting calm before a storm I couldn't see coming. I had searched all over Vegas for Aria and Dala, but there was no trace, no smell, no trail of where they were hiding. I had gone out to Paradise and Primm, but no sign of them in either city.

Patrick devoutly monitored Dorothy and Stella, texting me all was well. But Harvey was nowhere to be found. I had visited Bouchons, but Janna hadn't heard from him. His staff at Tao hadn't heard from him either. They were worried. As was I.

What happened to our dear friend Harvey?

I prayed he had been broken out of his trance. But if not, he was most likely under Sitan's influence. I put Patrick on high alert. Sitan might use Harvey's friendship with Dorothy and Stella for his benefit. But Patrick hadn't come across any drama. Dorothy was spending time with Meredith. Stella was packing in-between makeout sessions with Eric.

Anna and Gus said I looked more restless than usual. I deflected their concern by playing with the kids and spending time with Frank and Lilia. My heart ached at their sorrow when their oldest daughter died years ago. Little did they know her death saved their lives, and her love kept them safe.

Aria and Dala had vanished. Harvey was MIA. There was no doubt Sitan recognized Dorothy existed. The only way to keep her and Stella safe was to kill Sitan and get the girls to the Mandalagan gateway. But I didn't know what he looked like. We hadn't seen his face in years. He had become a legend, a character in a fable from long ago like Kolipulako and Urduja, heroes who had roamed the earth in the place of the gods.

Except Sitan was not a messenger of the gods. He was a Danag devil we should have killed decades ago when we had the chance.

CHAPTER 27: DOROTHY

ﻉﻉ

By the time night had turned to dawn, I was out of bed and staring at the Danag inscription on the back wall of my closet.

ᜇᜈᜄ

Da NaG

An Internet search confirmed the three symbols were Alibata, or the Baybayin alphabet, a writing system traced back to pre-Spanish Philippines. The first symbol sounded like *Da*, the second *Na* and the third *Ga*. Together they spelled *DaNaGa*. The combination translated in English to *Danag*, a term for vampires in the Philippines who lived in harmony with humans.

These were ancient tales to keep tribes entertained, but it was coincidental this happened to me, a Fil-Am girl whose father mysteriously vanished. I couldn't stop thinking that my father was somehow linked to the Alibata script in my closet even if there wasn't tangible proof. I was most likely projecting my need to know more about him, to know why he disappeared. But Filipino script was carved in my closet wall! It had to be more than a coincidence.

If there was a connection, there was one way to find out.

I opened my desk drawer and stared at my father's graduation card. Without thinking too long, I slit the top of it with my letter opener and pulled out the card.

My mom was mistaken. It wasn't a congratulations card, at least from what I could tell. Alibata script was written across it in black ink without a signature. I studying the card and ran my fingers over the symbols. I studied the symbols, afraid to know what the message read.

Adrian would know how to read this, but...no...I wasn't ready to go there yet. This was a card from my father who, after all these years, had sent a message in Alibata for my graduation. Why write to me in a long forgotten script? And what did it say?

I stared at the message before pulling up an alibata alphabet on the Internet. With shock and fear hitting me all at once, I matched the symbols with its English sounds. The first symbol represented the sound *Lo* and the second symbol *Bo*, spelling *Lobe*. When I heard mom's footsteps in the hallway and a staccato knock on my door, I stashed the card away and minimized my browser. I wanted to translate the message on my own.

"*Inday!* Wake up!"

I opened my door to my mother wearing her favorite fire-red robe, her hair tied in a bun. "Morning, mom."

"You should not eat diniguan so late!"

"I know, I know. Don't know what came over me."

"But I'm glad. I would have thrown it out today! Aren't you excited we're flying to Negros today?"

"Yes, of course I am. But before we go, can I show you something?" I motioned her inside my room and pulled her to my closet, pushing my clothes to the side.

"*Anak?* What is it?"

After moving a laundry basket out of the way, I revealed the Alibata script on the wall. "Have you seen this before?"

Da NaG

Mom's facial expression changed. She brushed her fingers over the carving and was lost in a thought before snapping back. She retreated and sat on the edge of the bed. "This brings back old memories."

"Memories of what?"

"Memories of your dad. He had a tattoo with those same symbols."

"He did?"

"Yes. He had it when I met him. When I asked him what it meant, he didn't answer; he changed the

210

subject instead. I remember one time I pushed him to tell me more. He ended up kissing me so passionately I got dizzy and we made love for hours."

"Mom! TMI!"

"*Susmaryosep!* What does it matter? You're sexually active now. It doesn't make a difference!"

"Mom! I'm not frickin' sexually active!"

She gazed out the window wistfully as if she didn't hear me. "That was the last time we made love. He disappeared days later."

Sadness tugged inside as more questions came to me like a mirage. My dad never answered mom when she asked about the tattoos, and since mom has no idea how to conduct a thorough Internet search, he chose to keep her in the dark.

A surge of energy rose through me. "Why would he do that?"

"He was a passionate lover," mom replied. "The things your dad did to me…"

"No no no! Not that! Why would he conceal the meaning of his tattoo?"

"I wondered myself until Yasmin helped me figure it out. Your father's tattoo is the word Danag in Alibata which signifies the number nine."

"The number nine?"

"Danag is significant with the astrological Life Path Nine. Through this life path, Danags are selfless and care for others to a fault. That was your dad in a nutshell."

"Life Path Nine?" I asked out loud, more to myself. I hadn't come across this astrological meaning in my own research. "How did he leave us?"

"One day he said he had to go. That it was life or death if he didn't leave. When I started to panic, he held me and told me he loved me, but he still had to go. He kissed you on the forehead while you were asleep and just left in the middle of the night."

"That must have been hard."

"It was...but...I wasn't alone. Your Tita Yasmin helped me. She had been close with him too. Yasmin said he visited them to say goodbye that same night."

"Did he send letters?"

"No letters. And I haven't spoken to him since he kissed me goodbye. But he communicates with money. Twenty-thousand dollars show up in my account every month."

"Twenty grand!"

"Since 2004." She swiped at her moist eyes. "I know this house is extravagant. But...I wanted you to be comfortable. And I got used to having the money there for us."

"So the cars, our lifestyle. It's not because of your real estate career?"

"It is partially," she said. "But the money has always been there."

"Why didn't you tell me this before?"

"You were so young. But it's out now, so it's a start."

"It would have been nice to know! Did you try to find him?"

"Years ago I tried to trace the bank deposits, but the routing number leads to a small bank in Brunei in the name of a non-existent corporation in New Zealand. The detective I hired didn't find anything in New Zealand except vacant office space in Auckland that hadn't been used in years. Whoever sends this money is untraceable."

"But you think it's my dad?"

"Who else could it be."

I considered her answer, the realization of my father being alive making my insides squirm capricously. "Mom. Do you know where he is?"

"I have no idea where he is. He's like a ghost."

"What did he do for a living?"

"He stayed at home while I worked my way up the real estate firm. We weren't rich by any stretch of the imagination. But it was happy times."

"He stayed with me twenty-four seven?"

"*Sus!* You, Stella and him..." She trailed off.

I squeezed her hand gently. "He helped watch Stella too?"

"Yes. He watched her too."

"When did the card arrive in the mail?"

"Just the other day." She reached for me. "I know it's a lot. But maybe he carved this in your closet for *you* to find."

"Maybe. But did we even live here when he was with us?"

"Construction had finished a few months before he left. We had just settled in."

"I didn't realize we were the original owners of this house."

"Yes. Somehow, we got this built with the income we were making at the time."

"I'm in shock at how he left. As if he didn't care anymore."

"That's how I felt for a long while. But as time went on, I remembered the good times. He was a good husband and father when he was with us."

"And now, you think he's sent this card to me?"

She stood. "Maybe he wants to see you? I don't know. Maybe that's what I want to believe. But his disappearance will be one of the greatest mysteries in my life." She stepped towards the door.

I reached for her hand. "Mom. Thank you for telling me."

"I love you, Cleng. And before you ask. Yes. I

took my meds and I'm feeling great today." She pulled me into a hug, my tongue tasting salt from tears dripping down my cheeks.

"You read my mind."

"How's that boy Christian?" she asked over my shoulder.

"I've been hanging out more with Adrian," I answered.

"Is that the boy who gave you a heart attack at school?"

"Yeah. I've been thinking about him a lot lately."

We disengaged and she fervently placed her hands on my shoulders. "All these years of not dating and now you have two boys fighting over you."

"They are not fighting over me." I sniffled and wiped my eyes.

"*Sus!* You are...how do they say it? Oblivious. But remember. Whoever you choose, never let them walk over you like your father did to us. Okay? They should always respect you."

"Okay, mom. I promise I'll remember."

∽

As soon as mom left my room, I took out the graduation card, wiping my eyes with a tissue. I was reeling from her story, the idea that my dad left in the middle of the night blowing my mind. What man deserts his family like that?

I'm glad mom told me, but...it was literally shocking how my father abandoned us.

I wanted to tell Stella, but she was spending as much time with Eric before our trip. I didn't want to bother her. I would have more than enough time with her in Negros. I hastily studied the card and searched Google for the Alibata alphabet.

The first two symbols spelled *Lobe*. I had translated the third symbol as the letter *y* when my phone vibrated. I pressed the green accept icon without paying attention to the caller ID.

"Dorothy?"

"Christian?" I stepped away from my desk.

"What's going on? Did I catch you at a bad time?"

"Oh no." I moved the phone to my other ear. "I'm glad you called. I've been wanting to talk to you."

"I wanted to talk to you too," Christian said.

"What you said at the dojo surprised me, but after I thought about it, I can see why you're upset."

"I'm not sure if that makes me feel better."

My heart sank. "After what you said, I thought about how I've been acting. I don't know why I ghost. I guess I've been caught up going clubbing with Stella."

"You've been going to clubs?"

"Yeah. That's why I haven't been at workouts the last few weeks."

"The last few months. But I haven't noticed."

I adjusted the phone to my ear. "My mom..." I hesitated about talking to him about my family issues. "Are you mad?"

"I'm not mad. I just thought you considered me more important in your life."

I didn't know what to say. He was my martial arts friend, but he wanted more. "You *are* part of my life and I appreciate you coming to my graduation."

"I appreciate your mom inviting us. You were about to say something about her. What was it?"

The burn of mom's story made me want to cry, but I held it in. "She told me to say hi to you, that's all."

"Tell her I said hello. And that I owe her an expensive meal. You have time to hang out today?"

"I'm leaving for the Philippines today."

"You are? You're going to the Philippines?"

"Sorry. A lot going on."

"I'm going to miss you which confirms how much I'm in love with you."

My heart started to race when he said the L word. "Okay," I said.

"Dorothy. Wait. That came out weirder than it should have."

"All right," I replied, my voice softer. "I have to go pack for my trip."

"Dorothy. Please. How long will you be gone?"

"Three weeks. Should be back by July. But I really have to go."

"Have a safe trip," I heard Christian say before I ended the call.

᠌

"He loves me," I said out loud. "He said he loves me."

Christian hardly knew me outside the dojo. How could he love me? It was nice to hear his voice, but I hesitated to talk to him about my mom's story about my father. And then he says he *loves* me? I wasn't ready for that.

The moment Christian said it, I imagined Adrian's impeccable smile and his consuming coconut scent. I remembered the first day I saw him at school, the day we met in the cafeteria, my graduation when he was ablaze, and the day he took me to the mosque, one of the best days of my life. But he had disappeared from my room and wasn't answering any of my texts. He was a mirage who slipped in and out my life at his own volition.

I remembered his face in my dream, his eyes fiery red, pushing me away when I attempted to hold the baby. I placed my hand on my chest to regain control of my breathing, a sudden need to see him overwhelming me just as a baritone voice I didn't recognize ricocheted inside the chambers of my brain.

You will see Adrian soon. It is destiny. You will see. Salaam. Salaam.

I opened my eyes. I am not hearing voices in my head. I tied my hair in a ponytail and said this over and over again. I am not hearing voices in my head.

I am not hearing voices in my head.

Without thinking, I stayed in continuous motion. I shadow practiced my crossover dribble and jump shot, wishing I had access to the Valley High gymnasium to shoot some hoop. I imagined swishing my step back three-pointers after my hezzy broke my imaginary defender's ankles. Basketball was my sanctuary, but a clear invite for the male voice to return. Guys *loved* basketball.

So I switched up and played "Chun-Li" by Nikki Minaj and "Run the World (Girls)" by Beyonce on repeat while I showered, songs that surely intimidated any male voice from wanting to enter my head. After toweling off and putting on Warriors sweats and my favorite Dubs halter top, I helped mom pack up the last balikbayan box and finished packing my luggage and backpack.

With Daya's "Sit Still, Look Pretty" blaring from my phone, I showered again after a text conversation with Stella. She confirmed she had been *busy* with Eric and had a lot of packing to do. I texted back to *not* give me details and that I'd see her at the airport.

Mom must have noticed my energetic behavior. She kept asking if I was okay and reminded me to eat. I told her I wasn't hungry and that I was fine, omitting the fact I heard a voice in my head. She didn't need to know her daughter was going mental. I wanted her to have a stress free trip.

As she poured herself a glass of water, I noticed how much smaller she looked. She was napping longer than normal these days and kept her fitness workouts short. But she never complained that she was tired.

I was about to ask if she took her meds, but instead, I told her I loved her. She said she loved me too and that our trip would be one to remember. I agreed as I helped her bring her luggage downstairs, pushing away my apprehension that something had changed the moment I heard the voice in my head.

CHAPTER 28: ADRIAN

కిండుండి

"You are as stubborn as caribou trying to enter the waterfall."

I let my brother's words take hold. Perhaps I was stubborn, but what did it matter? Kenneth was talking nonsense.

"I am not talking nonsense," Kenneth said defensively. "Don't forget we are kindreds, so I can sense everything."

"And vice versa. It's annoying how happy you are with your beautiful wife and son."

"I've tried to hold it back from you," Kenneth said. "I don't want you to be envious. But I cannot help it. I *am* happy."

"It's great to see you happy." Whenever I became consumed by my complicated Timawa existence, I tapped into Kenneth's emotions unobtrusively. I wondered if Kenneth even noticed.

"I know my current emotional state is contrary to my conflicted brother. But we are kindreds for a reason. I know you love this girl."

"There is no way I love Dorothy. There is a connection Timawas have towards those they protect. But that is all."

"I don't care what the legends say. What you feel is love. And you admit she is attractive," Kenneth said.

"Of course she's attractive. But that doesn't mean I love her. Pleasures of the flesh don't compare to those platonic in nature."

"Agreed. But you think about her more than you should."

I laughed. "Of course! I *have* to think about her on a daily basis. I'm her protector." I extended my laugh, hoping it would camouflage my apprehension at having my saliva running through her and Stella.

"So the happiness you feel is simply because you saved her and Stella at the Bellagio?"

"Yes. And Patrick promised to buy me In and Out. That makes me extremely happy."

"Your humor is worse than mine! *And* you're acting so unusual!"

"I am not acting unusual."

"Come on, bro. You just laughed like a madman!"

"Kenneth, I have to go."

"I love you brother, but be honest with yourself. That's all I ask."

"I heed your advice by saying stop being annoying. Goodbye, *kuya*."

I fluttered my eyelids, a zap of energy, and opened my eyes. My story to my brother was that I *didn't* love Dorothy and my only concern was to capture Sitan and bring her safely to Mandalagan. I'm not sure if he bought it, but I hoped my exceptional acting skills had convinced him.

And with my saliva in Dorothy's system, I sensed she wasn't in imminent danger. She was confused by something on her mind, but she wasn't emoting any lovey dovey feelings. Stella was also thinking, but I couldn't discern the details. These girls were constantly *thinking*. I imagined Bulosan laughing at me for having two beautiful girls in my mind.

I grabbed the keys to the Shelby, ready to help Eric and Anna watch the kids in the mayhem of Circus Circus, until Frank and Lilia's desperate screams had me bolting upstairs.

CHAPTER 29: DOROTHY

ﺏﺏ

As we waited for our Lyft driver, I vigorously nibbled on my nails.

Thankfully, I hadn't heard the voice in my head since earlier in the day. But the word *salaam* stuck in my head. It was a friendly word that meant "peace" or "greetings" in Arabic. The voice had said it twice, so I guessed it was friendly.

You will see Adrian very soon. It is destiny. You will see. Salaam. Salaam.

I had packed my dad's card in my backpack, hoping Adrian could translate once we met up in Negros. If it was a message from my dad, I should know what it says, but I hadn't had time to translate the last line of symbols. And I didn't want to take it out in front of mom. I didn't tell her I had opened it, not ready for another heavy conversation.

"Stop biting your nails." Mom's voice broke through my thoughts.

"Oh, I didn't realize."

"You look nervous, as if you haven't been on an airplane before."

"I haven't been on an airplane before!" I replied.

Mom laughed. "My God! You're absolutely right! Now why did I think you took a trip before?" She finished applying moisturizer on her hands and checked for her meds in her purse.

"Mom. Your meds are where you last saw them."

"I know, *iha*. Just making sure."

"And you're uptight about the time. But departure is five hours away."

"You never know with traffic, *diba*? It's better to

get to the airport early."

A loud car horn interrupted us from the front. Looking out the window, a black Escalade had pulled up to the curb. A young man wearing a Kangol hat, a blue flannel and khaki pants waved from the driver's seat when mom opened the front door.

"Hey there!" he yelled as he got out of the SUV. "Let me help."

I double-checked my app to verify his license plate and name. "Patrick, right?"

"That's me!" He picked up the balikbayan boxes effortlessly and placed them in the rear of the Escalade.

We rolled out our DKNY luggage and Patrick laid the cases on top of our boxes. I was about to get in the vehicle, but waited for mom to check our home security system was armed. She checked the security panel, set the alarm and rushed out of the house. I held the passenger door open for her.

"Sorry about the delayed arrival," Patrick said after we got in the Escalade. "Unexpected traffic."

"No problem," mom replied. "We have time before our flight."

The driver merged onto the street and picked up speed. "Off we go."

The airport was a half hour ride without traffic. But of course, there was frickin' traffic. Our Lyft driver looked vaguely familiar, his stocky build and Filipino features reminding me of a bunch of people I've seen randomly around town or at church.

He glanced at us once in a while with a warm smile and engaged in small talk about how much Vegas had grown from all the housing built in the last decade. Mom pointed out areas that hadn't been developed until a few years ago when builders came in like gangbusters. He agreed that Vegas had too many people moving here.

Eventually, the white noise made us drowsy. Mom leaned her head on my shoulder as Patrick navigated through stop and go traffic. I looked at the time, grateful for mom's OCD about getting to the airport early. If she wasn't so tired, she would be even more anxious being four and a half hours ahead of departure.

She snuggled against my arm, the weight of her body becoming heavier as she fell deeper to sleep. And as we pulled up to the McCarran International Airport, I gently woke her up, making sure not to put pressure on the side of her stomach.

CHAPTER 30: ADRIAN

ఉౕఴ

A moment of frustration of not sensing danger quickly gave way to my Danag duty to protect.

I was upstairs in less than a second to see a cloaked intruder holding Lilia over his head. The attacker was a blond-haired male with pale white arms emerging from underneath a hooded, black cloak. His face was indistinguishable, his blond hair covering his eyes, the distinct hue of pink lips against his porcelain skin. Lilia was screaming and flailing her arms. His grip held her in place like a doll.

I attacked with punches and kicks that rocked him off balance momentarily, but not enough to release Lilia out of his grasp. I hit his arms and kicked his elbow, which loosened his hold on Lilia, giving her a chance to wriggle away. She fell to the floor, her scream changing from fear to physical pain, but luckily, her fall wasn't fatal. I motioned her to run away.

I pulled the intruder's blond hair, his blue eyes turning red as he tried to squeeze my neck. I pushed his arms and pushed him to the ground. I crouched in a fighting stance and waited for him to make the next move.

"I'm glad I got your attention. I had no intention of killing the woman," he said as he stood up.

He could have killed Lilia easily, but used her as bait to lure me in. "I figured," I replied.

"I am much stronger than my sister Aria. But probably not as strong as you."

"I think that's a fair assessment."

"But perhaps all of us might take you down."

The late evening light that had streamed through the windows had suddenly turned black. With a hand motion, enemies appeared out of nowhere and surrounded me.

They all had blond hair and pale arms, their bodies covered in similar black cloaks to Aria's brother. Filipinos called them *aswangs*[*], while Danags simply called them Sitan's evil defectors of Mandalagan. I assessed my enemies and calculated the probability of surviving this encounter, surprised there was a chance I could die if I didn't stay focused.

"Are you sure you want to take on a Timawa warrior?" I asked.

"Perhaps you should ask yourself if you want to take us on," the blond-haired leader answered.

"It's guaranteed most of you will die," I replied. "Maybe even you." I sensed a flash of fear in his eyes. "What is it that they say? Timawas only appear when we kill. Yes, I believe that's what they say."

An enemy to the far left stepped forward. He had dead white skin like the others, except his hair was gray. "Where is Dorothy!"

"I ask you the same thing. I haven't seen her in days!"

"You lie!" the gray-haired being yelled. "You think we should bow to you because you are Timawa! What about us? You forgot about us!"

"You forgot about your true purpose!" I yelled. I tried to hold back the anger, but it had already

---

[*]   *In Filipino folklore, **Aswangs** are shapeshifting white beings during the day, monsters by night, one of the most feared creatures of Filipino mythology. Term #8 in Terms of Consequence.*

boiled to the surface. "You left Mandalagan on your own and your leader, Sitan, chose to use mortals for his own selfish reasons. The way you are now is against the very fabric of our existence!"

"Humans exist to serve us!" he answered. "They are the weaker species in body and mind! This is the new world order! And if we do not kill you, Sitan will!"

"Where is the coward!" I yelled. "Have you asked yourself why he isn't here himself? Why are all of you here instead of him? He's using all of you!"

"We are here of our free will!"

"So you think! He has convinced you it's your free will, but it's obvious to me he sent you to your deaths!" And with passion running through me, I attacked.

The blond-haired leader fought me off with quick defensive moves. He showed his grotesque fangs for the first time when he tried to bite my neck. When he lunged, I got both my hands on his ears. He kicked me below the belt as his eyes filled with fear at the realization I had him in my grasp. With a mighty scream, I turned his head to one side, twisting it like a vinyl record on a turntable. In an instant, his body turned to ash.

I was immediately choked from behind. I positioned my feet for leverage and flipped my enemy over me. I grabbed the attacker's ears and twisted the head. Within seconds, another black cloaked *aswang* killed. Two others attacked, but even together, they were no match for my Timawa quickness and power. I turned their heads with each hand, killing them instantly.

More attacked at once. I warded off two while holding another, pulling the enemy into me. One was a follower and no match for me. I turned my attention to the others. One had its fangs inches from my neck while the other punched me in the chest. I avoided the neck bite by dodging his open fangs and slamming his head violently against the floor. The stunned male had no time to defend himself as I grabbed his ears and turned his head. The other one stopped punching me once the other was killed, giving me an opening. I lifted him off the ground by the neck and popped his head like a balloon. I had turned them to ash, leaving the room eerily silent.

I took a long breath as I assessed the damage to the house. Miraculously, the vases and picture frames on the walls were in place and the furniture hadn't moved. I heard the pitter-patter of human feet from the other room. I scrambled to find Frank and Lilia hiding behind a bookcase. When I approached, Frank stepped in front of Lilia, his hands trembling.

"Who are you!" Frank yelled.

"It's me. Adrian."

"Who were all those white beings?"

"Please, you have no reason to fear me. They're dead now."

Frank didn't move as his wife crouched behind him. "Yes, I see that! But where are their bodies?"

"Their bodies are now dust."

"Dust?" Frank shielded Lilia from me. "Did they mean what they said? They said they were going to kill us in the name of *Satan*."

I reached out my hand. "Please. There is nothing to fear. You probably heard *Satan*, but they said *Sitan*, an evil being I'm trying to find."

"Who are you?" Frank asked. "What you did…they…they weren't human! Adrian! You aren't human!"

"Tito Frank. Please give me a chance to explain."

Lilia slowly stepped out from behind him, wiping tears from her eyes. She reached for my arm. "Thank you for saving us," she said in a shaky voice.

"You're welcome. You're my Vegas family. I would die for all of you."

The natural hue of the house had returned, except for piled gray ashes in random places in the kitchen and living room. I went to the pantry and found the broom. I swept up the ashes and dumped them into the garbage bin. I vacuumed the floor. Lilia and Frank tried to help, but they were in terrible shock and were undoubtedly shaken.

Danag protocol was to wipe their memory. It was for their own safety, to protect them from hysterical panic. But they had endured so much with the loss of their daughter years ago.

I had to be fair to them.

I loved them like my own family and it was time to be fair. And that's when my phone vibrated with a blue text message.

> **Patrick:** *I've tracked Aria and Dala to the airport! They are with another!*

I hugged Frank and Lilia and told them someone would watch them while I was away. They asked where I was going. I told them the Philippines with Dorothy. Lilia approached and hugged me. I told them to stay home and not to contact the police.

And when Lilia answered they wouldn't, I left their memories intact, knowing Patrick would help them understand that their research wasn't crazy after all.

CHAPTER 31: DOROTHY

〰〰

McCarran Airport's international terminal bustled with impatient passengers. The Lyft driver had taken our balikbayan boxes out of the Escalade. When he finished piling our luggage and boxes on carts, he politely declined the tip we insisted on paying him. I thanked him and promised a five-star review on the mobile app.

Mom's small bladder forced her to go to the bathroom, but I managed to push our carts near the check-in counter by myself, privately thanking basketball and martial arts for keeping me in shape. I took my place in line and submitted my rating on the Lyft app as I hummed along to Anne-Marie's "2002." The chorus was just starting when someone tapped me on the shoulder.

"Hey, Dorothy."

I turned to see Christian in fitting Levi's jeans and a khaki polo, a serious look on his face. I removed my earbuds. "Christian? What are you doing here?"

"I needed to talk to you before you left."

"How did you know where to find me?"

"There's one flight a day from Vegas to Manila, so it was easy to figure out."

I moved with the line. "Yeah, I guess it would be."

"Listen. I didn't mean for you to freak out when I said I loved you. I didn't mean to be scary."

"I didn't mean to be so weird about it," I replied. "I was surprised."

"I know. So to clarify, I'll miss you while you're on your trip. And when you come back, I hope we get to know each other better outside the dojo. And if you give me that chance, I'll never, ever say I love you again."

I laughed. "Christian. You said the L word again."

He put his hands up. "But not in *that* way."

The line moved, a part of me melting. "You're right. I'll excuse it one more time."

"Thank you, Dor." He revealed a small box from behind his back. "And as a parting gift."

"Christian. What is this?"

"It's your graduation gift."

"You didn't have to get me a graduation gift."

"It's a gift from one friend to another." He shifted from one foot to the other.

I opened the box revealing a hand-crafted amulet with a picture of me speaking at graduation. The picture wasn't a mobile device photo. The vibrant white and red gowns dominated the photo of my fellow students gazing at me during my speech.

"Christian. It's beautiful. But this is...."

"Too much. But...you look adorable. I thought you should see how you looked on stage. It's a momento of your graduation day."

"I love it."

"Now you're the one using the L word," he teased.

I quickly circled my arms around his waist before the line started moving again. Christian helped me push my carts and I zipped up his gift in my backpack, thanking him again for being so thoughtful.

"You don't have to wait with me," I said.

"I don't have anything better to do, except teach a class in thirty minutes."

"Christian! You'll be late!"

"So I better go. Can you tell your mom to have

a safe trip for me?"

"Of course."

Christian came in for a hug. "Can't wait to hear about your trip. Be safe."

"Thanks again for the necklace."

"I'm glad you *loved* it." He smiled affectionately, stepping aside when a Filipino family took their place in line between us. Christian waved and disappeared from view once he turned towards the parking garage. I moved with the line, incredulously perplexed he cared enough to see me off at the airport.

CHAPTER 32: ADRIAN

ఌ౿ఌ

It might have been a mistake keeping Frank and Lilia's memories intact. But I had made my choice and now, I focused on Dorothy.

Patrick had disguised himself as a Lyft driver and transported Dorothy and Meredith to the airport without incident. From behind a ticket booth kiosk, I watched Dorothy standing in line while talking to Christian, the Filipino guy I sparred with the other day. I had no idea he knew Dorothy. And from the looks of it, he was apologizing.

I held sparks of jealousy at bay as Patrick met with me in one of the airport breezeways. He reported that Aria and Dala had been in the terminal. They were close, but I still didn't sense them. I told Patrick to stay close to Stella and her mother who had arrived at the airport an hour earlier. We agreed the attack at the house was a diversion. The main event had to be at the airport.

I told him to go directly to Frank and Lilia after the flight departed, and it was his responsibility to keep the entire family safe. He was not to wipe their memories, but to help them understand the big picture. And I ordered him to find Harvey. We still didn't know where he was.

No one knew.

Once I confirmed he understood everything, we bro-hugged. I wished him luck, and he did the same in my mission to get Dorothy into Mandalagan. With a final salute, he left to monitor Stella and Yasmin until takeoff. I made my way to Philippine Airlines, my Timawa instincts on high alert.

CHAPTER 33: DOROTHY

ﺑﺴﻢ

Christian had left before I was face-to-face with Bong, the overly polite customer service rep with a frozen smile on his face. "How many bags are you checking in, ma'am?"

"Three bags and four balikbayan boxes." I pointed at our carts.

"Tree bags, ga ling!" Bong clasped his hands and looked at me with a lifted eyebrow.

"Yes, *three* bags and four balikbayan boxes," I repeated deliberately, emphasizing the *th* in three.

Bong's smile disappeared, his other eyebrow lifted. "You don't have to give me attitudes, deary." His tone of voice turned from sweet to sour.

"Oh, I'm sorry, I wanted to make sure—"

"I know what you wanted to make sure ob." Bong waved an index finger at me. "But lucky por you, I'm a propessional, despites your attitudes. That will be pipty dollars per extra bag and box."

Are you kidding? Airlines were hurting, but fifty dollars per bag? I wished mom could've waited to go to the bathroom. I had $200 dollars cash on me, but I wasn't ready to spend it thirty minutes into our trip.

"I got it," a smooth voice said behind me. A graham-cracker-colored hand effortlessly passed three bills to Bong over my shoulder.

"Oh, well I see you hab a berry, berry handsome priend!" Bong's voice rose and fell like ocean waves. He looked past me ardently, his cheeks flush. The smell of coconut assailed my senses as Adrian leaned in from behind.

"Adrian. What you are doing here?" I asked.

"I happen to be on the same flight. Crazy coincidence, huh?"

I didn't answer, instead letting Adrian reply to Bong's sudden interest in his lack of check-in baggage. Adrian spoke affably in Tagalog and when Bong handed us our boarding passes, he waved us off after Adrian tipped him.

"Thanks for taking care of the luggage." I unzipped my backpack and took out my father's graduation card. "I was wondering if you could help me translate this card. The message is written in Alibata."

Adrian studied the envelope parchment. "Where did you get this?"

"My mom said it came in the mail. Supposedly, it's from my father."

"Your father?" Adrian started to take the card out, but tucked the card in his inside jacket when my mom approached.

"*Anak!* I asked you to wait!" Mom exclaimed.

"The line moved faster than your bladder. You took forever in the bathroom."

"*Iha.* I'm an old lady," she said, looking at Adrian. "Looks like you took care of everything. And don't be rude, Cleng. Whose your friend?"

"Mom. This is Adrian."

"Oh *diba*? *The* Adrian! Nice to finally meet you!"

"The pleasure is all mine." Adrian picked up the back of her hand and placed it against his forehead, offering the traditional Filipino sign of respect.

"Adrian is on the same flight," I said.

"*Really?* And you had no idea?"

"No, I didn't." And I wasn't lying. I really didn't know. I thought I was meeting up with him in Negros. I handed our boarding passes to her.

Mom placed the passes in the bright pink fanny

pack she insisted on wearing around her waist and zipped it up. "Adrian. Where are your parents?"

"I'm traveling alone," Adrian replied.

She looped her arm through his. "So we'll get to know each other."

"I look forward to it," Adrian said.

The bustle of airport activity continued. Parents chased after kids who played hide and seek in the airport terminal. The distant arguing over the weight of balikbayan boxes rose from the ticket counter.

Mom rubbed Adrian's bicep, noticing how strong it was no doubt. "Cleng. Did Stella text you yet?"

"Mom! Stella and Tita Yasmin are already at the gate. We should get through security."

"I didn't know they were here already. *Sige na!* Let's go!"

We entered the security line, showing our passports and boarding passes at the front. We took off our shoes and placed our carry-on bags through the security scanners. Mom and I got through without incident, but the TSA agents chose Adrian for a random check, patting him down heedlessly and searching his backpack. Once the inspection ended, he gathered his carry-on and we walked by the duty-free shops. Once on the moving sidewalk, we stood on the right side, letting other passengers pass by. Mom moved a few steps ahead, giving me and Adrian some privacy.

"I thought you were leaving weeks from now?" I whispered once mom was a safe distance away.

"I did too, until my dad told me to get on tonight's flight. I'm completely at his mercy in some ways."

I wondered what he meant by being at his father's mercy. "Is everything okay? You seem distracted."

"I'm fine."

I swept my hand across his arm. "I haven't seen you since you disappeared on me the other night."

"Sorry about that," Adrian replied abjectly. "We were not our rationale selves."

"I don't know what came over me," I said disconcertingly. "But please don't ghost on me anymore. I worry about you."

"I'll try for now on. But if I'm being forthright, it'll be hard to forget how stunning you looked that night."

The bold move of stripping to my undies made me incredulously abashed. I tucked a stray hair behind my ears. "I'm curious how you got out of my room."

Adrian averted my eyes. "That's not important."

"For once, can I decide what's important?"

"Dorothy. Please try to understand."

I took a step, a swell of frustration rising inside me. "I should dismiss your behavior? You glow like gold, you appear out of nowhere, then disappear. And you expect me to follow along? And you ask me to trust you?"

Adrian reached for me before speaking in an conciliatory tone. "I know it's difficult." His voice made my frustration burst like air from a popped balloon.

"Yes, it's difficult to say the least." I turned and walked a few paces ahead.

Adrian caught up to me and squeezed my hand earnestly. "Listen. When we get to Negros, you'll see why I'm acting this way. I'm hoping it all makes sense to you in the Philippines."

I hesitated and didn't answer.

"Okay?" he asked, his magnificent smile begging me to agree.

My stomach lurched sideways and my hands

were suddenly sweaty. I found him impossible to resist; I trusted him implicitly. "Okay, Adrian. I trust you. For now."

The whiff of coconut and his minty breath made me lean in and kiss him lightly. The touch of his lips made my eyes roll to the bridge of my nose. The pounding of my heartbeat slowed and my stomach stopped rolling. I stepped back, dizzy from the kiss. It wasn't until I looked up that I realized mom, Stella and Tita Yasmin were staring at us, along with everyone in the entire terminal.

I had just kissed Adrian in public in front of my mom!

Adrian's jaw clenched, the muscles showing on the side of his neck.

"Adrian," I whispered.

"Yes."

"Did we just do that?"

"Yes. And it's probably not appropriate, especially with your mom and best friend watching our every move."

"I agree."

"Let's try to control ourselves. Okay?"

"Agreed," I said.

We walked over and I introduced Adrian to Tita Yasmin. Stella gave me funny looks, but I deflected them by avoiding eye contact. Mom asked Adrian questions about his family, nodding admiringly when he spoke to her in Visayan. Stella had taken a call from Eric, the shock at seeing us kiss still prevalent on her face.

Tita Yasmin excitedly showed me a poster image on her phone for the upcoming summer flick *Crazy Rich Asians*. We debated if a movie with an all Filipino American cast would succeed in America. *The Debut* was released before I was born, but there hadn't been another since. Mom and Adrian joined in the conversation and everyone agreed Hollywood needed to open their frickin' eyes to the diverse stories that had never been made into movies. We held out hope for more Filipino American stories to be told.

Stella had ended her phone call with Eric just as the airline announced they were ready for boarding. We slowly moved like cows being corralled for the Philippines Airlines ground personnel to scan our boarding passes. Once we entered the gate and into the cabin of the Boeing 747, we found our seats in the first row of coach, which offered more legroom than the rows behind us. I took my window seat and mom sat next to me. After buckling my seat belt, I glanced at Stella and Tita Yasmin a few seats over in the same row.

Once I looked out the window, it hit me. I was leaving the United States for the first time in my life. And Adrian, a guy I had met less than a month ago, a guy I had kissed in public, was sitting in the aisle seat behind me. I peered at him, his head back and his eyes closed, his earbuds dangling from the phone in his hand.

Was this what love felt like?

Once the pilot announced we were ready for departure, the plane reversed onto the tarmac. The flight attendants began the lap belt and life vest presentation. With this being my first ever flight, I paid close attention to the choreographed demonstration. I suddenly felt claustrophobic, so I turned the air vent to full blast, the hiss of air soothing my face.

The engines revved and the airplane gathered speed. As the plane ascended, I put on my earbuds and listened to "Reminisce" by Malyssa, a song that eased my nerves. I watched the Bellagio, MGM Grand and Luxor casinos shrink as the plane elevated. I closed my eyes, focusing on the song lyrics and uptempo beats, trying to keep my stomach from jumping into my throat.

CHAPTER 34: ADRIAN

ぢぢぢ

I managed to sit close to Dorothy, Stella and their mothers, never too far if anything went down with Sitan. I zoned in on the intentions of passengers on the plane, having to do it now before the wind goddess, *Anitun Tabu*, exerted her power and relegated my Timawa senses to mush.

The majority of passengers were Filipino and Asian, which made it easier to notice if someone had porcelain skin like Aria and Dala. I had pulled Dorothy close to me at the airport when we kissed in front of everyone when two white women looked at us suspiciously. Once I got a better look at them, I knew they were harmless. The young women boarded a flight to Jakarta on another airline, oblivious to Dorothy's importance.

Surprisingly, our flight was on time and the plane was already on the runway for takeoff. We watched the flight attendants' safety presentation, my senses heightened, ready to defend Dorothy at a moment's notice. The flight attendants were all Filipinas dressed in khaki tops and skirts, their shiny black hair and appropriately made-up faces showcasing the essence of Pinay beauty. They reminded everyone to stay in their seats for takeoff.

Once the pilot announced we were cruising at thirty-five-thousand feet, the flight attendants scrambled to start the first beverage service. When a flight attendant named Maritess reached my row, I asked for ginger ale, the same as Dorothy and Stella, while their moms ordered margaritas. It wasn't long before they were sharing sips of the margaritas, their laughs growing more animated. When the meal service started, I passed on the beef and fish, content with my ginger ale to stay focused for any sign of Sitan and his granddaughters.

Dorothy flipped her hair from her forehead and twirled a stray hair with her finger. She bounced between conversations with Stella and their mothers. She commented on the margaritas being yummy, which led to jokes about her finding a new alcoholic pastime. I smiled, knowing she was enjoying her first time on an airplane.

Stella had looked back a few times with an inquisitive look on her face, but I pretended not to notice. I hadn't talked to her since the perilous kiss that broke Aria's trance. She often looked back when Dorothy talked to her mom, my Danag reflexes giving me the advantage of avoiding eye contact.

After Filipina rapper Ruby Ibarra's "Us" ended in my earbuds, I spoke amiably in Tagalog to an *Manong** at his mention of visiting his daughter and grandchildren and looking forward to fresh *buko*† in the Philippines. The Ilocano family in the row behind me made all sorts of noises, the energy of their three young boys boosted by the Sprites they had ordered. A few rows back was a white woman next to her *mestizo*‡ adult son, a pleasant sight compared to the older French man holding hands

---

*	*An Ilokano term of respect for a person older than you like an uncle or grandfather. Also can be used for older brother, although not used as regularly as the term **kuya**.*
†	*Tagalog term for "young coconut." Buko juice is a popular drink served throughout the Philippines.*
‡	*Term used in Spanish speaking countries for a person of combined ethnicities. For Filipinos, it's commonly used to describe someone who has at least one Filipino parent.*

with a young Filipina a few seats over.

I took out the graduation card Dorothy gave me to translate from my jacket pocket and opened it. I deliberately read the symbols, the realization of the meaning a confounding revelation.

I repeatedly the English translation in my head incessantly, the meaning hitting home. I peered at Meredith and Yasmin, the mothers who had raised their daughters the best they could. If this card was indeed from Dorothy's father, her life would astonishingly shift by the secret Meredith and Yasmin shared.

This message confirmed there was more at stake than I realized. If Sitan and his granddaughters attacked, it would be on this flight. The Danag phenomenon of *Anitun Tabu* minimized my Timawa instincts at higher altitudes. I silently prayed to Allah my instincts wouldn't fail me.

With an astounding appreciation of Dorothy and Stella's friendship, I stretched my muscles in the aisle, empathy pouring from my heart for the four women who had endured so much.

The cabin lights dimmed as the flight crew encouraged passengers to watch a romcom starring Filipino celebrities Sarah Geronimo and Jericho Rosales. I waited my turn for the lavatory, my internal radar unaware of any threats, even as tension grew in my chest. Once I returned to my seat, Dorothy was in a conversation with Stella. They paused when I walked by before laughing at a scene in the movie. Other passengers had already dozed off.

So far so good. So far, so good.

By the time the flight attendants had distributed all the meals and drinks, the featured had ended and passengers had switched to other entertainment.

The pilot emerged and engaged in flirtatious conversation with the flight attendants before he went down our aisle and politely greeted passengers. He was lanky with black shoulder-length hair, his face a rosy hue against his white skin tone, his bangs covering his eyes. He said hello to Dorothy, Stella and their moms. He tipped his pilot cap and swiped at his hair, revealing his face. I was instantly filled with rage at the sight of the pilot's sacrilegious smile.

My instinct to protect surged through me as Sitan said something in Dorothy's ear. She leaned in and laughed. I stepped towards them, conscious we were in public with mortals for Sitan to use as leverage. I clenched my fists, imagining myself crushing his head. I took another step until he gestured for me to stay where I was.

Or else.

He must have anticipated my presence when he devised this plan. He had kept a low profile in Europe and emerged only when he had the advantage. We had forced him underground during World War II, when he used the ravage of war to kill humans for blood. At the time, I was filled with rage after his vampires had killed my grandfather and youngest brother. My Timawa warriors had to imprison me in Mandalagan to keep me from chasing after him in the Afghanistan mountains.

Now, with his granddaughters, he had sacrificed his grandson and his little army who had attacked me at the house. But he had to know they would be no match for me. So what was his ultimate plan? And that's when it hit me.

Sitan wanted Dorothy for himself. That's why Aria didn't kill Dorothy in Vegas. They wanted to bring Dorothy to Sitan. The way he smiled reinforced this theory. He didn't want to hurt her. He wanted to mate with her.

If he had a child with Dorothy, he could enter Mandalagan with less resistance from Timawa warriors. The child would be royalty and, for better or worse, Sitan would be the baby's father! If he compelled Dorothy, he would have the most powerful bargaining chip to return to Mandalagan. He knew *Anitun Tabu* minimized my Timawa abilities and he had the threat of crashing the plane at his disposal.

Suddenly I heard screams from the other cabin.

I turned to see Aria dressed in a khaki stewardess uniform and pointing an AK 47 rifle at the head of a toddler girl holding her Pokemon

Pikachu doll. Passengers screamed, their high pitches begging Aria not to kill the girl.

Another stewardess emerged brandishing the same weapon, butting the heads of passengers as she stomped through the cabin. I recognized Dala, the quiet partner of Aria.

"We're hijacking this flight in the name of King Sitan of Mandalagan!" Aria yelled. "Do what we say or you will all die!"

Sitan motioned at them and pointed his pale index finger towards the floor. The plane started to change directions until a wave of turbulence came out of nowhere, knocking me off balance. I found myself at the edge of the first-class cabin. Another vortex forced me towards the cockpit.

One of the lavatory doors slammed as I was hit in the face with furious punches. I had a brief moment to see a female in a stewardess uniform winding up for another punch to my head. I hit her with jabs that slammed her against the cockpit door. I was on top of her in an instant, my forearm on her neck, giving me a chance to see into Aria's blue eyes.

Aria lunged at me, her fangs inches from my neck. I punched her. She looked at me with hate while jabbing at my face. I grabbed her fist in mid-punch and pushed it against the cabin wall as the plane hit another round of turbulence. We stumbled. I pressed against her neck and applied more pressure with my forearm.

I squeezed her neck and grabbed her hair. She swung side to side while trying to punch me in the face. I moved my palms to the top of her head. I pushed down on her and tried to turn her head like it was on a swivel. She waved her arms frantically and clasped my shoulders, her strength making me loosen my hold.

Dorothy and Sitan emerged out of nowhere, his white arm around her neck. He rushed to the cockpit, the door slamming behind him.

"Aria! Please! You cannot kill me! Join us in stopping your grandfather! You will see the value in living a Danag life the way it was meant to be lived!"

Aria responded by kicking me in the back and and in the groin. A searing anger flowed through me.

I grabbed hold of her ears and screamed into a powerful twist of her skull. She grabbed at my neck to no avail, her blue eyes turning gray just before her body collapsed into dust forever.

ॐ

I crumpled Aria's clothes in my hands and pounded on the cockpit door. I pulled back the door enough to see Dorothy in the co-pilot seat and bodies of crew members on the floor. The plane jerked right to left and up and down, making me lose my grip. The plane leveled. I struggled to stand but was suddenly tackled at my feet. A powerful hand slipped underneath my chin and pushed to turn my head. I used my strength to flip on my back.

Dala, the brunette from Vegas, held a spiteful stare. She threw her elbows into my face, causing a searing pain to resonate through my spine. I yelled as more pain missiled through my midsection. I kicked my legs and landed one to Dala's back, giving me a chance to slip my legs out from under her. I kicked her face, forcing her to fall on her side. I jumped on her and punched her multiple times. She was helpless against my superior strength.

I stopped punching. "Dala! You can still be

saved. Do you want to be saved?"

"I'd rather die!" Dala twisted her body, trying to scramble away.

I held her down as she tried to grab my neck and push my chin. I wrangled her arms from me, hating there was only one way to stop her completely.

"Dala! Please stop!"

But she didn't stop. She made another attempt to turn my head. I held her down, my strength surging as she struggled to get me off her.

"Dala! Please! Submit to the Danags. You would be welcomed if you do. You could live in Mandalagan and see the beauty of protecting humans, the beauty of protecting mortals! It's a life worth living!"

Dala stared at me, the hate turning into curiosity. "Did you offer the same to Aria?"

"She wouldn't give me the chance! But you're different! There is kindness inside you!"

Dala loosened her brow, until she grabbed my neck and squeezed. "There is no way out for me!"

I gasped for air. "Why do you say that! I'm offering you a way out!"

"Sitan will take over Mandalagan! All Danags will be ruled by him!"

She was running on adrenaline, her strength zapped. I pushed her arms and held her down. "I apologize, Dala. But you leave me no choice."

And with regret resonating in my heart, I lifted her body off the floor and twisted her head three-hundred-sixty degrees.

CHAPTER 35: DOROTHY

ﷺ

I had no idea what just happened. The distinguished-looking pilot had looked at the hijackers like he knew them and suddenly grasped me around the neck when turbulence forced the plane upside down. Stella reached for me, but the plane's change in cabin pressure pushed my momentum away from her. She tried to hold our mothers in their seats before the pilot had somehow pushed us safely in the cockpit where he strapped me in the co-pilot's seat.

But now my mind was swirling at the sight of crew members' dead bodies. My stomach was in my throat when the plane suddenly changed altitude again, the nose of the plane pointed towards the ground. I tried to scream, but my voice was muted by intensifying cabin pressure. The plane continued its sharp decline, my eyes moist as the plane leveled off.

I heard someone's muffled yelling from the other side of the cockpit door. And that's when I heard a voice clearly in my mind. The yelling stopped and I closed my eyes. Adrian's baritone voice echoed through me.

He's trying to kill us! Stop him any way you can!

And without hesitation, I tried to reach the pilot's arm until the plane jerked up, forcing my body to reel back. Somehow, I grabbed his bicep as the plane started on another sudden descent, using every ounce of strength to resist his attempt to crash the plane.

CHAPTER 36: ADRIAN

౨౨౨

I threw my body against the cockpit door. It slowly gave way, dents forming in the middle of the steel barrier. I took a few steps back and ran into the door as the plane spiraled down. With the force of my running start and the plane's sudden descent, the door crashed open.

Dorothy was pulling on Sitan's arm. I jumped over the the pilot and co-pilot's bodies on the floor and took hold of Sitan's neck and pinned his arms behind his back. His ice-cold skin made me shudder. I tried to turn his head clockwise, but he was strong. Dorothy let go of his arm and backed up.

"Grab his arm!" I struggled against Sitan's strength, but had him locked in his sitting position. "Grab his arm!" I repeated to Dorothy.

I heard her voice in my head. *I'm so confused.*

"He's trying to crash the plane!" I answered out loud. "Grab his arm!"

Dorothy didn't move.

I tried to turn Sitan's head, but our combined strength had us in a stalemate. I pushed my elbow into his Adam's apple, making him wheeze. I started to get leverage when he tried to move his arms. His head slowly turned clockwise.

Why are you trying to kill him?

"He's trying to kill us!" I yelled at Dorothy.

"Don't believe him!" Sitan managed between breaths.

Dorothy's eyes changed as soon as she heard his voice. She approached. I held on tighter to the back of Sitan's neck and arms.

Stop hurting him, I heard her say collectedly in her mind. *Stop.*

I searched for her eyes reverently, but she was locked in on Sitan.

"Dorothy!" I yelled as I squeezed his Adam's apple impetuously. She reached out and caressed Sitan's cheek with her index finger.

"Your skin is so cold," she said.

"Dorothy, do not fall for him! He's evil!"

I know you're evil, I heard her say. *Do not hurt him!*

"Dorothy! No!" I yelled as my heart deflated. Why does she think I'm the evil one? "I'm trying to save us!"

She placed her palm on Sitan's cheek. "You're the infamous Sitan. The one who killed his grandfather and brother?" She brought her lips close to Sitan. "Why are you here?" She cupped his face with her palms, her lips inches from his chin. I was starting to lose my grip.

"You are beautiful," Sitan said.

"Are you here to kill me?" Dorothy asked.

Sitan laughed. "On the contrary," he managed to say as he fought me off. His lips searched for hers. "I may not even be who you think I am."

Dorothy didn't waver and squeezed his cheeks. "You're Sitan and I've met your granddaughters. Where are they?"

His chin was now over his right shoulder and Dorothy moved with him. He grabbed for my ears and skidded his fingertips against my jaw. He clasped my neck and pinched. I wrangled his chin over his right shoulder. Dorothy held on to his face.

"Where are your granddaughters!" Dorothy yelled.

Sitan squirmed as his face became red. "They...

had to be sacrificed!"

I still couldn't turn his head, his strength holding me off. "Sacrificed? What kind of game are you playing!" I responded. "Why would you sacrifice family! They did not deserve to die! I could have saved them!"

Dorothy leaned dauntlessly towards him. "You kill your own family!"

Sitan managed to move the throttle, causing another acceleration towards the ground. "They're not my family!" He yelled malevolently. "More are coming! I am only one Sitan!"

Dorothy squeezed his cheeks, her eyes connecting with his, no doubt a conversation taking place between them in their minds. I held on to his head precipitously, my strength dissipating the longer they stared.

Until without warning, Dorothy violently turned his face over his shoulder, his body disintegrating once his eyes stared at me in painful despair.

ॐ

I jumped into the pilot seat and struggled with the controls. The plane was nosediving. I heard air traffic control through the headphones yelling for our coordinates. Alarms were ringing spasmodically. I grabbed the controls with two hands and pulled back, the plane not responding until I forced the controls into my chest.

Slowly, the plane leveled into a stable trajectory. I looked at Dorothy holding on to the legs of the seats. I reached for her and assured her everything was okay.

You saved us, Adrian. You saved me.

"It's the other way around, Dorothy! You're the one who turned Sitan's head! You saved me! What did he say to you in your mind before you killed him?"

A look of dismay grew on her face as she hesitated and fidgeted with her hands.

I just killed him?

It didn't occur me that this was the first time she had ever killed anyone. I emoted compassion through my mind, and before I could react, she kissed me lustfully, her saliva and her tongue exploring my throat, a kiss that made a burning jealousy flare out knowing she had caressed the face of Sitan.

I broke our kiss in shock, not only at how passionately she kissed me, but at the sudden realization that Dorothy had somehow tapped into her ancestral strength to turn Sitan's head. She shouldn't have had the ability to kill any supernatural being until *after* living in Mandalagan. From what Kaptan told me, she would understand how to harness her newly discovered strength only in Mandalagan. And not before.

For the first time, I didn't question Dorothy being a true descendant of the great warrior Urduja, making the Alibata message from her father even more of a revelation. If I had translated the message correctly, Dorothy's family ancestry was more complicated than anyone imagined. And if it was true, I was more honored to be her Timawa protector, even as frustration boiled to the surface at not being told the full story.

CHAPTER 37: DOROTHY

بسْمِ

After Adrian had reassured air traffic control everything was okay, he looked frustrated in the pilot's seat. I had just kissed him and now I wasn't sure what to think.

Adrian. Sitan spoke to me in his thoughts.

"How did he do that?"

I don't know. I told him not to hurt you.

"I thought you were talking to me."

I held his hand. *You're mad I touched him. I had to distract his focus.*

Adrian squeezed my hand. "You realize you're speaking through your thoughts?"

His jealous sensibility passed through me. *I am?*

"You are."

I brushed my hands over my mouth. I pondered what to say next, unsure how to control what Adrian heard me say in my mind. *There was a voice in my head before we left for the airport. Was it Sitan?*

"Maybe."

The voice was friendly though.

"I'm sure he was being nice. He wanted you to fall for him."

How did he get on the plane?

"I have no idea. But now he's dead. Same with Aria and Dala." Adrian assessed the dead bodies of the pilots and stewardesses. "They're all dead."

"What about mom! Tita Yasmin! Stella!" The panic in my voice surprised me. I scrambled out of the cockpit. Gray ash fluttered around me as I ran past first class and into coach, my heart palpitating at Stella sitting fearfully between mom and Tita Yasmin.

A foul odor had me gag as Stella held on to Mom and Tita Yasmin.

"Stella!" I knelt down to her level.

"Are they dead?" Stella asked dolefully. She had our mothers wrapped in the glow I remembered her having at graduation.

"Yes. They're all dead!" I replied.

"No!" Stella clasped our mothers' hands. "Mom can't be dead!"

"I thought you meant Sitan! Our mothers are fine!" I lied.

"They are?" She slumped her shoulders. "I threw up," she whispered. "What's happening to me, Cleng? I don't feel very good." Here eyes rolled back, her radiance disappearing once she closed her eyes.

"Stella!" I held her face and patted her cheeks. "Stella! Stella! Wake up!" I looked around for help, but all the passengers were unconscious. "Stella! Wake up!"

Her face hung forward and sideways. I patted her neck and wrist for a pulse. I did the same with mom and Tita Yasmin. I checked again and again.

But nothing.

Adrian! None of them have a pulse! Stella was awake and glowing, and now she's not breathing! I started to sob.

I heard Adrian's voice. *She was glowing? Check for a pulse on her upper thighs!*

I broke my embrace and placed my hand up Stella's skirt and rubbed her thigh. I touched higher, then lower. Left. Right. Nothing.

I heard Adrian's voice again. *Be patient! You're looking for the femoral artery. Hold your thumb over her upper thigh. Slowly feel for the artery.*

I rubbed her beautiful golden thigh slowly. I checked different spots of both thighs, but still nothing.

I think she's dead! There isn't a pulse!

"Let me try." Adrian hovered behind me.

He gently released my hand from Stella's leg and touched the front and back of her upper thigh. He closed his eyes and emitted a strong light from his body. The light became stronger and expanded over Stella and our mothers.

Adrian leaned closer to Stella and kissed her lightly on the lips. He kissed her a second time, his hands searching for a pulse throughout her thigh. And after the third kiss, he looked at me, his face red.

"There's a pulse." His hands were pressed on Stella's inner thigh. He moved my hand over his thumb and released his hold. "Do you feel it?"

Yes, I feel it. I scrambled to mom and Tita Yasmin and felt delicate pulses, a wave of relief sweeping through me. They were alive!

Stella coughed and opened her eyes briefly before falling back unconscious. Adrian checked her pulse again, his body illuminated.

"They're going to be okay. Once the altitude lowers, they'll wake up."

I held my mom's hand and caressed her face. I moved to Tita Yasmin and Stella, my panic that they had died alleviated.

Stella was awake! She was glowing like you and had our mothers wrapped inside the light. How did you know to look for a pulse on her thigh?

Adrian's expression had changed. "Because she was glowing."

"Because she was glowing," I repeated out loud. "She said she didn't feel very good before she went unconscious."

Adrian took my hand and pulled me into his warm aura. "She saved your mothers."

"How did she save our mothers?"

He pointed at their waists. "Notice they aren't wearing lap belts. She held onto them herself."

Adrian was right. Mom and Tita Yasmin didn't have a bruise or scratch on them. Stella had somehow kept them from careening out of their seats by clasping onto their hands. Stella had the strength to keep our mothers from being pulled into the turbulence.

Adrian. What does this mean?

"It means Stella is more than we know."

I tried to look him in the eye. "Why did you kiss her again and again?"

Adrian didn't answer, but held me tenderly until he detached and kissed Stella's forehead, his eyes moist. He stepped around me towards the cockpit. "I have to take autopilot off to land the plane," he said through his sleeve.

I looked between Adrian and Stella, wondering why he had covered his tears. He was crying as if he was overcome with grief. But Stella and our mothers hadn't died. He had saved them, kissing Stella numerous times in the process.

I gently placed Stella's hands on her lap and ensured her pulse was constant. She was unconscious, but gloriously alive. I hugged her and our mothers incessantly, thankful to Adrian for saving them, the shock of my new reality taking hold.

I had killed the pilot after Adrian pleaded with me in his thoughts. The pilot was Sitan, and I didn't think twice about turning his head. A sudden wave of nausea hit me that pushed against the jealousy that had resonated inside me the moment Adrian had touched Stella's thigh. And that's when I vomited, shocked at my willingness to kill.

CHAPTER 38: ADRIAN

ಹಲಹ

I landed the plane at the Bacolod-Silay airport on the Philippines island of Negros. The captain was dead, along with his co-pilot and all the flight attendants. Some of the passengers were also dead. I would have to dispose of the bodies and make the authorities believe or, more accurately, *forget* there had been an incident. I hated this part of the clean-up, but knew I wouldn't be alone. Timawa warriors would be welcoming us home.

I was shell-shocked that I had kissed Stella so many times, and still jealous that Dorothy touched Sitan's face. Stella had died and, in that moment, a new sensation had emerged inside me. After I revived her pulse, I kissed her again, and that's when I was barraged by an urge to hold her. I pulled Dorothy close to me instead, only to succumb and kiss Stella on the forehead.

I went back to the cockpit to land the plane, my mind swirling. As I slowly lowered the controls to start our descent, Dorothy had joined me in the cockpit cautiously, her thoughts difficult to interpret.

The first whiff of the tropical climate hit me as Timawas surrounded us. I led Dorothy out of the cockpit and to the plane exitway. The hot sun blinded me as I peered at the Filipino males and females with tattoos on their bodies assisting passengers onto the tarmac. I nodded conspicuously at the Timawas disguised as airport workers.

Some were opening the luggage bay. Others waved passengers towards the terminal repeating, "Hello sir, hello ma'am." Another Timawa warrior held the airport terminal door ajar as the first set of passengers entered the airport. They gave me their silent salute, ready to help escort Dorothy and Stella into Mandalagan. This help meant making the surviving passengers *forget*. With a warrior's polite welcome and touch of the skin, each passenger's memory bank was wiped clean.

I held Dorothy's hand, resisting a nervous energy inside me. I tried to push my emotions away and focused on her and Stella's hidden ancestry. They had no clue Urduja had planted Tawalisi traditions into the blood of future generations. They didn't know that, over time, Urduja's people had become known as Danags through the metamorphosis of language and that Danags protected mortals. I smiled at Dorothy with the same desire to protect. But a sudden swarming urgency to see Stella made me abrade my tongue in a million directions.

Meredith and Yasmin stood near their seats as Dorothy emerged. They didn't look frightened, so a Timawa must have touched their hands. Meredith jovially commented on the smooth flight and her excitement to see her brother. Yasmin followed her down the stairs, both accepting the hands of Timawa warriors helping them step off the plane.

I patted my jacket pocket, confirming the graduation card was still there, the last two alibata symbols a proclamation of Meredith and Yasmin's unusual bond.

ᜐᜒ ᜆᜒ

se te

The vowels sounds translated to *sister* in English. Dorothy had correctly translated the other symbols in the message as *lobe y*.

Together, the message read *lobe y sete*.

This message was written in ancient Alibata without Spanish modifications, making it difficult to translate to English. But I knew the translation to mean *love your sister*.

From what Dorothy told me about her family history and her mother's close relationship with Yasmin, I was convinced the sister her father referred to was Stella.

Dorothy and Stella had to be half-sisters.

Did Stella receive a card of her own? I didn't know the answer. But Dorothy's card was evidence of their father believing Dorothy had reached enlightenment, while Stella was mistakenly disregarded.

How did I not consider the possibility after Dorothy descried her glow at graduation? Or when she had found my burner Twitter profile? Or after the kiss to break Aria's trance? The signs were there that Stella was experiencing a metamorphosis.

Her aura emerged only when I had caressed her velvety thigh to revive her pulse. She had somehow used *bioluminscence** to protect her mothers, a talent not easy for any Danag being. Dorothy hadn't even reached this level of enlightenment!

Stella had been the *one* all along.

Meredith and Yasmin had kept Dorothy and

---

*   *When organisms biochemically emit light from their bodies.*

Stella close all these years. I wasn't sure if they had agreed to share the same male, but I had a strong suspicion they cooperated with each other and loved him in their own unique ways. From what I could tell, Dorothy and Stella had no clue, but would definitely find out in Mandalagan. They were at Mandalagan's doorstep and it was my responsibility to get them safely home.

But this important responsibility became a distant thought when Stella came out of the lavatory. She hugged Dorothy, not knowing their bond was deeper than chosen friendship. The half-sisters held their embrace until Stella reached for my hand. An onslaught of emotions spiraled through me when she smiled.

Lust. Passion. Joy. All wrapped into one.

ॐ

Dorothy stepped onto the tarmac and hugged Meredith and her second mother, Yasmin. I sensed fear of her mother's cancer and apprehension being in a country that held deep, family secrets. I craved to touch her when she glanced back at me. And that's when my desire to be closer intensified.

I moved quickly, hoping to catch up to her and their mothers. I had to tell Dorothy face-to-face that my pledge to protect was unconditional. Through her thoughts, she thanked me for defending her and consoled me over my jealousy when she had touched Sitan. I perceived her confusion, her fear, her love. I coveted her ambiance.

Until the touch of Stella's soft, golden hand vanquished me. A new sensation besieged my body.

I shivered as if hit by a thousand bolts of lightning. I became dizzy. My legs wavered. When I heard Stella's tired voice, she pushed Dorothy's sensibilities to the side. An astounding happiness deluged my soul, mesmerized by Stella's amiable resonance, her beautiful aroma, and her astonished confusion at hearing us talk to each other in our minds. I zealously urged her to stay calm as I tried to keep myself composed. She had a temperate glow around her hands, so she had also discerned something prodigious. Stella's mahogany eyes connected with mine, her aura permeating in my soul. I took a breath and another, amazed at her exquisite beauty.

ॐ

Stella and I stepped down from the plane, the hot sun a catalyst to hold hands. One of my Timawa warriors patted me on the shoulder and grabbed my carry-on that I had apparently dropped on the tarmac. With a reverential nod of her head, she understood that something had changed. She moved ahead and motioned another Timawa into the terminal. I knew her to be a *Kinalakian* Timawa, but in that moment, I had forgotten her name. Was it *Anagolay*? I couldn't remember because I was literally dizzy.

My Timawas had already started disposing dead bodies while making sure surviving passengers

---

*   *The goddess of lost things in Filipino folklore, ever-present in the fabric of everything and is said to never abuse her powers.*

remembered the flight as being uneventful. They would have a vehicle ready the minute we left customs and were clearing our path to Mandalagan. All of these things were at my command, but immediately didn't matter when Stella caressed my hand.

She stared intensely at me as we approached the terminal, her eyes akin to mine. She asked questions in her mind at a hundred miles per hour, seemingly not waiting for answers. Why did she hear my voice in her head? Why was her body warm? What did it mean to be someone's *kindred*? What did it mean to be Danag?

I vehemently explained that kindreds tapped into each other's thoughts and emotions. I explained there was no mention of Danags in history books except through the hidden passages in the Bible and Quran. Sitan had led a faction out of Mandalagan and into Europe where they lost themselves through the evolution of war and greed. Over time, these Danag defectors became known as *vampires*: souls always looking for home. I told her when I was young, I had hoped vampires would remember to protect mortals. But too many generations had passed for rehabilitation.

I gently squeezed her iron-hot hand. Her breathing steadied, her voice softened. And that's when a ravenous craving to taste Stella's skin ravaged through me. I let go and clenched my fists, not wanting to hurt her.

But Stella encased her arms around me, the warmth of her body unleashing another onslaught of emotions. She absorbed my vulnerability, my jealousy over Dorothy and Sitan and my underlying sadness as an unbranded being. She cradled my burgeoning affection for her and my unrelenting adoration of Dorothy.

Her empathy almost brought me to my knees.

She swiped a tear falling from the corner of my eye. I discerned her sadness at how hurt Eric would be by her transfigured disposition. I discerned her compulsion to talk to Dorothy. I tried to assuage her worries, affirming we would go through it together.

Her questions gradually became statements, her doubts nullified by the glow around us, our hands intertwined. I kissed her with passion from my heart, my mind, my lungs, my *Anito* spirit. Stella extended her lips and straddled me. I held her by the thighs, my emotions under siege by the touch of her skin. And as we kissed, a bubbling energy made me uneasy, knowing she would be introduced to Danag life *only* if she entered Mandalagan safely.

ॐ

After our lips separated, Timawa warriors slipped Dorothy, Yasmin and Meredith through our secret exit at customs. I did the same with Stella while thinking back to Sitan's last scream. He had proclaimed himself to be the one and only Sitan and had sacrificed himself and his grandchildren. This meant something bigger was coming.

But why didn't he care his family had died? What kind of being doesn't care about his family! He was a monster, his last words proving it.

They're not my family! More are coming!

And what else did he say? Didn't he say he was the only Sitan? But that didn't sound right. I held Stella close as I remembered his exact words.

I am only one Sitan. He was only *one* Sitan.

One.

He didn't care about Aria or Dala because he was a martyr himself, one of Sitan's evil agents. And more were coming.

So this meant Sitan was still alive.

With a surging sense of urgency, I picked Stella onto my back and sprinted. In my thoughts, I yelled orders to my Timawas to get the half-mortal sisters to the Mandalagan gateway. Sitan's evil agents were in the Philippines. I felt it in my bones.

And then my brother Kenneth emerged. He reminded me that Dorothy and Stella had reached *enlightenment*, a profound consciousness to see the world's true realities. He told me to stop panicking and to calm the fuck down.

I thought of *Urduja*. The great *Kolipulako*. My Timawa warriors. My Danag people. I started to think more clearly and slowed my roll. I gently let Stella off my back and held her beautiful, soft hand as we walked to the pickup area.

I silently prayed to Allah that Stella and Dorothy embraced their new existence, finally at the cusp of a prophesized new era in Danag history. I was a witness to the ancient prophesy of *half-sisters* with mortal mothers returning home to Mandalagan. I was always skeptical of this prophesy. Until now.

Dorothy interrupted my thoughts to ask how close we were to Mandalagan. I answered that it depended on the water and the sun; it would make sense once we arrived.

But when Stella whispered my name in my ear and kissed me, Dorothy's voice gradually faded with Stella's breath in my mouth. For the first time in my life, my spirit was filled with unbridled joy at the realization I was no longer an unbranded Timawa. I had found the female I was destined to love.

URDUJA OF TAWALISI
1357 A.D.

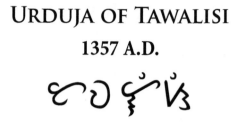

EPILOGUE

Somewhere in The Sulu Sea

بسم

Urduja and her Kinalakian warriors had been at sea for days. They ate tuna, swordfish and marlin from the ocean, thanking Amanikable, the god of the sea, for the sustaining gifts.

On the seventh day, Urduja recognized the island of *Java** hovering in the horizon. She was thinking of ways to approach the islands without looking weak and feeble, when she noticed dozens of vessels approach. Within the hour, her proas boats were surrounded by majestic paraw sailboats with hulls triple the size of any in her Tawalisian fleet.

A handsome man with light brown skin, a youthful beard and a batik shawl covering his shoulders emerged from the middle boat. Urduja noticed the gold amulets hanging from his neck.

"I am *Muhammad Shah†*," he said in her Malay language.

Urduja was shocked the handsome sultan had spoken in her native tongue.

"And why should I care?" She replied in the dialect she knew he spoke.

Muhammad hesitated. How did she know his

---

* *An island in modern-day Indonesia said to be center of Hindu-Buddhist empires in ancient times. Jakarta, the capital of Indonesia, is in northwest Java.*

† *The first Sultan of Brunei from 1368 to 1402 A.D.*

mother tongue? "I am Muhammad Shah of Brunei, in line to be the first sultan of Brunei. Who is the leader of these three boats?"

"I am," she said in her dialect.

"And your name?"

Urduja remembered her father's orders. "I am Urduja of Tawalisi."

Muhammad took a step back. "You are outside of Tawalisi! No one has seen your people at sea in years."

He had heard of Urduja's beauty from *Ibn Battuta**, the Moroccan infidel who had traveled through the Arab route. A gold necklace with a talisman hung from her neck and down the crevice of her beautiful, voluptuous breasts. She had gold bracelets on her arms and golden circle earrings. Her long black hair was like a snake wrapping itself around her shoulders and waist. She looked like a goddess.

"Urduja. I am here now. You will be my wife once we land in Brunei."

Urduja's insides squirmed. "Ha! With no proper proposal I will be no one's wife!"

"You dare go against my wishes? By Bruneian law, you must die!"

"Not if I kill you first!" Urduja stepped forward and exposed the knife and bolo weapons she had hidden underneath her robe. The Kinalakian warriors behind her exposed their javelins.

Muhammad held his ground. "I believe you need some convincing to see things my way."

"I will not be the wife of someone I can kill!"

---

*   *The only historical figure to have written of Urduja and Tawalisi.*

Urduja proclaimed.

"Then we must fight. I'm sure you have heard of *Pencak Silat*?"

"Kaliradman is the art of my people!"

"I have heard. But everyone in Brunei is trained in Pencak Silat. I believe you will see Kalidradman is no match to our artform. But we don't have to fight," Muhammad continued in Urduja's native language as his paraw ships surrounded her proas boats. If Urduja escaped, she and her Kinalakians would have to fight their way out.

"I agree we don't have to fight. So why are you insisting we do!"

Muhammad couldn't stop staring at Urduja's hypnotizing aura. "Because you won't agree to marry me!"

"You are not worthy if you cannot defeat me!" As a little girl, Urduja had promised her father and brothers she would never love a weaker man. Many suitors had tried, but not one had been successful. Her Kaliradman skills had become her test for any man who wished to win her heart.

"You leave me no choice but to show you the beauty of Pencak Silat." Muhammad crouched into a fighting position.

"May the best warrior win," Urduja said calmly.

She jumped onto Muhammad's boat and charged with an array of kicks and punches of a seasoned warrior, ready to die in the name of Tawalisi.

---

*   *A martial art encompassing a full-body fighting form and weaponry. Historically, **Pencak Silat** collectively describes the martial art influences of the Malay Archipelago. Today, this term is used primarily to describe an Indonesian martial art.*

END OF BOOK ONE

MAP OF THE VISAYAN REGION - PHILIPPINES

Mandalagan is somewhere in this region!

What island is Mandalagan located?
Is Mandalagan fact or fiction?
Is Tawalisi fact or fiction?

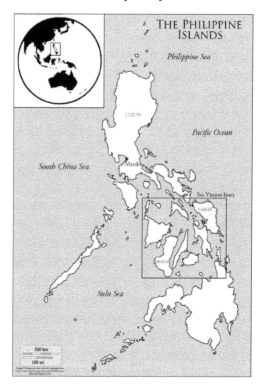

Map courtesy of JenniferHallock.com
Map vector image by D-Maps

EARLY SPANISH MAP OF THE PHILIPPINES

Factual or Fictional characters and places?

Urduja

Kolipulako

The land of Tawalisi

Historians argue over the location of Tawalisi.
What province claims Tawalisi and Urduja in present day Philippines?

What is the significance of Ibn Mattuta's quote at the beginning of this novel?

Map courtesy of Project Gutenberg's *A History of the Philippines*
by David P. Barrows
ebook published December 11, 2011
(http://gutenberg.org)

ALIBATA / BAYBAYIN ALPHABET

True or False Questions

1. Was Alibata the Philippines original writing system prior to Spanish rule?

2. Was Adrian's description of Alibata to Dorothy fact or fiction?

3. Did the Spanish colonize the islands in 1521?

4. Did Alibata survive Spanish colonization?

VOWELS

1st set basic consonants nds with "a" sound	ba	ka	da	ga	ha	la	ma	na	nga	pa	sa	ta	wa
2nd set ds with "e" or "i" sound	bi	ki	di	gi	hi	li	mi	ni	ngi	pi	si	ti	wi
nds with "o" or "u" sound	bu	ku	du	gu	hu	lu	mu	nu	ngu	pu	su	tu	wu

ORIGINAL BAYBAYIN SCRIPT

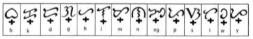

b	k	d	g	h	l	m	n	ng	p	s	t	w	y

SPANISH MODIFIED

LAGUNA COPPERPLATE INSCRIPTION
Monday April 21, 900 A.D.

Discovered in 1989 near Laguna de Ba'y,
Philippines

Is the Laguna Copperlate described by Adrian <u>fact</u>
or <u>fiction</u>?

What language is the Copperplate written?

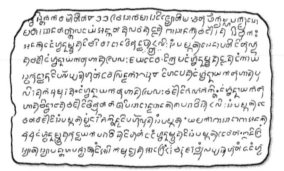

Photo courtesy of *http://Paulmorrow.ca*

ACKNOWLEDGMENTS

To my family for tolerating my far-off gazes.
Lynette, Alyssa, Reilyn and Noah - I love you unconditionally.

To my parents Concordio & Lily - thanks for your
sacrifices and endless stories.

To my sister Joanna, Sheraan, Anyse and Lucien - thank you.
To the Calilungs and Zamoras in California - thank you!

To the Dizons of West Bloomfield, Michigan - thank you family.
To the Philippines family - Salamat!

To the real life Dorothy - Thank you for your presence in my life!
To the real life Stella and Adrian - surprise!

I could not have written this without the encouragement
from these fine people and organizations! Thank you!

Jim Dempsey	*National Library of the Philippines*
Catheryn Wynn-Jones	*Filipinas Heritage Library*
Charlie Sutherland	*Alameda Science & Technology Institute*
Joselito Sering	*San Francisco Area RWA*
Mirene Benitez	*San Francisco Writers Workshop*
Nina Bautista Paddit	*The Lalala sisters writing group*
Rakia Clark	*The AswangProject.com*

IN YOULOGY OF FILIPINO AMERICAN SCHOLAR
DAWN MABALON
(1972-2018)

To all the readers - Keep imagining the possibilities.
And to the Philippines, my motherland
Your history is my obsession

ABOUT THE AUTHOR

Reno Ursal

A Filipino American author in California who believes in
self-discovery and education through
the power of storytelling.

Social Media
renowrites - Instagram
reno1107 - Twitter

Email
info@renowrites.com

Website
http://renowrites.com

Advanced Praise